THE MYSTERY OF THE BLUE STONE

A Dr. Brett Carson Thriller

KEITH WILSON

Published by Hallard Press LLC.
www.HallardPress.com 352.460.6099

Cover and book design by Eliza Osborn.

Library of Congress Control Number: 2022923382

Publisher's Cataloging-in-Publication data

Names: Wilson, Keith D., 1943-, author.
Title: Mystery of the blue stone / Keith Wilson.
Series: Dr. Brett Carson Thriller
Description: The Villages, FL: Hallard Press, 2024.
Identifiers: LCCN: 2022923382 | ISBN: 978-1-962326-25-4 (hardcover) | 978-1-962326-24-7 (paperback) | 978-1-962326-26-1 (ebook)
Subjects: LCSH Havasupai Indians--Fiction. | Indians of North America--Fiction. | Grand Canyon (Ariz.)--Fiction. | Physicians--Fiction. | Murder--Fiction. | Mystery fiction. | Thrillers (Fiction) | BISAC FICTION / Action & Adventure | FICTION / Mystery & Detective / General | FICTION / Thrillers / Domestic | FICTION / Thrillers / Political
Classification: LCC PS3623 .I57 M97 2024 | DDC 813.6--dc23

ISBN: 978-1-962326-25-4 (Hardcover)
ISBN: 978-1-962326-24-7 (Paperback)
ISBN: 978-1-962326-26-1 (Ebook)

To my wife Cathy

My best friend, my best editor, and my favorite poet

ACKNOWLEDGMENTS

There are many people to thank for helping this book become a reality. A very special thank you to Katy D'Amico, Maureen Blunt, and Jody Perkins Bramel for their incredible suggestions, corrections, and insights to keep the book on track. And to Millard Johnson and all the gang in the writers' critique group for their continued support. As always, a special thank you to Gary Provost and the gang at WRW for their support during my early writing career. And my continued gratitude to my publisher Nancy Hellekson, editor Eliza Osborn, and to J. Flowers-Olnowich, copy editor. The team at Hallard Press are the best publisher and editors anyone could have.

And finally, to my first-line editor whom everything is filtered through before anyone else — my wife Cathy.

SPECIAL NOTE

Several names are used in this book, all of whom are friends of mine. The characters that they are named for in no way reflect on them personally. If your name appears in the book, it is only with the best of intentions to my friends.

1

What the—?

What had he just seen? Had he just imagined it? Were his eyes deceiving him? Something caught his eye. Leaning against the cliff, he glanced down.

His breath caught in his throat as he stared in disbelief at a deep cerulean blue rock—the bluest mineral he'd ever seen. He shed his backpack and knelt beside it. He brushed his gloved hand over the rocky ground again to wipe away the dust, revealing a brilliant blue stone. What the hell was it? He knew for certain he'd never seen anything even remotely like it before in the Grand Canyon—or anywhere else, for that matter.

Dr. Kevin Horton, professor of geology at the University of

Colorado, spent his summers exploring mountains and cliffs, studying rock strata that encapsulated eons of time. Today, he was in one of the narrowest canyons within the Grand Canyon, so narrow that it seemed as if the land had simply split open. Of course, it hadn't *split open*. A stream surging through the floor of the canyon had gouged and carved it out over millions of years. The gorge was so precipitous and narrow that the canyon floor remained locked in a permanent shadow except for a brief time during every summer solstice when the sun reached its highest point north. Only then did sunlight manage to reach the canyon floor for a few minutes each day.

The Havasupai called it the *kúuchil yéek'joch'e'en*, meaning "the valley of darkness."

Its official name was the Black Canyon.

Today, that brief passage of sunlight into the canyon would change everything. It was mere luck that he'd happened to glance down when the light landed on a rock near his feet. He brushed his gloved hand again over the rocky ground to wipe away all the dust, revealing the brilliant blue layer that lay buried beneath compacted strata a mile high. He knew it had to be some kind of ancient rock, millions—maybe even *billions*—of years old. Without question, he needed a sample to study.

Concentrating on the task at hand, he ignored the deafening roar of the stream beside him, swollen with spring run-off that churned downhill to join the Havasu River and then on to the Colorado. As the sun moved on, the once-brilliant blue rock became indiscernible as it retreated into the shadow.

He grabbed his rock hammer from his pack, then took a huge swing and struck the blue rock. The hammer bounced back, ringing as though it'd encountered steel. He ran his finger over the surface. The hammer hadn't made a scratch. He swung over and over with increasing intensity. No results. Horton had no idea what it was, but what he did know was that he wasn't leaving without a sample of it. Setting to work, he pried, chipped, and hammered—again with no success.

More than two hours later, sweating and exhausted, Horton dropped the hammer, slumped to the ground, and drank the rest of his remaining water. He rubbed his sore arm and paused to consider his options. Daylight in the canyon faded, and it grew darker. He had no intention of spending the night in the canyon. But he also had no intention of leaving without a sample.

He had to try something different. Change tactics. Instead of hitting the layer directly, he attacked the ground and rocks pressing against it. After exposing a small section of the rock, he swung hard. Strike after strike. A fine fracture line appeared. The muscles in his arms were burning. Gritting his teeth and with his last bit of energy, he struck again as hard as he could. Finally, a thick, smooth piece of the rock broke free.

He picked up the piece and noted several things beyond its unique blue color. It was dense and heavier than iron ore. Its surface was glassy smooth, and the exposed edges razor sharp. He wondered briefly if it could be radioactive, which would be one of the first things he would check for in the lab. Now it was time to get moving. He slid the piece into his backpack, gathered his supplies, and began the treacherous hike out of the canyon— trying to be careful not to slip on wet rocks or fall into the torrent of water racing beside him.

As he worked his way down, the realization hit him that it was going to be very difficult—if not impossible—for him to find the exact spot again since the blue rock layer had been hidden in shadows and covered with a layer of dust. He'd spotted it just by blind luck. Now he realized he should have left some kind of marker because he knew for certain he would be coming back. And he would bring a lithium flashlight with him when he did. Convinced he'd found something that had been unknown until now, he began listing in his mind all the testing he needed to do on the sample.

Moving downstream, he slipped on a wet rock, twisted his ankle, and fell. He gasped as sudden pain shot up his leg. He slowly moved his ankle from side to side and tested his weight. Convinced nothing was broken even though the pain was intense, he continued on. There was still more than a mile to go, and night was descending. Now, he just had to get out of the damned canyon alive before dark.

Buried for over two billion years, crushed beneath strata of rock rising more than a mile above it, a small, fractured piece of the strange blue stone was leaving the Black Canyon.

2

TEN WEEKS LATER

MINERAL TESTING LABORATORY
GEOLOGY DEPARTMENT
UNIVERSITY OF COLORADO AT BOULDER
SEPTEMBER 5

Kevin Horton had done every test that was possible in the University of Colorado's mineral lab and was now reviewing his notes and test results. So far, he'd learned nothing definitive about the rock he'd found. He'd called the Colorado School of Mines a few times because he was anxious to hear what they'd found regarding a small sample of the strange blue stone he'd sent them.

His phone rang. It was from an area code he didn't recognize. "Hello."

"Are you Kevin Horton?"

"Yes. May I ask who's calling?"

"This is Mark James, with the Lawrence Livermore lab in California."

Horton was familiar with the 'LLNL' in California: it was a modern state-of-the-art research laboratory. Their diagnostic facility included streak cameras, neutron detectors, X-ray imaging and spectroscopy, and the world's most energetic short-pulse laser. Their Electron Beam Ion Trap facility was composed of X-ray and UV diagnostics, including high-resolution crystal and quantum calorimeter spectrometers used to measure photon emission, laser spectroscopy, a Nova Blue Laser Plasma Fusion reactor, 3D X-ray, micro-array imagers, electron microscopy, linear accelerators, a broadband heterodyne infrared detection system, and a dozen other testing systems he'd never heard of. Basically, everything that his lab at the university couldn't afford. *Why were they calling him?* "Livermore?" he managed to say. "How can I help you?"

"The Colorado School of Mines sent us a small portion of the sample you gave them when they realized it was beyond their ability to do a complete analysis. Since we received it, we've been studying it very extensively. Do you have any idea what you've discovered?"

He hadn't *discovered* anything—he'd just stumbled onto a strange blue layer of rock at the bottom of the Grand Canyon. Why in the world would Lawrence Livermore be interested in it? "The blue rock, you mean? So, what did that turn out to be?" he asked. "Some kind of gemstone?"

"Hardly. As you probably know, we here at Lawrence Livermore first created and identified element 117, tennessine. That element was produced in our fusion reactor and existed for just a few milliseconds before it decayed. Every element beyond 117 is only theoretical, and none could ever actually be created or identified until now—using our Nova laser plasma fusion."

"Sorry, but what are you talking about? I'm a geologist, not a theoretical physicist. I'm with you so far, but where is this going?"

"As far as we can tell, it seems you have discovered unbiquadium with atomic number 124, also called 'eka-uranium.' Until now, it was considered only a purely hypothetical chemical element, thought to have never existed, nor could it ever be created in a fusion reactor. As the physicist Richard Feynman proved, no element having an atomic mass of 137 can even exist. What you have found is one of the rarest and most valuable discoveries on the planet."

Horton was too stunned to think of a response. His mind was reeling, trying to figure out what this could possibly mean.

James continued. "Of course, people in Washington are now all over this. There is so much more about this element, but we can't discuss this further over the phone."

"Wha—what are you talking about? What people in Washington? Why would they have any interest in a rock layer in the Grand Canyon?"

"Well, for starters, they want to know exactly where you discovered this rock. Don't discuss what I've told you with anyone. And people in Washington would prefer that you don't discuss the rock, its location, nor any information about it that we share with you."

Horton couldn't fathom what the hell James was talking about. What could be so secret about a rare rock layer in the canyon? "What's going on? Why does this have to be kept secret?"

"We can't discuss any other information over the phone. Don't discuss any of this with anyone. People may try to get information from you during a conversation or over drinks. Don't tell them anything. Watch your back."

Click.

Lawrence Livermore National Laboratory had just ended the conversation, leaving many more questions and all unanswered.

None of what he'd just heard made any sense. He put the phone down. He was mad as hell that he'd been left out of what was happening with the stone until now. What was going on? Who in Washington was interested in a rock layer? Why was the rock and its location supposed to be so secretive? And the question that bothered him the most—who else would want information about a rock? What was he involved in?

A dark pit of anxiety knotted in Horton's gut as another worry formed in his mind.

Watch your back? Was he in any kind of danger?

Just then, there was a knock at his door.

3

THREE WEEKS LATER

PEDIATRIC WARD
QUEEN ELIZABETH II HOSPITAL
HALIFAX, NOVA SCOTIA
SEPTEMBER 29

They were standing at the nurses' station on the pediatric floor, reviewing patients' charts.

"Glad you made it back, Brett. But god, man—you look awful. When was the last time you slept?" Dr. Ross Solt asked. The dark circles under his friend's eyes told Solt what he had suspected. As usual, Brett had driven himself to the brink of total exhaustion. He was still trying to save the world.

Dr. Brett Carson flipped through lab results in one of the medical charts he was holding. "They're still dying, Ross. Especially the kids."

"We do what we can. You can't save everyone."

"Not good enough," Brett said. "I've been in our toxicology lab the last twelve days. Once we were able to identify the molecular structure of the toxin, I think we may have found a way to save them. There's a slight risk, especially in children, but it just might work."

"What did you discover, some miracle anthelmintic?" Solt asked.

"No, that would take too long. Testing the effectiveness of various agents could take weeks, or possibly even months. And we don't have that kind of time. And that would do nothing to those already sick and dying from the toxin. Instead, I knew if we could identify the chemical makeup of the toxin, maybe we could figure out a way to neutralize it."

"So, what'd you come up with?"

"I made a synthetic antitoxin I think might work. I used carboxylic acid to bind with the acrylic acid portion of the toxin. That forms a harmless acrylate polymer that can be excreted in bile. There's just one caveat."

"Yeah? What's that?"

"I'm not sure how well it will be tolerated in children, but we're going to find out. It might be their only chance."

Brett Carson and Ross Solt were doctors with the Epidemiological Investigation Service, or EIS, a very selective and specialized field investigative branch of the Centers for Disease Control and Prevention in Atlanta. Over the last six years, they'd worked together on difficult and often dangerous assignments around the world.

They'd been in Nova Scotia the last two and a half months, tracking down a deadly illness that had quickly spread along the coastal towns from Nova Scotia, up along Prince Edwards Island, and most of the eastern seaports of Labrador. Not only was it causing severe illness and death among many of the people along the coast, but it was also threatening their vital fishing industry. When the Canadian Health Service couldn't find the cause, they contacted the CDC for assistance.

The CDC sent its two best EIS agents, along with a small support team consisting of a virologist, an epidemiologist, and a marine biologist, to tackle the problem. After spending several weeks trying to solve the mystery, Brett discovered the answer they needed. They'd finally uncovered the cause of the illness, then worked furiously to find a treatment. Thanks to the work Brett did in the toxicology lab, they finally had an antitoxin. Unfortunately, seven children died before Brett and his team had arrived in Nova Scotia. Their deaths hit him hard. If only he had been contacted sooner...*if, if, if.*

Now he was doing everything in his power to make sure no more children died. And now it seemed they might finally have the antitoxin they needed to save them. The next few days would be critical.

4

STEWART LEE UDALL BUILDING
DEPARTMENT OF THE INTERIOR
C STREET
WASHINGTON, DC
SEPTEMBER 25

It was what could be described as a nearly perfect autumn afternoon in the nation's capital. A warm breeze sent showers of golden-yellow leaves into the air and carpeted the sidewalks. But the silver-haired man, sitting in the back of a black government Suburban as it wove its way along Dupont Circle, was feeling anything but peaceful. His lunch meeting with Phillip Fox, the director of the Bureau of Indian Affairs, had been a total failure. Nothing had gone as planned, and he was growing impatient. His ability to focus on the problem at hand had gotten him this far, and he wasn't about to let some remote Indian tribe get in his way now.

They sped around Dupont Circle and later, near the monuments, they passed crowds of tourists enjoying the beautiful autumn. The Suburban turned onto C Street and stopped in front of the Stewart Lee Udall Building. The Secretary of the Interior, Donald Wainz, stepped out. Wearing an Imperial Tailored Armani suit and imported Italian shoes, Wainz was the image of distinction, power, and wealth—an image he carefully fostered. As Secretary of the Department of the Interior, he was in charge of both the BLM and BIA—the Bureau of Land Management and the Bureau of Indian Affairs—along with the Geological Survey office, the National Forest Service, and the National Park Service. The Secretary of the Interior was a member of the cabinet but reported only to the President. Congress had little, if any, oversight or control over him. In short, Wainz held a powerful office with a great deal of latitude.

An aide rushed down to the Suburban, grabbed the Secretary's briefcase, and followed him up the steps and through security.

"Good afternoon, Mr. Secretary," the guard said. Wainz gave him a quick nod and walked down the long corridor. As he entered the large workroom, several staff members greeted him. "Good afternoon, Mr. Secretary," they said almost in unison.

"We'll see if it's good or not," he shot back.

As he approached the door to his office, his personal secretary stood and handed him a note. "Good afternoon, Mr. Secretary. Here's a message marked urgent. He requests that you call him as soon as possible."

"Thank you, Karen," he said, snatched the note, and after a quick nod to the marine guarding the door, entered his spacious and elegant private office. The Department of the Interior received dozens of requests daily for his time and help. Karen and her staff did a superb job of sorting out most requests and passing them down to any one of his multiple Deputy Secretaries and assistants. Any message that managed to get through to him personally he knew had been carefully scrutinized, appropriately filtered, and would be important.

Once inside, he sat down at his large, polished desk, read the note, then pushed the intercom bar. "Karen, get me Chief Jack on the phone." Chief Jack's given name was *Jacq-teh Kwa-ki*, which roughly translated as *Path of the Bear*, but he was simply known by everyone outside the Havasupai tribe as Chief Jack.

After several minutes, Karen's voice came over the intercom. "Chief Jack is on line one, Mr. Secretary."

Wainz punched the blinking button and picked up the phone. "Chief, what do you have for me? Good news, I hope. Have they signed the mining lease?"

"No. As I tried to explain to you before, that's not going to happen. The tribal council wouldn't go for it. They still remember the uranium mining fiasco. They don't trust you."

Thirty-five years previous, the federal government obtained a lease for a small portion of the canyon from the Havasupai in order to mine uranium. But that project had turned out poorly for everyone. First, the amount of high-grade uranium was minimal and did not warrant the effort and expense to dig it out of the canyon. In the process of trying to mine the uranium, a large portion of the Havasu River was polluted with dust and tailings, which killed off fish and wildlife. It had taken the river more than a decade to finally wash away all traces of the mining. The Havasupai tribe had suffered a high cost because of it.

"*Me?* What do you mean, they don't trust me?"

"Not *you* specifically—it's the entire federal government. They don't trust anyone in Washington."

"God damnit!" Wainz said. "Aren't you the chief of the tribe?" he snapped, struggling to control his frustration.

"Yes, I'm the chief of our nation, but the tribal council has the last say about everything that concerns the entire tribal nation."

"What about their relocation? How is that going?"

"That's also another problem. The tribal council blocked that also. There was total opposition to the idea. It just isn't going to happen. If we leave the canyon, we will lose forever the sovereign nation rights to the land. Because of that, they'll never leave."

"Then let them know we are prepared to—"

"No. It's not going to happen, no matter what you promise them."

"Basically, you have no good news on your end!" he yelled into the phone.

Silence.

The Secretary slammed the receiver down. It seemed the lease wasn't about to be signed, and the tribe's relocation apparently wasn't going to happen without more pressure. He went over to a cabinet, took out a bottle and glass, and poured himself two fingers of twelve-year-old Macallan scotch. He sat back down and sipped his scotch while trying to decide what his next move would be.

It had become a top priority, and the White House was pressuring him to get it done. He'd assured them he could take care of it. But so far, that hadn't happened.

It was time to take more decisive action. And he knew just how to do that. It was a desperate and dangerous plan, one with big consequences.

He knew that once set in motion, there was no turning back.

He punched in a number on his secure line and called.

5

The person on the other end of the phone was a thirty-eight-year-old man who'd lived the last three years completely under the radar of every country. A trained killer, he had worked for one of the most dangerous and violent Mexican drug cartels along the border and had seen and done more than most men twice his age. Three years ago, his luck ran out, through no fault of his own. And he'd found himself in the dark hole of the maximum federal security prison in Florence, Colorado.

Its official name was the ADX—Administrative Maximum Facility. The "Alcatraz of the Rockies." It held some of the world's most dangerous criminals. These were the world's most psychotic and vicious animals.

But prisoner 47-130-US Fed was not some uncontrolled animal. He was, however, ruthless, cunning, highly skilled, and lacked any sense of conscience. No one knew his real name. Few knew his history, other than he had been a skilled assassin for the dangerous drug cartel. Until three years ago. That was when things changed catastrophically for him.

While in Mexico, he'd had a short but torrid sexual affair with a beautiful young woman who, he found out later, was also the girlfriend/mistress of the head of the powerful rival Treque drug cartel. They'd killed the girl for being unfaithful, then they came looking for him. They placed a high price on his head. They wanted him dead. He knew the Treque cartel would never give up looking for him. While sneaking out of Mexico through a tunnel at the border, a US federal officer stopped him as he stepped onto US soil. He knew he couldn't risk going to jail, or worse, to prison—the cartel would have him killed within hours. He easily overpowered the federal officer, then killed him with his own gun. But before he could make his escape, he was surrounded and captured by a dozen other federal agents.

For the murder of a federal officer, prisoner 47-130-US Fed was sentenced to die by lethal injection. The government knew the cartel would try to kill him in prison, and the feds couldn't let that happen. They'd locked him away in solitary confinement for his own safety.

Solitary in ADX was a place where a person lost essentially everything—they lost track of time, their dignity, sense of self, and most of all, any sense of hope. Insanity slowly seeped into the soul of even the toughest person. Many prisoners underwent total mental breakdown, even more tried to kill themselves in various grotesque ways. His seven-by-twelve-foot cell was mostly void of outside sounds and was never in total darkness. A dim light remained on, even at night. Food was shoved through a slot. He ate alone, without human contact of any type. He tried to guess how long he'd been locked up, but eventually realized it was hopeless. Along with everything else, he'd lost all track of time.

Despite his strong willpower, he realized he was starting to crack. He began to hallucinate about being outside, about being free. There was no observable way out of his misery. The needle would be his freedom from the hell that crushed in on him. So, he thought he was beginning to hallucinate again one night when he heard footsteps of several people approaching his cell. He bolted upright when he heard the key in the door. *In the middle of the night?* Something big was going on. Had the Treque cartel somehow managed to get to him, even in here? Was it already time for the needle? Whatever was going on, it wouldn't be good. A cold fear paralyzed him.

His cell door burst open and four men in tactical combat gear charged in, grabbed him, and pulled him out of the cell without a sound. They practically ran down the corridor with him, past several guards and gates at checkpoints, never even slowing. Suddenly he was outside, the cold Colorado mountain night air fresh in his face, and he sucked it in.

They ran a short distance and practically threw him into a helicopter with blades already spinning and ready for takeoff. Before the doors were completely shut, it shot up, banked into a steep turn, and disappeared into the night.

A well-placed person in DC had learned that prisoner 47-130-US Fed being held at Colorado's ADX had unique skills that certain people within government might have need of from time to time; tasks that were either too dangerous or too difficult for others to even consider. After extensive arguing and discussing the possibilities, a plan was devised, then put into action. Exactly sixty-one days and eleven hours after being placed in solitary, they came in the middle of the night and extracted him.

That was three years ago.

Now, an elite group of unknown government people owned him. They gave him his freedom in exchange for his services. He was a man living under a death sentence, both from the cartel and from the law. He was never sure who he was working for on any given assignment. Over the past three years, he'd received text assignments from at least six different phone numbers, so he assumed at least six men were involved. When a need for his unique abilities arose, they provided him with a temporary credit card, cash, a passport if needed, and detailed instructions at drop places which varied and were never used twice. There was no worry of him disappearing. His family had also been targeted by the cartel.

In exchange for his unique services, his family had been flown out of Mexico by the US Federal Marshal Service. Once they were safely placed in the WITSEC, they were provided with a place to stay and monthly cash payments to allow them a comfortable—if not lavish—lifestyle at an undisclosed place in America.

He knew he was merely a valuable tool, but he also knew he was expendable to the feds, to the cartel—basically to everyone. He was a ruthless killer; he felt nothing but saw everything.

He'd learned years ago as a young boy living on the brutal, dirt streets of Mexico to make himself invisible—to blend in, to melt into his surroundings. His ability to remain "unseen" had kept him alive. With years of experience, he'd honed his skills to near perfection. More like a brief shadow or a vapor, there one minute, gone the next. Never leaving a clue. Nothing. He didn't even seem to disturb the air when he moved through it.

No one would ever pick him out of a lineup or could even describe him. He could walk into the middle of a small group and later nobody would remember having seen him. If he was in line for coffee, the barista would often ask the person behind him what they wanted, seemingly unaware of his presence. He had medium brown hair kept short, wore casual clothes, and was of average height and weight.

He didn't look threatening; he didn't look friendly; he didn't look anything definable. He walked and moved without a sound, his presence so silent, his appearance so plain and average, that he almost didn't exist. His exact whereabouts were unknown. Passports and various driver's licenses were all fake. There was no way to trace him. He was a man with no name, no past traceable background, no definite future. He simply *was*. He lived one day at a time.

A virtually invisible killer, he was simply known to a few select people in Washington as "The Ghost."

He never called them under any circumstance. The only communication allowed was when they called him. Those were the rules.

Secretary Wainz had just called him.

"We have a new assignment for you. I've sent you a text with detailed instructions. As usual, delete this text after you've copied all the instructions. Call me as soon as you complete this. If you manage to pull this off successfully, there will be a small bonus sent to your family this month, along with their usual payment."

The ghost texted back to Wainz:

Received

He read the text with his instructions three times to make sure he understood exactly what was expected of him. This would take some preparation, and he had a long trip ahead of him. He wondered how involved it would be.

He chugged the rest of his Bud Light, grabbed his keys, and left.

The ghost melted into the night.

6

Pediatric Ward
Queen Elizabeth II Hospital
Halifax, Nova Scotia

It had now been twelve days since the patients started receiving the new antitoxin. It had proven to be very successful, with no more deaths since they had started using it. Only five patients with the illness remained hospitalized, and four of these were children, ages six to eight. Brett was making his last visit to Queen's Hospital: a trip through the pediatric unit to see how the four children were doing and to say goodbye.

As he passed the nurses' station, several nurses working there waved and said, "Hi, Dr. Carson." They were attracted to the handsome American doctor with unruly dark hair, a tanned face, and a quirky personality that made them want to know more about him.

"Good morning," he said and smiled at them. "I'm just

making a quick stop to check up on my kids and to say goodbye before I have to leave. How are they doing?"

"All four will be going home soon," one of the nurses said. "We're just waiting for their latest liver test results before they can be released. I know they'll be excited to see you."

He grabbed the four charts then headed down the corridor to their room.

After ten kids had been admitted and started on the treatment he'd devised, he'd visited several times to check on them. Six had already gone home.

The antitoxin he'd developed neutralized the toxin with complete recovery of the patients. His initial concern was what the new antitoxin treatment might do the liver in children because they were so much more vulnerable. So far, that hadn't been an issue. He reviewed the liver functions, urinalysis, and CBCs—complete blood count—of the remaining four young patients, relieved that everything was normal. Then he entered the pediatric ward to see them.

He spent time with the kids, asking about their pets, how they were feeling, and were they anxious to get back home? He took a group picture of four grinning faces, gave them each a sucker, and said goodbye. "I'm going to miss all of you," he said, wanting to leave before he got too emotional.

"Thanks for the suckers."

"Goodbye, Dr. Carson."

"Thank you."

He dropped off the charts as he passed the nurses' station on his way out. One young nurse with a broad smile on her face stood and said, "Dr. Carson, some of us are going over to the pub for some beers after our shift. Would you like to join us?"

"Thanks. I'd like nothing better than to have a few beers with all of you, but I'm meeting one of my colleagues in Meat Cove."

"Dr. Solt?" one of the nurses asked. "Are you going to see Dr. Solt?"

"Yes."

"Tell him Sarah says 'hi.'"

"Will do, Sarah," he said and waved goodbye to everyone.

———

Chowder Hut Restaurant
Village of Meat Cove,
Nova Scotia

Two hours later, Brett and Solt relaxed on the sunny patio of the Chowder Hut restaurant in the quaint Village of Meat Cove, located on the northern-most tip of Nova Scotia. They dined on hot clam chowder, cold beers, and a plate of large chilled Atlantic shrimp while enjoying the sweeping view of the northern Atlantic. The air was filled with the sound of waves crashing against granite boulders and seagulls cawing overhead. A large dog rested on the patio at Brett's feet.

Solt, sporting a well-trimmed beard and thinning silver hair, had an almost Hemmingway-esque appearance. He'd been an EIS agent for twenty years when Brett arrived and had teamed up with him for Brett's first assignment.

Entirely different paths led to them eventually working together.

Solt had been a brilliant internist and at age thirty-five, he became the youngest man to become chief of the department of internal medicine at Columbia University's medical school. Shortly after his appointment, his young wife, whom he adored, died from a brain tumor. Devastated, Solt sank into a deep depression and became withdrawn. On the advice of worried friends, he took a leave of absence from Columbia. Finally, after much soul-searching, he decided to resign from his position at Columbia and join the EIS division.

Brett became an orphan at age twelve, when a horrible crash killed both his parents. After that, he'd been raised by his aunt and uncle on a ranch in the foothills of Colorado. Growing up on the ranch, he'd had lots of space and independence and learned to become self-sufficient. But he was driven by an irrational inner need to succeed at any cost. That drive had served him well in college and medical school, but it also served to shut out others. His total focus and commitment to his job had left a string of relationships that hadn't worked out—doomed by his lifestyle.

Six years ago, to everyone's shock and surprise, Brett had suddenly resigned mid-year as chief surgical resident at Duke University Hospital and went to work for the EIS division of the CDC. Solt, nearly twenty years older than Brett, had been his mentor when he arrived, and they eventually became best friends.

Their current assignment was successfully completed, and they were enjoying the quiet sunny afternoon before leaving. The support team had already returned to Atlanta.

"What wild goose chase do you suppose Quinn will send us on next?" Solt asked as he sipped his beer. Dr. Mitchell Quinn was the director of the EIS division. "Never stops, does it?"

"Nope," Brett said. "Solve one problem, another one always pops up."

"Has it ever occurred to you," Solt asked as he sipped his beer, "that each assignment is more involved and a bigger tangled mess than the last one?"

"Yeah, why is that?" Brett asked. "I remember the old days of cholera, meningitis, dysentery, the plague, even Ebola," Brett said. "Now everything is new, unknown, artificially created, and then somehow politically and socially involved. Yep, one big, tangled mess that we always seem to get stuck in the middle of."

"I'm anxious to get home," Solt said. "I'm going to try to get tickets to the next Falcons home game. Ya wanna come?"

"Yeah, sounds great. But I can't get really excited about the Falcons. You know I've always been and will always be a Broncos fan."

They watched a fishing boat, burdened down with a fresh load of flounder and poles sticking up like whiskers, pass in front of them on its way in from the Atlantic, with dozens of seagulls following in its wake.

When a man at the next table stood and stepped back toward their table as he turned to leave, the dog instantly raised his head in a defensive posture. The man saw that and jumped back.

"*Quedar*," Brett commanded the dog, and scratched its head. "Sorry he scared you. He's very friendly and harmless."

The man nodded and left.

"Friendly and harmless?" Solt said. "That monster dog's not going to let anyone near you that you don't want to be nearby. Tequila is stuck to you like Velcro."

"We've been through a lot together in the short time I've had him. I saved his life, and I think he's trying to return the favor. Leader of the pack and all that ancient instinct."

Solt took out his pipe, pushed a fragrant cherry blend into it, and lit it, sending puffs of smoke into the breeze. He did his little routine when he had something important to say or just needed time to think. It seemed incongruous that a doctor would smoke a pipe. But as he always retorted, he never inhaled. After several minutes of silence, with both men lost in their own thoughts, Solt finally asked, "What do you want out of life, Brett?"

"Well, that's a hell of an open-ended question."

Solt continued. "Where do you see yourself in ten or twenty years? Family? Kids?"

"Don't know. Been too busy to stop and think about it. How about you?"

"Fair enough," Solt said and puffed his pipe more vigorously, no answer forthcoming. He'd remained single and hadn't really dated since Alice died.

Brett knew what was tearing at his friend, afraid to let go of the past, of letting go of her memory. "Alice would tell you to move on with your life. That was almost twenty years ago. Time to let go and move on, Ross. She would want you to be happy."

"Well, you suddenly have answers. What about you? How are you and Kari getting along?" Solt asked.

"Okay, I guess."

"What does that mean?"

"It means that it's hard to maintain a relationship when we're more than seven hundred and fifty miles apart. And by the way, a cute nurse named Sarah said to say 'hi' to you. Do you care to fill me in on her?"

"It's none of your damn business."

"Oh, I see. It's okay to inquire about Kari and me, but not to ask about what's going on with you."

"Fair enough," Solt repeated and settled back, puffing on his pipe.

Kari Wheeler, the beautiful young woman whom Brett had rescued in Guatemala, was an associate professor of anthropology at the University of Chicago. She and Brett had had a passionate love affair during their hazardous adventure and daring escape from killers in the jungle of Guatemala. Since then, they'd struggled to maintain their long-distance relationship between Atlanta and Chicago.

Solt shook his head. "That can't work forever. Something has to change, or you're going to lose her."

Brett laughed. "What the hell are you talking about, Ross?"

"Kari is beautiful, intelligent, interesting. You have to know every grad student and half of the faculty at the University of Chicago are pursuing her."

"Probably right. But I'm not worried."

"Well, for Pete's sake, you should be," Solt shot back. "Women need security, a home, companionship. While you're out saving the world, someone's gonna snatch her up."

"Yeah, like you would know."

But Solt did know him too well. Brett *had* left a trail of broken relationships. Solt knew about Brett's parents' tragic deaths and his growing up in Colorado with its wide-open spaces on his relatives' ranch, which afforded a freedom that fostered an independence born of isolation and the need to cope with being raised—largely—alone.

Finally, Solt said, through a small cloud of smoke, "You know what your two biggest problems are?"

"I'm sure you're about to tell me."

Solt grabbed his pipe from his mouth and pointed it at Brett. "You drive yourself too damned hard. You can't accept failure, even when it's not your fault. You try to take responsibility for everything. Problem is Brett, the world isn't like that. Things don't always work out like they're supposed to—the way we want them to. Sometimes bad things just happen. Sometimes they can't be fixed."

Solt was probably referring to the incident that caused Brett to suddenly quit his surgical residency. Brett was senior surgical resident at Duke when it happened—the event that changed the direction his life was to take. On Christmas day, a twelve-year-old girl, on her new sled, slid into the street and under a moving car. With massive internal hemorrhaging, she was rushed into surgery. Brett and his surgical team repaired her torn kidney, removed a ruptured spleen, sewed a torn diaphragm, and stabilized her with no more visible bleeding. However, they'd missed a small tear in an accessory splenic artery, and she'd quietly bleed to death while in recovery. On Christmas night, Brett resigned from surgical residency and left.

Solt knew Brett had never gotten over it and drove himself unmercifully—whether to make amends or punish himself, no one really knew.

"And...?"

"And," Solt continued, "you can't commit to anyone."

"Maybe it was because I hadn't found the right girl. Until now."

Solt leaned back, tamped down his pipe, and relit it.

"Listen, Brett. Kari is the best thing that's ever gonna happen to you. Don't screw it up. That dog there is the only being you've allowed yourself to really commit to. Kari deserves the same love and commitment you've given Tequila."

Tequila. The large abandoned, injured, and starving dog that Brett had rescued in Guatemala. Since then, the man and the dog were inseparable. Tequila never left his side. Brett and Tequila were both lonely souls, and they had found each other. It was hard to know who had rescued whom.

He'd dated several girls in high school and college but hadn't developed any serious or long-term relationship with any of them.

Until Kari Wheeler. Everything changed for him after that.

Puffing on his pipe, Solt continued. "Kari is not going to wait forever. Don't let her slip away."

"We're together as much as time permits. We'll see how things work out. I'm going to see her this weekend on my way back to Atlanta."

"You obviously haven't talked to Quinn recently, have you?" Solt asked.

"No, why?"

"Because you're not going to Chicago, not just yet anyway. In two days, you're scheduled for an interview on television with the CBC," Solt said and smiled.

"Well, Sigmund, that was an enjoyable lunch," Brett said sarcastically as he finished his beer.

"Don't forget your interview with the TV reporter," he said. Knowing how much Brett hated doing interviews, Solt added, "Maybe we should order another beer."

An hour later, Solt tapped his pipe clean, stood, and turned to leave. "I'm flying back early tomorrow, so I have to go pack. See ya back in Atlanta. Let's have dinner at Murray's. Enjoy your interview," he said and smiled at him as he left.

———

Ross was right. Brett's life had been a series of broken relationships, victims of his demanding job. Why didn't it ever work out? What was it he really wanted?

He hoped it might be different with Kari, but they'd both learned that long-distance relationships were strained and difficult at best. Things always seemed to pop up to keep them apart, things neither one of them had any control over. Such as this unexpected television interview.

He began to wonder if he would ever be able to have to a permanent relationship—something he'd never really had in his life. The one thing he knew for sure, he wanted Kari Wheeler. His previous more-or-less carefree lifestyle had become progressively more complicated with Tequila and Kari.

Kari's life was at the University of Chicago as an associate professor of anthropology. The Forrest Wheeler Museum of Archaeology at the university was named after her father, who had been killed in Guatemala. She and her father's name were forever a part of the University of Chicago. She had grown up around the university. It had been the only life she had known. She could never leave the university, and Brett would never ask her to.

How could he have a life with Kari? One of them would lose everything—their career, friends, their very lives. They'd never talked about marriage, kids, settling down. Maybe they avoided talking about the future because they both knew a future together didn't seem possible.

So...where did that leave them?

Seven hundred and fifty miles apart.

Maybe it was more than his job that was to blame.

Brett was tired. This had been a rough, demanding assignment. As Solt noted, often they were sent into dangerous areas of political upheaval, rebellions, or civil war, since polluted water and diseases were always the by-products. He wasn't physically or mentally ready to tackle a new assignment. He needed rest, and he desperately wanted time with Kari.

In college, he'd had to make a difficult decision, one that would affect the rest of his life. He loved playing classical guitar, and he'd chosen music as his major in college. But at the start of his senior year, he thought about going to medical school. Music or medicine? He'd struggled with that decision for weeks until he made his choice—and switched courses to pursue a career in medicine.

Was he now facing another serious crossroads in his life? His work as an EIS agent or a life with Kari? If he couldn't have both, which would he sacrifice in order to have the other? He didn't think he could live without either. In essence—he was *screwed*. He reached down and scratched Tequila's neck and stared out at the vast empty Atlantic.

Solt was right about one thing: life only became more complicated with time.

And he really hated interviews.

7

Near the village of Porton Down
Wiltshire County, England
October 5
1:30 a.m.

A chilling, dense fog blew off the English Channel as cold night air settled into the hilly county of Wiltshire in Southwest England. Clouds and fog blocked the feeble light of a small crescent moon, blanketing the night in murky darkness. A shadow-like figure slipped across a field and stopped short of a chain-link fence. He had sprayed himself with an earthy-smelling spray used by hunters to mask human scent, then sprawled in the grass to wait and observe. Razor-sharp concertina wire coiled along the top of the fence. He spotted cameras on poles inside the fence, spaced. He estimated one positioned every three hundred meters. On the other side sprawled the seven thousand-acre compound of the UK's most secretive and controversial military research facility, the Defense Science and Technology Laboratories, known as the DSTL.

No one outside the DSTL knew exactly what went on there, but it was reported to be a CBRN facility, the military acronym for "Chemical, Biological, Radioactive and Nuclear Weapons," which included chlorine, mustard, ricin, sarin, and other deadly gases in addition to numerous deadly biological agents. Building 5 was the most secretive and secure building in the complex, because the entire third floor housed the Biological Level 4 Laboratory, known simply as "Bio-4." It held some of the world's deadliest organisms. Only a handful of people knew the security codes to the doors. It was the nucleus of the DSTL.

The dark figure lay in the damp grasses and studied the compound. Flood lights lit the buildings and the grounds near them. After ten minutes of watching, two guards leading a dog circled the compound, then went through a door into a small building, probably a security center for the entire compound. After observing the place over the last two nights, he knew he had approximately thirty minutes before the guards made their next loop.

From his tactical backpack, he pulled out a small, sharp spade and dug a short trough under the fence, then spread a black plastic sheet in the hole. The fence had sensors that prevented him from cutting or even touching the wire. He carefully snaked himself under the fence and dragged the backpack through. The plastic made sliding easier and kept dirt off his clothes. He then raced across the lawn to Building 5 and crouched down against its brick wall.

There was no way to penetrate the multiple layers of the secured, locked doors into Building 5, but he had no intention of going through any doors. He had a much better plan. No one anticipated an intrusion from above. He assembled a small but powerful titanium crossbow, uncoiled a long thin nylon rope with a grappling hook attached, and looked up. His target was a daunting four stories up. He aimed the compact titanium crossbow and fired. On the first attempt, the grappling hook bounced off the brick wall with a loud *clank*. He recoiled the rope for another attempt. He knew he had a short window of time before the guards made their next rounds.

He waited a few seconds to make sure the sound had gone undetected, then aimed and fired again. It flew to the top and held. The black nylon rope hanging down was virtually invisible in the deepening fog. In less than a minute, he climbed to the top and settled on the roof to wait for the next round by the guards and dog. He heard the door to the security building open, then close. He knew he had thirty minutes to complete his next task.

He measured off thirty-five feet from the south corner, secured the hook, then slipped over the edge again. He slid down twenty feet of rope to a window located on the third floor. He pulled two items from his pack, then sprayed the edges of a large window with a lubricant to help raise the window and to eliminate any scraping noise. Using a diamond glass cutter, he made a thin slit in the bottom of the window, slid a wire through the slit, and unlocked the window. He raised it and slipped in. He silently closed it just as two guards and a dog passed by beneath him. Except for very rare circumstances, nobody would be in the extremely hazardous and secured the Bio-4 laboratory at night.

After confirming that the entire floor was vacant, he went to the four-inch-thick secured main outer door to the Bio-4 laboratory. It took an intense ten minutes to open the lock and disarm the sophisticated alarm system. He moved through the decontamination area without bothering to use proper procedures for safety and sterilization, then unlocked the secure inner door leading into one of the most dangerous biological labs in all of Europe and entered.

Once inside, he pulled on a surgical mask, snapped on sterile surgical gloves, and looked around. The room was huge and well-lit, even at night. Multiple microscopes, culture tubes, petri dishes, centrifuges, and several other pieces of equipment filled the counters. He knew where to go and headed to the freezer marked "H." Making quick work of picking the lock on the freezer, he opened the locker and carefully pulled out a tray of tubes from the top shelf. A frozen mist swirled around the tubes, which were stored at −40 degrees Fahrenheit, using liquid nitrogen coolant.

He slipped on a thick thermal glove, then pulled three tubes from the eighth, ninth, and tenth slots, and checked the labels twice to make sure they were correct. He carefully placed them in an insulated, padded pouch containing dry ice. He then pulled three identical-looking vials from his pouch, placed them in the empty slots, and slid the tray back into position. When he closed the door to freezer H, it made an unexpected loud click as the lock snapped into place. The man froze for a minute and listened. The main door to Bio-4 was still open, but he didn't think the sound was loud enough to be heard beyond the room.

———

Jonathan McRury, known as "Jon" to everyone, was one of three night shift guards assigned to Building 5. McRury had been a special forces paratrooper in the British military.

At sixty-five, he had only three months and two days to full retirement. After completing his tour of the corridor of level two, he sat down to continue tying the perfect green-face nymph, winding the fine nylon strand around the hook. Feisty brook trout would be searching for food in the cold spring streams in Scotland. He smiled as he thought of the fight they would put up on the other end of his line.

Click.

McRury paused, slowly put the green-face nymph down, and

listened. Had he heard something? Was his mind playing tricks in the quiet of the night? Or had he...?

He slipped up the stairs, unlocked the door to the third floor, and quietly stepped into the hallway. Even in the dark, he could tell that the door to Bio-4 was open! He pulled out his 9mm Glock-19, then reached for his two-way radio for backup. Before he could press the button to speak, a gloved hand clamped down over his mouth. In the next instant, he felt a tiny prick in his neck. In seconds, his muscles went slack, and he slumped to the floor.

In the faint ambient light, the dark figure saw the old guard's face turn red as he struggled to breathe. Slowly, his body gave up the struggle, and in the final moments of life, his shoe beat a soft staccato against the floor, then relaxed. After checking to make sure the guard was dead, the dark figure retraced his steps to close and lock the doors to Bio-4 and reset the alarm. He glanced at his watch. He had less than five minutes before the guards made another sweep around the compound.

He quickly slipped through the window and closed it, slid down the rope. After snapping the rope to release the hook from the roof, he coiled the rope, then raced across the huge lawn and melted into the night. After slipping under the fence, he pushed the dirt back into the hole and rolled up the plastic and sprayed the ground again, leaving no sign of him having been there. He darted into thick brush outside the compound and dropped down.

The ghost lay motionless in the grass at the edge of the woods, watching two guards and a dog doing their rounds. The dog stopped once, lifted his head, and sniffed the night air. The guards paused and swept their flashlights around, looking for anything suspicious. Then they moved on. The ghost turned away from the compound and melted into the fog. The small disturbance in the ground by the fence would be impossible to notice in the thick fog and darkness of night.

When the tray of frozen vials on the top shelf of locker H inside of Bio-4 were eventually checked, all would appear to be accounted for.

The small slit in the base of a window would go unnoticed. Nothing seemed out of place.

Except for a dead guard on level three.

————

The following morning, the body of Jonathan McRury was found on level three just outside the large, secure Bio-4 laboratory, presumably a victim of a heart attack. There was no hint of why he had been on level three. There had been no radio transmission from him that would have suggested trouble.

Initial examination revealed no obvious trauma. His body was transported to King's Hospital for a limited autopsy. The strap on his holster was unsnapped and his Glock was partway out of the holster. Presumably, it became partially dislodged when McRury fell to the ground. An examination of level three showed nothing out of the ordinary. The doors to Biological Level Four Laboratory were found locked and secure.

————

Secretary Wainz had just settled into his favorite leather chair in his library at home, with a glass of Macallan in his hand, when a one-word text arrived on his private phone:

Done

"Tell me you have good news," Wainz said after calling back.

"Three vials, just liked you asked."

Wainz had to admit—the man was as rough as they come,

ruthless and cunning, but he always got the job done. "Any problems?"

"None—it went smoothly. Just one little hiccup."

Wainz sat up in his chair. "What kind of 'little hiccup?'"

"A guard spotted me just outside their Bio-4 lab. I had to put him down."

Wainz nervously took a drink from his glass, then said, "I told you I didn't want any comebacks. Nobody is supposed to even suspect the vials are missing. I told you this had to be clean."

The rough voice on the other end grew even rougher. "It was clean. There's no evidence I was even there. His death will most likely be considered a heart attack."

Wainz took another drink of scotch, thought a moment, then said, "It's time to put the rest of the plan into action. Exactly like we discussed. Spread it out over a few days. Not all at once. It has to confuse them, but also force them into some kind of action."

"When do you want me to start?"

"Now. As soon as you can get out there."

Click.

And like that, the ghost was gone. Vanished.

Wainz took a large swallow of his Macallan. This next phase was the trickiest and carried the highest risk. But he was sure it would work.

It had to.

$$8$$

The University of Chicago
Cobb Hall
Friday afternoon
October 7

Kari Wheeler looked out over her anthropology class. "Don't forget your term paper on theories of the lost Mayan civilization. They're due on Monday." A collective moan rose from the class. "Have a great weekend."

She gathered her notes and slid them into her messenger bag. She inwardly smiled when she noticed the boys in the class checking her out and, she noted, they were also the last to leave class. Even though nearly every grad student and several of the faculty had hit on her, none of the undergrad students had yet dared to ask her out.

Kari was used to all the male attention. At five-seven, she was a stunning statuesque beauty with black hair and dark eyes. She had dated several men but had never had a serious relationship. Then less than a year ago, she met Brett Carson—the adventuresome, crazy, brilliant, and incredibly passionate man who saved her life and rescued her from the jungles of Guatemala. He would be arriving here in Chicago within the hour. They hadn't seen each other since he was sent to Nova Scotia on his latest assignment more than two months ago. Thinking of him always made her smile and her heart beat a little faster.

"Dr. Wheeler—"

"Yes, Richard?"

"Ah…our fraternity is having a dance tomorrow, and I was wondering if—"

"Sorry. Not possible. I'm all tied up for the weekend. Besides, you are an undergrad in my class. That's strictly prohibited."

She watched as Richard was leaving. *So, an undergrad actually took a chance.* She turned to leave just as George Pettit walked in.

"Hi, gorgeous," he said. "If you don't have plans, I was wondering if you'd like to go grab dinner somewhere."

Dr. George Pettit was an associate professor of geology. Both their fathers had been professors at the University of Chicago, and Kari and George had grown up together around the campus. They had been close friends since junior high school, and she was aware that he had always had a crush on her. He was attractive—face it, George was handsome—and all the undergrad female students were falling all over each other to be in his classes.

But Kari knew he couldn't come close to matching Brett. In anything. Brett was wild, reckless, daring, as well as a brilliant physician. He majored in music in college and played classical guitar, had a large dog he'd rescued while in Guatemala and drove an old Jeep full of bullet holes.

George was cautious, reliable to a fault, steady, orderly, always well-dressed in Land's End, and drove a new Mini Cooper. He was solid, no secrets, no former life—or wife. And she knew he adored her. Over the past several weeks, she and George had had dinner together several times while Brett was away on assignments. It had become almost routine on the weekends when she was alone.

"Sorry, George. Maybe some other time. Brett is coming here for the weekend." She grabbed her messenger bag, smiled at him, and said, "Come on, you can walk me partway home."

They walked across the campus quad, now crowded with students and faculty anxious to get somewhere on a Friday night. Fading late afternoon sunlight flickered through yellow and golden leaves as the breeze made dancing patches of sun on the sidewalk. Kari's cell phone rang. "Hi, Brett. How was your flight?"

His voice was almost raspy. "I can't make it this weekend. I've been scheduled to give an interview on CBC television. I swear, Quinn has something against me. I'm so sorry. I miss you."

She stopped and blew a painful sigh. "Wow, that's a shock. I was really looking forward to seeing you, Brett. It's been more than two months—"

"Next weekend, I promise I'll be there. I can stay for the entire week, and we can do dinners and movies after your classes."

"I'll look forward to it. Next weekend it is. You know, this is going to be a long, lonely weekend for me. I was so hoping to spend it with you."

"Starting next weekend, we'll have an entire week together. Nine days for just us. And, of course, your classes."

"Be careful, Brett."

They continued walking. Finally, George said, "So, how about that dinner tonight? I really don't like eating alone, especially on Friday nights."

Kari was still struggling with what had just happened. Another weekend alone, without Brett. She walked faster, trying to sort out all the emotions. Since her father's murder while they were in Guatemala, she found herself all alone. Her mother died from cancer when Kari was in high school. She didn't think she could bear another lonely weekend.

George said, "Look if you'd rather not—"

She stopped and looked at him. "Oh, George, I'm so sorry. I was just trying to figure out the sudden change in plans. Thanks for asking. Yes, I would love to have dinner with you tonight."

"Great," he said with a big smile. "It's too late for reservations, especially on Friday, so we won't be able to get seated in any decent restaurant."

"Let's just go to Jimmy's. I'm fine with hamburgers and beer tonight. Any place will be better other than being home alone," she said. Jimmy's Grill was the popular and always-crowded beer 'n burgers hangout near the campus.

With a big smile on his face, George said, "I'll pick you up at 6:30."

———

Kari and George worked their way through the noisy crowd at Jimmy's and found a booth that had just been vacated. After ordering burgers, fries, and a pitcher of draft Amstel Light, George looked at her for a moment, then said, "Look—whenever you're lonely and want some company, you know you can call me anytime."

She reached across and put her hand on his.

"I know. And thank you. That means more to me than you can ever know."

The waitress arrived with two glasses and a cold pitcher of beer. George poured both their glasses, clicked his against hers, and said, "Here's to great friends. And thank god, it's the weekend!"

Kari took a large drink from her glass, then inwardly sighed.

Where the hell are you, Brett Carson? I need you.

9

As instructed, Brett arrived at the television station a half-hour before the scheduled live interview. He was still fuming that he wouldn't be able to be with Kari this weekend. He hated interviews and was sure that Quinn, the director of the EIS Division, was punishing him in some way. Quinn knew Brett handled himself well in interviews. But Quinn also knew he had a short fuse. As long as the interviewer didn't cross any unforeseen line or ask stupid questions, the interview should go fine.

Brett originally thought the interview was going to be a quickie five-minute filler between the weather and sports. He was steaming when he learned the show was called *News Digest* and was the equivalent of *60 Minutes* on CBS in the US. He was scheduled for a twenty-minute segment to talk about the recent health crisis that occurred on the eastern shores of Nova Scotia and up along Labrador. Quinn really owed him for this one.

He was taken to a studio room and took a seat while production adjusted the lighting, placed microphones, and tested the audio. A girl slipped in and quickly powdered his nose and forehead before he could protest. Then a sharply dressed, attractive young woman entered the room, walked up, and shook his hand. "Dr. Carson, I'm Simone Benoit with the CBC in Quebec," she said with a slight French accent, "and I'm here for your interview tonight." She was immediately struck by his penetrating blue eyes that seemed to take in everything, missing nothing.

He stood and shook her hand. "Nice to meet you, Simone."

She glanced at him and said, "You did know that this is a live televised segment, didn't you?"

"Yeah, that's why I dressed up." He was wearing his usual "dress" clothes of jeans, a pale blue oxford button-down shirt, a hand-painted tie given to him by the Alaskan Inuits, Dockers shoes, and a navy blazer. He self-consciously ran his hand through his unruly dark hair and sat back down.

She smiled at that. "Do you have any questions before we start?"

"No, not really. I'm fine."

Simone took her seat, flipped through her notes, and waited for the production staff to give the signal. The producer held up four fingers and started a countdown, finally pointing to Simone, and the cameras went live.

"Good evening, everyone. I'm Simone Benoit, and this is *Weekly News Digest*. We are broadcasting this special edition from our sister station, CBHT Channel 39, in Halifax. Tonight, I'm interviewing Dr. Brett Carson, who is with the Communicable Disease Center in Atlanta.

"Three months ago, a mysterious, deadly illness struck the Atlantic coastal towns and villages of Nova Scotia," she said as the monitor now showed aerial views of coastal towns, "and eventually spread north along the coast of Labrador from Fox Harbour northward to Nunavut. Eventually, forty-three people would die from the illness, which included twelve children. More than two hundred people had been hospitalized, and five still remain in the hospital as of today."

Simone crossed her legs and turned to face a different camera. "When our Canadian Health Service investigators were unable to identify the cause or stop the spread of whatever it was, they contacted the American CDC for assistance. And that's where you come in, Dr. Carson. You are one of the most renowned and highly respected investigators in the EIS division—and after your recent work solving the epidemic in Guatemala among the Mayan ruins —now also the most famous. Can you tell us what you found here and how you went about discovering it?"

The cameras turned to him. "First, let me clarify that I didn't single-handedly solve this. A top-level investigative team came with me, and as a team, we were able to identify and hopefully stop the spread of the illness."

"From what I've learned, you're being too modest, Dr. Carson, but please proceed."

"Our first task was to identify the cause of any illness. And that proved to be very tricky indeed. The symptoms initially were severe abdominal pain, fever, vomiting, bloody diarrhea, and dehydration. Several victims progressed to seizures, severe headaches, and eventually some type of paralysis."

The monitor now showed several patients in the hospital.

He continued. "Sadly, as you know, several of them died. The early symptoms were nearly the same as cholera, which can be fatal within hours. We ruled that out almost immediately. We also, in short order, ruled out other causes of dysentery such as shigella, amoeba, leptospirosis, and giardia, just to mention a few. The list is quite extensive."

"So, what was your next move, Dr. Carson?"

"We also wondered if this might be caused by a deadly illness known as PAM—primary amoebic meningoencephalitis, popularly known as 'brain eating amoeba.' Tests on the spinal fluid and brain biopsies of patients that had expired were negative, so another dead end."

"How did you finally go about finding the cause of the mysterious illness?"

"We began testing insects, water and soil samples, food sources, and of course we did extensive evaluations of the patients. We were unable to isolate any suspicious organism such as bacteria or a virus, and all our tests and cultures came back negative. It was at that point that I knew we had to change our focus. We began to do chemical analysis of blood samples. We finally identified a deadly toxin that is produced by a rare Asian parasite called Spargana."

"Where did this parasite come from? Why did it suddenly appear along our coast? It was responsible for the deaths of dozens of people and nearly wiped out our fishing industry."

"This is a rare, highly toxic parasite. Until now, it's only been identified in the much warmer waters off Korea, China, and Indonesia. We were able to trace it to the McKindren barrier reef fishing area sixty miles offshore, where surprisingly, the waters were found to be warmer than ever previously recorded there."

A microscopic image of the parasite was shown on the screen briefly while the interview continued.

"You said this parasite is Asian. How is it possible for something from the other side of the planet to make it to our shores?" Simone asked.

"Exactly how it made its way all the way here is anyone's guess. And that very question is what threw us initially. So, I wondered what conditions would allow this to occur. Thinking it might have something to do with water temperatures and currents, I did some investigating.

"According to the National Oceanographic Institute, during early spring this year, a very unusual variation in ocean currents created a much warmer trough in the Pacific, which eventually joined with the Gulf Stream, pushing water temperatures in a narrow current significantly higher. Before you ask—no, this is in no way related to global warming. This is strictly a geo-thermal phenomenon caused by underwater thermal vents created by shifting tectonic plates."

"So, once you identified the organism responsible, what treatment did you use that saved countless lives of those who were already sick?"

"We first gave the usual regiment of drugs for parasites called anthelmintics, but it became obvious they had no effect. I realized it wasn't the organism itself, but rather the toxin it produced that needed to be neutralized. And at that point, there was no known antitoxin. Children were especially very susceptible. We had stopped the spread after identifying the parasite, but we still had the toxin and its effects to deal with. And we had to do it quickly. There were more than a dozen kids in the hospital, very sick and dying."

"And how did you manage to do that?" Simone asked, now leaning forward in her chair. "That seems like it was a nearly impossible task, at least to accomplish it in a short timespan."

"Without getting too technical, after much experimenting in our toxicology lab in Atlanta, we devised a combination of compounds that bound two free radicals which neutralized the toxin. After we did that, most of the patients quickly recovered." What he didn't say, and what only a few other people knew, was that he had worked night and day for nearly two weeks to finally come up with an antitoxin. His efforts to find the compound that would work had nearly killed him. He couldn't stand the thought of another child dying before treatment could be devised, so he had driven himself relentlessly to find a cure.

"What can we expect going forward in the future?" Simone asked. "Is this going to be an ongoing problem for us?"

"No, it seems very unlikely that this would occur again. The very warm, narrow oceanic current has never been recorded before, and it has already disappeared. Fishing in a large area surrounding the shallow barrier reefs region has been temporarily banned for now. The parasite should be completely eradicated as soon as the colder Atlantic water returns."

Simone turned to the camera. "More than twelve weeks ago, our coastal towns were suddenly hit with a deadly disease which turned out to be caused by an extremely rare toxic organism, known only to occur nearly halfway around the world."

The reporter sat there a moment, then turned to Brett. "It seems like a miracle that you were able to basically invent a specific antitoxin within such a short time, which saved countless lives. No wonder you're considered the go-to person at the CDC. You also solved the Mayan virus outbreak, but that is a topic for another interview. I know I'm speaking for every Canadian when I say thank you, Dr. Carson, and to your team, for your brilliant work here."

She then turned and smiled at the closeup camera. "This is Simone Benoit, with Weekly News Digest, saying good night, and thank you for watching. Be sure to tune in next week."

The sound man, wearing bulky headphones, signaled that they were off the air.

Simone stood and shook Brett's hand. "Thank you, Dr. Carson. That was a great interview. There's a pub right around the corner. Would you like to go get a drink? I'm buying."

"Thanks for the offer, Simone, but I'll have to pass. I've been ordered back to Atlanta, and I have a long trip ahead of me. I'd love to have a drink with you the next time I'm up this way." He smiled, shook her hand, then turned and left.

Simone watched him walk away, thinking he was unlike any man she had ever met.

10

SUPAI VILLAGE
THE BOTTOM OF GRAND CANYON NATIONAL PARK
ARIZONA

The night was dark, the air cold and still, without a breeze. Steep canyon walls made the deep canyon even darker. The distant howl of a coyote briefly broke the otherwise silence. It was well after 2 a.m., the time of night most people would have fallen into their deepest sleep.

He found the cabin he was looking for and moved inside without a sound. A young couple occupied the cabin. This was the eighth cabin he had visited and would be his last until further instructed. He knew that a young woman and man slept in the bedroom.

Moving silently as a shadow through the cabin, he slipped into the bathroom. Wearing latex gloves and a mask to protect him from the deadly virus, he carefully put the last few drops of

the vial he carried onto each of the two toothbrushes. That guar-
anteed it would be ingested.

He left without a trace.

Like a vapor, the ghost melted into the dark night.

———

Twenty-year-old Daniel Ortage was a Native American member of
the Havasupai tribe. He lived in Supai, the Indian village located
at the bottom of the Grand Canyon at the end of the Hualapai
Trail. As he made his way to his favorite fishing spot along the
blue-green waters of the Havasu River just before it flowed into
the Colorado, he noticed a man walking away from the village and
heading downstream. The thought briefly entered his mind that
something was off. Nothing about the man was of note. He was,
in fact, very nondescript. Daniel wondered what had caught his
attention.

Then suddenly, he knew what bothered him. Because of the
illness that had spread through the village in the past two weeks,
the area was in total lockdown. All tourism, including hikers and
backpackers coming into the canyon, had been canceled and all
visitors already in the canyon had been evacuated more than two
weeks ago. No one from outside was allowed into the canyon, the
village, or onto any of the trails. Only the Native Americans living
in Supai Village remained.

Daniel glanced down the trail along the stream, but the man
had already moved on. He seemed to have vanished. Daniel
shrugged his shoulders and set about getting ready to fish the
river. He wanted fresh rainbow trout for dinner. His father had
shown him how to fish the rapid, twisting Havasu River as it
tumbled and smashed over rocks on its way to join the Colorado
River. Daniel looked forward to teaching his own son someday the
intricacies of fishing the untamed river.

He had just cast his fishing lure into the torrent river when it suddenly hit him like a brick to the head. His vision blurred, he broke out in a cold sweat, became dizzy, then nauseated. He slumped to a sitting position on the ground; his fishing rod and reel fell into the dirt and weeds beside him. He spread his hands on the ground to keep himself upright. Despite being a strong, fit young man, he was suddenly struggling to sit upright. His mind raced as he tried to make sense of what had just happened.

Had he just had a stroke? Was he coming down with the flu? Then he was struck with a horrible thought. Had he somehow contracted the same thing that had killed nine others in the village in less than two weeks? Their deaths had spread panic throughout the village. Fear could be seen on everyone's face.

His body was trembling—and he grew more miserable by the minute. And he was scared. The cabin he shared with his girl-friend was a mere two hundred yards away, but for him now, the way he felt, it may as well have been miles instead of yards. Daniel struggled to his feet, stumbled a few steps, then crumpled to the ground.

Using the last bit of strength he could muster, he yelled, "Cochica!" then fell, unconscious, face-first, to the ground.

———

The sound of the small medical transport helicopter landing outside the small hospital meant something bad was about to arrive. Dr. Pamela Martin had spent the past two years as a Public Health Service physician in the medical hospital at the edge of the Grand Canyon on the upper South Rim. She had treated heat strokes, life-threatening injuries from rock climbers that had fallen, snake bites, broken limbs, and the usual medical problems to be expected from visitors to the massive canyon.

Cliff walls over a mile high lined with thousands upon thousands of layers of various rock deposits were a magnet to a huge assortment of people. There were seasoned climbers who challenged the cliffs, many to end up with broken backs or legs, a few each year even falling to their deaths. And there were always the inexperienced day hikers wearing flip-flops or sneakers, carrying one small bottle of water, who thought they could just hike down and back up in a few hours.

Most of them, of course, never finished their poorly planned trip, leaving Dr. Pamela Jo Martin to treat them for blisters, dehydration, heat stroke, and often complete exhaustion and collapse.

She had seen it all, and it had almost become a daily routine of "break it—then fix it" for her as she dealt with all the visitors to the steep, dangerous, beautiful, deadly Grand Canyon.

That is, until recently.

Over the past two weeks, nine people from the Supai village at the bottom of the canyon had died suddenly and mysteriously. She had been unable to find any cause for their deaths. She had called in the Arizona State Health Investigative Department for help. After a week of intensive testing and examining insects, water, and blood samples from those who died, they'd found nothing.

While the state lab had been there looking into the situation, another two people died.

That was when Dr. Martin decided it was time to get more help, so, on her own, without consulting first with the director of Indian Health Service, she contacted the CDC in Atlanta. That was three days ago, and she still hadn't heard from them.

But in the meantime, she'd heard from the director of the IHS, and he was furious that she had contacted the CDC without his permission. How had he even found out she had contacted them? And why was he upset because she had?

The shift in the sound of the copter blades told her they had landed. The ER doors flew open, and two gurneys were pushed into the hospital.

"We received an urgent call from Julie at the medical clinic," the flight nurse said, "and we found these two. The man is Daniel Ortage, age twenty. His blood pressure is 60 over 20 and failing rapidly. We started an IV and gave him O2. His PO2 was only 40 percent. The other one is—was—his girlfriend. She died almost immediately after we got to her."

Martin knew both Daniel and his fiancée, Cochica. She also knew that neither she nor the small hospital was equipped to handle this kind of escalating situation that was spreading out of control. Something had to change and soon or they would have a huge problem on their hands.

And that was only part of the problem. It was so much bigger than that.

Damn, she didn't need this right now...

11

Brett and Tequila made it back to his condo well after dark. Both he and the dog were exhausted after driving two long days back from Nova Scotia. He fed Tequila and threw a frozen dinner in the microwave for himself, then called Kari's number while waiting for it to cook.

A sleepy voice scratched, "Hello?"'

"Hey—did I wake you?"

"It's nearly midnight, so yeah."

"Sorry. I just wanted to hear your voice and let you know I made it back."

"Everything go okay?"

"Sure. I'm looking forward to this weekend. We're still on, right?"

"Can't wait." Kari yawned, then said, "Good night, Brett. I love you."

Brett made quick work of his dinner, then collapsed on his bed and slept soundly, with Tequila already asleep on the floor beside him.

———

After a brisk morning run with Tequila, he showered, started a load of laundry, then headed to his office on the CDC campus. He had a small corner office with two windows, but barely enough room to work, but he considered the windows more important than a larger office. There was a desk with a computer, a lamp, and a new leather chair he'd 'confiscated' from the second-floor conference room.

He shared a common printer in the hall with several other offices. As the team leader, he had a report to write, along with several emails to answer. He was on his second cup of coffee and working his way through a long, detailed report on Nova Scotia when the phone rang.

The EIS director, Dr. Mitchell Quinn—"Mitch" to those who knew him — was on the other end. How did the man always seem to know where he was? Quinn always seemed to be involved in some sort of medical crisis somewhere in the world. Brett didn't envy the man.

"Morning, Mitch. How did you know—"

"Welcome back, Brett. Something has come up and I need to see you in my office."

"Sure. But you should know I already have plans to see Kari this..."

Click.

Quinn had already hung up. Brett grabbed his report, which was only partially completed, and headed toward C Building, which housed the EIS administrative offices.

The large CDC complex was spread out over four acres. With

an annual budget of over 1.5 billion dollars, it employed more than six thousand people, including renowned scientists in microbiology, virology, immunology, epidemiology, and biochemistry. The Epidemic Investigative Service, the 'EIS,' was the elite division within the CDC: doctors and other specialists who specialized in tracking down some of the world's deadliest diseases.

Brett took the elevator to the eighth floor, knocked once, and entered Quinn's office. The large corner office had two walls lined with large windows. The director sat at a large, polished wooden desk that held multiple computer screens. Quinn's appearance never changed—tie loosened, shirt sleeves rolled up, and reading glasses parked on the bridge of his nose—he seemed anything but the director of the elite EIS division.

Quinn stood to shake his hand. "Welcome back, Brett. You and the team did a great job in Nova Scotia."

"Thanks. It was complicated and took longer than we thought it would. And too many people died before we finally figured it out. I'm ready for a break."

Quinn looked at him, nodded, but said nothing. He stood and walked over to the coffee pot, and poured himself a cup. "Coffee?" he asked, holding the pot out toward Brett.

"No thanks. I just had some."

Quinn dumped in a packet of NutraSweet, took his pen from his pocket and stirred his coffee, tapped the pen to shake off drops, then continued. "How did the TV interview go?"

"Yeah, I want to thank you for that. No more interviews. I'll quit first."

Quinn smiled. "You've handled hostile rebels, corrupt army officers in Guatemala, and a bunch of crazy monks in a monastery, but you're afraid of some perky little TV reporter?"

"Perky? Who said anything about perky?"

"They're all the same. Let me try—about five-seven or -eight, blonde or dirty blonde, slender but has nice curves. How close am I?"

Quinn was spot on, as if he were looking at her. "I don't care if she's six feet tall and naked. No. More. Interviews."

Quinn held up a paper document with a red maple leaf embossed on it. "Here is an official tribute to you from Prime Minister Trudeau recognizing the work you did in the eastern provinces." He handed it to Brett. "As usual, you and Solt, along with the rest of the team, did a fantastic job. Brilliant, in fact. I still can't believe you and the guys in the lab were able to patch together some type of antitoxin in such short order."

Brett smiled, took the document, glanced at it, and turned to leave.

"Hold on. I didn't call you here just to give you a piece of paper. Have a seat." Quinn then slid a folder across to him. "Ever been to the Grand Canyon?"

"No, but it's on my to-do list. Why do you ask? Are you sending me on a vacation or something?"

"Afraid not. Something more serious than that. Got a strange one here. Do you know anything about the Havasupai Indians?"

"Nothing really, other than I believe they are one of several tribes located in Arizona."

"Well, it seems there's an outbreak of something on the Hava-supai reservation down in the Grand Canyon. There have been at least ten deaths out there so far."

"Hantavirus or the plague, most likely," Brett said.

"Yeah, my thoughts too, initially," Quinn said, "but all the cultures and serologies so far have come back negative."

"And...?"

"And I want you to go check it out." He slid a folder across the desk to him.

"No way. Sorry, can't do it. I just got—"

"I know, you just got back. However, before I can give you a week or two off, I need you first to make a quick trip out west, spend a few days checking this out, and get back to me. I'm not sure what's going on out there. They requested help, so we're obligated to check it out. I want you to go."

"You know, every time you send me for 'a short trip to check things out,' it usually turns into a major shitstorm. The last time you sent me alone to check something out, I got caught up in a civil war in Guatemala, as well as an artifact smuggling ring. I have plans to see Kari and spend the week in Chicago with her. So, I can't help you."

"Brett, this is not a request," Quinn said after taking a sip of his coffee. "This will only take a few days. She'll understand."

Brett didn't think so. "Anything else?"

"Yeah," Quinn said. "Don't get yourself killed. You're always walking on the edge, tempting disaster. That damned Jeep of yours has more bullet holes in it than Custer's horse did." Quinn was referring to the old Guatemalan military Jeep that Brett had 'confiscated' and driven all the way across Mexico back to the US with half the Guatemalan army after him. Ever since the *Atlanta Journal-Constitution* had done a large feature article about his exploits and escape from Guatemala, his bullet-ridden Jeep had become somewhat iconic around Atlanta whenever he drove it.

Brett took the commendation document, along with the folder of information about the situation in Arizona, and left.

12

Brett went back to his office to fret over the situation and to get angry at Quinn. But he knew Quinn was just doing his job. There had been nothing personal about his assignment to go to Arizona. He was just pissed at the timing. Damn, he wanted to see Kari.

Before he'd met Kari, he'd never had a problem with taking on new assignments. In fact, he had always looked forward to it. Now—now it was different.

Now he wanted to be with Kari. That was a major change for him, and he wasn't comfortable with it, nor did he know how to handle it. It seemed that his job as an EIS agent and finding time to spend with Kari were always at odds with each other. He picked up his phone and called Solt.

"Ross, can you meet me at Murray's tonight? I need to talk." Murray's Irish Pub was their go-to place to hang out with food and beer.

"Sure," Solt said. "Six o'clock work for you?"

"Yeah. See you then," Brett said and hung up. He half-heartedly looked through the information from Arizona. He didn't want to call Kari and cancel yet again a date to be with her, but he knew he had to. He picked up his phone, then paused. He was dreading this call more than the assignment ahead of him. There was no way to soften it. He prayed she'd understand. For the first time, he wasn't so sure. He called her number and took a deep breath.

"I've been waiting for your call," Kari said, excitement in her voice. "I'm all set for your visit. I moved some classes around, and I have a grad student taking two of my classes for me. So, we should have lots of time to see some things around Chicago."

When Brett didn't say anything at first, her stomach knotted up. She feared what was about to come.

"Kari." He stumbled, trying to find the right words to soften his message. "I'm being sent to Arizona—to the Grand Canyon, actually—but I should only be gone a few days."

That was met with a painful silence on the other end. He wasn't sure she had heard him. But he was more afraid that she had.

"Brett, I've made arrangements to be free for most of next week when you said you were going to be here. It's been more than two months since we've seen each other."

There was silence for a few moments while he tried to find the right words.

"And..." she continued.

"And?"

"And it will be my thirtieth birthday at the end of that week. A big milestone for me. I hoped I'd be spending it with you."

"Kari, I'm so sorry. You've no idea how anxious I am to see you. I'll definitely be there with you the weekend after next. No matter what the hell is going on in Arizona. Maybe you could fly out to Arizona and spend the weekend with me."

"Nothing I would love more than to do that. But flying out just for the weekend is out of the question. I've got work to finish, and besides, I would be spending most of Saturday flying out there, and most of Sunday flying back. And that won't leave much time together. Not a plan." She blew out a sigh. "I'll switch things around—again—and try to get some time off for that week. And by the way, what's going on in Arizona?"

"Do you know anything about the Havasupai Indians?"

"You *have* been gone a long time. I'm an anthropologist, remember? And it's not Indians."

"I'm sorry. Native Americans."

"Wrong again, but getting closer. At the present time, the correct term is 'Indigenous People.' And yes, I do know a lot about the Havasupai tribe. I did my doctoral thesis on the tribes of the Southwest."

"Well, Pocahontas, me see you in ten moons."

"Once again, Cowboy, you're way off. Ten moons is ten months and you better not be gone that long, or Pocahontas won't be here. You mean ten suns. And Cowboy—"

"Yeah?"

"Be careful. This squaw wants you back safe and sound. And soon!"

"I miss you. This is killing me."

"Just be sure that's not literal, Brett. Be careful."

"Aren't I always?"

"No, you're not," she said in a more serious tone.

Click.

"Happy birthday," he said to a dead phone.

13

When Brett arrived early that evening at Murray's Irish Pub, Solt already had a table outside on the heated patio and was sipping his beer. "Long time no see," Solt said.

"Yeah, what's it been, three days?" Brett answered and laughed.

A waitress arrived, and they both ordered large cheeseburgers and fries, and Brett ordered himself a beer.

"Did Quinn call you?" Brett asked.

"About what?"

"Some situation out in Arizona."

"Arizona? No way. We just got back. We can't—"

"Oh, yeah?" Brett shot back. "Well, guess what? I'm being sent out west."

"Wow, a TV interview and then this. You get all the luck."

Brett stared at him. "Seriously? You call that luck?"

"So, what's going on in Arizona?"

"At least ten Indians have died recently on one of the reservations," Brett said.

"Hantavirus or bubonic plague, best bet," Solt said.

"That was our initial thought also, but apparently it seems more complicated than that. Cultures and serologies are all negative. And if I learn that I need your help, you're going to find yourself in Arizona also."

"Not going to happen," Solt said. "Someone's coming to visit me."

"Wouldn't be Sarah from Nova Scotia, would it?" Brett asked.

Solt smiled. "Maybe."

"You old dog," Brett said, and slapped him on the shoulder. "Good for you."

Their cheeseburgers and fries arrived, along with fresh beers.

"Weren't you going to spend next week with Kari?" Solt asked while stuffing a french fry into his mouth.

"That was the plan. Thanks to Quinn, that's been put on hold for a few days."

While they finished their burgers, Solt asked, "How'd that go over when you told her you couldn't make it?"

"Just as you might expect. Not so good."

Solt pushed his plate aside, packed fresh tobacco into his pipe and lit it. "That's the second time you've canceled on her in the last week. Better tread carefully," he said through a growing cloud of cherry-blend smoke.

"I'm afraid that sometime in the future it will come down to choosing between Kari or my work here. I worry I may have to quit my position here if I want to be with her."

Solt puffed away and just watched his friend for a minute. Then he said, "That's one hell of a situation you've got there. The question is—which do you think can you give up and still have a satisfied life?"

Brett sat there, thinking of 'what if's' and wondering what the future would look like.

Solt continued. "So, let me ask you this. If you asked Kari to marry you, would she agree? How certain are you that she would say yes, or have you just assumed she would?"

Brett was silent. Until now, he hadn't considered that she might not want to get married.

Solt pulled out his pipe and shook his head. "Just as I thought."

Brett looked at his friend for a few moments, then said, "I have to ask. What's with you and that pipe? Why is an intelligent physician like yourself smoking that thing?"

Solt pulled out his pipe and said, "You really want to know?" He paused a moment, then said, "It's because of what happened to Alice."

"Need more context here," Brett said.

"I was devastated after she died. I was so depressed I couldn't function, skipped most meals. I was a total wreck. I was in Kenya, alone, and for a brief moment, even considered suicide. In one of the villages, I spotted three men sitting together, each smoking their pipes. They weren't talking, just contently smoking their pipes. At that moment, smoking a pipe seemed an easier alternative to suicide, so I went to a store and bought one. Then I went out and joined them.

"I love everything about my pipe," he continued. "The smell of the tobacco blend, watching the smoke swirl in the breeze, the feel of the pipe in my mouth. What I'm saying is, in a sense, this pipe saved my life. You've got your guitar; I've got a pipe."

Brett looked at his friend as they drank the last of their beer, then they both stood to leave.

Solt said, "Take care of yourself, Brett. Keep me up to date on the situation out west."

"Yeah, sure. Say 'hi' to Sarah."

Brett walked home in a funk, even more depressed and confused. He was angry and almost ready to quit his job. His life was at a serious crossroads. And whichever choice he made, somebody would still be the loser. He had a lot to discuss with Kari when he saw her next.

Whenever that would be.

14

After two days of hard driving, Brett pulled into Parker, Arizona, late at night. Both he and Tequila were tired, hot, and needed both a good meal and a full night's sleep. He would check in at the clinic first thing in the morning. He found a large hotel that resembled a Spanish mission, called The Laredo Inn, and got a suite for one week. He needed the extra space a suite provided in order to allow Tequila room to move about, and it would give him room to spread out papers, maps, his laptop, medical charts, etc. Besides, Quinn would be stuck with the bill.

After a short run with Tequila, he showered, ate two of the hamburgers he had grabbed coming into town, fed Tequila his meal, then stretched out on the queen-size bed and was asleep in seconds.

The next morning, after taking Tequila for a morning run, he showered, grabbed a breakfast sandwich and coffee, then drove to the Parker Indian Health Center. It was a small but clean and tidy seventeen-bed hospital/clinic that served the villages of Parker, Supai Village, and Havasu Lake. He walked in and went to the receptionist.

"I'm here to see Dr. Joe Martin. Is he in?"

"As you can see, we're quite busy this morning. Do you have an appointment?"

A voice behind him said, "Can I ask what you want?"

He turned to see an attractive young woman with her hair in a ponytail, wearing scrubs and a white coat with a stethoscope around her neck.

"Yes, I need to speak to Dr. Martin."

"Is this an emergency?" she asked. "We're very busy and I—"

"I'm Brett Carson with the CDC. Please let him know I need to speak to him."

She held out her hand. "Hello, I'm Dr. Martin. Jo Martin. Thank you for coming. I can't tell you how happy I am to see you. I'm the one who sent for you. I wasn't sure anyone was going to come. Did you fly in last night?"

"I drove, got in late last night."

She glanced out and saw the Jeep parked near the front. "You didn't come all the way out here in that, did you?"

She turned and stared at the Jeep again, then shook her head. "Just when you think you've seen it all." She continued to stare at the Jeep with its multiple bullet holes. "You get shot at often?" she asked.

"Occasionally," he said, smiling.

"What's that in the back?"

He looked out. "That's Tequila," he said.

"I had the real stuff in college and I can assure you that's not tequila. That's some kind of huge animal."

"His name is Tequila."

"That's a dog? What kind of dog is that?"

"He's huge and he's furry. Other than that, your guess is as good as mine as to his lineage."

"Why did you name him Tequila?"

"When I found him shivering in an alley in Guatemala, he was malnourished, thirsty, flea-infested, and suffering from a badly infected paw from a rusty wire stuck in it. In order for me to be able to remove the wire and drain the infection, I gave him tequila to drink until he relaxed enough that I could fix and dress his paw." In the ensuing days and weeks in the jungle, they'd formed an inseparable bond.

She took in his words, nodded, and looked at him. He was wearing jeans, a canvas bush shirt, and a well-worn leather jacket. She noted his piercing blue eyes and untamed dark hair. He was not what she had expected. After the initial shock, she saw that he was handsome, tanned, and fit-looking. She glanced at the Jeep again, shot full of bullet holes, then said, "You are from the CDC, right? You're not some kind of secret agent or crazy mercenary they sent out here, are you?"

He laughed and said, "No, nothing like that. I'm actually with the EIS, the Epidemiological Investigative Service, which is a special division within the CDC. We're the field people they send out to try to track down problem sites around the world. Nothing more glamorous than that, I'm afraid."

"Come with me to my office, such as it is." She started to walk, then stopped and pointed to the Jeep. "Will it be okay out there?"

"What, the Jeep?"

"That, and the dog."

Brett just smiled. "He's just fine, and so is the Jeep."

They walked down the hall and stepped into a small but tidy office with Indian artifacts on the bookshelves, along with medical texts. There was pottery, woven baskets, and three or four arrows tied together. A Two Grey Hills Navajo blanket hung from the far wall. She saw him look at her medical school diploma.

Pamela J. Martin, MD.
College of Medicine
Duke University

"My name is Pamela Joanne. Growing up, my mom always called me PJ, but my friends preferred 'Jo,' so that has been my nickname forever."

"We received your request for assistance, so they sent me here to do an initial investigation. Can you fill me in on what you know so far?"

"Again, thanks for coming." Then she let out an exasperated sigh. "Well—it's a complete clusterfuck out here. I don't know how much you know about the Havasupai Indian tribe here in the canyon. Somewhere between nine hundred to a thousand Havasupai live down in the canyon, in Supai Village, more than a mile below from the top of the mesa here. Most of the tribe live up here on the mesa, all of which constitute just one reservation. So far, twelve of the Havasupai down in the village have died unexpectedly over the past two weeks."

He noted that already two more had died since they had been first contacted. He had many questions, but did not want to interrupt her train of thought.

"You would think that the death of twelve people would be a big enough problem to deal with, but no. The problem is much bigger than that. The director of the BIA—that's the Bureau of Indian Affairs, and my boss, by the way—wants the remainder of the tribe below to be moved out of the canyon village immediately 'for their own safety'."

"That sounds reasonable to me."

"You'd think so. But it's much more complicated. There is a geopolitical aspect as well as a medical part of it. The Havasupai tribe refuses to leave the canyon village and move up here onto the mesa, even if only on a temporary basis."

"Why's that?"

"The Havasupai have lived in the valley at the bottom of the Grand Canyon for more than a thousand years. The federal government let them keep the valley as a part of their reservation while Native American tribes were being assigned their lands. Nearby are the Navajo—the largest reservation, by the way—as well as the Ute, Hopi, and several other Indian nations. The stipulation was that the Havasupai must continue to inhabit the canyon permanently. It is their land and not part of the national park system.

"If the Havasupai evacuate the valley down below completely —even if only temporarily—then that part of the reservation reverts back to the federal government and becomes part of the Grand Canyon National Park System. Then the Havasupai would lose the land in the canyon their ancestors had lived on for over a thousand years. So, they refuse to leave. And then there is the medical aspect."

"And what is that?"

"Here's my dilemma and the main reason I wanted your help. Only a very small part of the tribe lives down in the canyon. The largest part of the Havasupai reservation both in land area and in population is up here on the chaparral mesa. Nobody up here has gotten sick or died. If it's contagious, I don't want to bring more than nine hundred people up here and possibly carry along with them whatever pathogen we are dealing with. Right now, the canyon village acts as a natural quarantine to keep anything from spreading to the mesa up here.

"On the flip side of that," she continued, "we don't know what is killing them, so if it's something in the valley itself that is the cause, then I want them moved out immediately for their own protection. So, I'm caught between a rock and a hard place. And I've got the BIA yelling at me to clear them out of the valley, and a tribe that refuses to leave." She turned and looked at him. "I think the exact quote from the BIA director Phillip Fox was, 'get them the hell out of there now.' So I sent for you."

"Is that all? I thought you had some kind of real problem out here." After staring at him in shock at his response, they both burst out laughing at the absurdity of the situation.

"It seems like you have one hell of a political-territorial-governmental tangled mess on your hands," Brett said.

"Yeah, well, welcome to my world," Martin said. "You'd think that providing medical care for the Indians and treating all the stupid problems of tourists would be enough. Instead, I find myself and this clinic in the middle of some deadly outbreak causing a power play which I don't even begin to understand."

"Okay, let's start at the beginning and you tell me everything you know so far."

She stood, walked over, and opened a file cabinet, pulled out several files and handed them to him.

Just then, a tall young woman with tousled ash-blond hair stepped into the office. "Would either of you like something to drink? Coffee, water, soda?"

"Yes, black coffee please," Brett said.

"This is my nurse, Kit. But she's so much more than just my nurse. This clinic couldn't function without her. Kit, meet Brett Carson from the CDC."

"Nice to meet you, Mr. Carson."

"I'll have the usual, Kit. Thanks," Dr. Martin said.

Brett stared at the door after the nurse left. "I know I've never met her before, but she looks so familiar——"

"Amelia."

"What?"

"You do recognize her. She could be Amelia Earhart's twin. We sometimes jokingly call her 'Amelia.'"

Kit returned with two coffees.

"Thank you," Brett said, and took a cup.

The nurse handed the other to Dr. Martin, then left.

"What happens to the victims when they get sick?" Brett asked, sipping the hot coffee. "How do they get transported up here to the clinic?"

"It's more than a vertical mile drop to the bottom of the canyon. There are three ways to get down to the village of Supai. By mule, on foot, or by helicopter. Mules are how supplies and the US mail are carried down. By the way—the only place in the United States that has mail delivery by mules. They use mules rather than horses on the trail because they are more sure-footed than horses. Or you can go on foot—not recommended if you really need to get there in a hurry, because the cutback trail is steep and over eight miles long, then even more miles to get to the village. And the trip back up on foot is hellish. Lastly, you can get there by helicopter. The copter is not a taxi service and is used only for emergencies. Or to take me down once a week.

"There is a small walk-in medical clinic in the village, more of a first aid station for the local villagers, and is mostly used to treat the tourists, hikers, and climbers who find new ways to hurt themselves each season. Any serious accidents or medical conditions must be airlifted out by helicopter and brought up here. Julie is our clinical nurse practitioner and works there full time. I make a weekly trip down to review everything, inventory medicines— just routine matters."

"I see you went to medical school at Duke," he said.

"Yeah, it's a tough curriculum, but a great medical school."

Brett smiled. He had been the chief surgical resident there

when she'd just started medical school. "How long have you been here at the clinic?"

"Forever. Actually, I've been with the IHS—the Indian Health Service—for over two years. It just seems like forever."

"I take it this isn't where you'd like to be to practice medicine."

She paused for a moment to think, then said, "This is exactly where I want to be. I think I can do some good here. They really need medical help and it's in very short supply here. After medical school, I did an internal medicine residency at Methodist in Houston. No, I didn't intend to make this a career. Just never got around to looking for another place to set up practice. I race through my days and catch sleep when I can. In addition to the Indian tribe, I have a million clueless visitors crowding into the canyon. Did you notice the waiting room?

"And now, to top it off, I have the recent deaths and all the problems they have created. Then you look up one day, and two years of your life have passed. I feel like I'm at my breaking point. I'm working at full capacity, and that's not enough." She paused to catch her breath, took a sip of coffee, then said, "What's your story?"

"I've been with the CDC for six years. Nothing really exciting to tell." Which, of course, was anything but the truth. The past six years had sent him around the world, into some extremely dangerous situations. Devastating epidemics in the midst of natural disasters, civil wars, and terrorists. He had been shot at, injured, infected, battered, and bruised during those six years.

She sipped her coffee and stared at him. There was obviously more to the strikingly handsome man than he was revealing. "I presume you're either an epidemiologist or virologist, so you're obviously an expert on infectious diseases. How much general medical knowledge do you have?"

Taken aback by her forthright question, he paused for a moment, then smiled. She hadn't realized he was a physician.

"Well, I finished medical school eleven years ago—also at Duke, by the way—and then spent the last six years with EIS."

Dr. Martin's face flushed deep red in horror at her mistake. "I'm so sorry, *Dr. Carson*, I...I mistakenly...I just assumed...you were probably a virologist or epidemiologist," she stammered.

"An honest mistake. And just call me Brett." He opened the top folder and asked, "So, what is all this about? Bring me up to speed on what you are dealing with."

"Let's see..." She fumbled with the files, still flustered and embarrassed. "The first case was more than five weeks ago. An elderly woman suddenly became violently ill and then died within the first day of her symptoms. Since then, there have been a total of twelve cases. The last two were a young couple engaged to be married in a few weeks. I knew them both, and they were great kids. They both died within a few hours of each other. The victims' ages have ranged from a fifteen-year-old girl to an eighty-eight-year-old woman."

"How did they present? What were their symptoms?"

"Five of them were already DOA. The others complained of sudden, severe headaches, blurred vision, and dizziness. Some had seizures. Whatever is going on obviously involves the central nervous system. It hits them like a brick. In addition to the headaches and seizures, they lost a sense of balance, even eventually the inability to walk or remain upright. Delirium and confusion, then comatose. All this within a few hours or less."

"What did you find on physical exam?" Brett asked.

"As I said, loss of balance, weakness. They had no muscle reflexes, their pupils were pinpoint, and they couldn't focus. Blood pressure and PO2 were all dangerously low, and they had tachycardia. I noticed the mucosa of their mouth was dry, and they seemed flushed—reddish."

"Sounds like a classic anticholinergic syndrome. I'm guessing something is blocking the acetylcholine. Now, the question is, what?"

She stared in amazement. "Wow, that was a fast diagnosis."

"That's my first guess. Of course, a few other pathological conditions could also cause the same symptoms. Now comes the difficult part—finding out what we're dealing with. What is the cause? Maybe an airborne pathogen, toxins, poisons, or possibly a vector carrying a virus? Several known drugs can cause it, such as phenothiazines, scopolamine—even jimsonweed. The list is extensive. Basically, we know what the result is; now we have to find the cause." He flipped through a second folder. "Other than flushing and redness, any other changes to the skin? Blotches, petechiae, hemorrhaging, or a rash?"

"No, nothing like that. The ultimate cause of death? Your guess is as good as mine. As I said, their PO2 levels were always low, but they were already near death or dying by the time I saw them."

"A fulminate anticholinergic effect on pulmonary and cardiac function. Have any autopsies been done?"

"Look around. See any facility or pathologist to do autopsies? There's no money for that. I did extensive blood cultures and looked at spinal fluids. I sent everything off to the Arizona State labs. Everything was negative. I asked for viral testing, toxicology screens, and anything I could think of. Zilch. Desperate for answers, I contacted the CDC." She paused and let out a slow sigh. "And as I said, that may cost me my job here. Neither the IHS nor the BIA want you here."

Brett frowned at her last statement. "The first two things that came to mind when I heard about your situation here were that you were dealing with either hantavirus or the plague. But it looks like you ruled these out already."

"Hantavirus, the cause of the 'Four Corners' outbreak a few years ago. Yeah, nothing has been identified so far. But the plague? Do you mean bubonic plague, as in the black death of Europe in the seventeenth century?"

"Yes, one and the same. Bacteria *Yersinia pestis* is endemic in the prairie dog population out west here, and every few years there is an outbreak that kills pets and sometimes a few people. But it's easy enough to rule out."

The door opened and the nurse poked her head in. "Sorry to bother you, Dr. Martin, but Chief Jack is on the phone, and there are three patients waiting to see you."

"Thanks, Kit. I'll be right there." Martin turned to Brett. "Chief Jack is the Havasupai tribal chief. He's a good man, but he can be a pain in the ass sometimes. When he focuses on something, he can't let go until he gets his way. Currently, it's about some lease or moving the tribe out of the canyon. I've got the BIA and Department of the Interior on my back, and I don't know which way to turn. That's where you come in. Now you'll have to excuse me. I've got patients waiting for me."

"Go take care of things," Brett said. "I'm going to read through these charts and take some notes."

Dr. Martin grabbed her white coat and stethoscope, took a last sip of coffee, and went to the door. Before leaving, she turned and said, "Thanks again for coming." Then she hesitated, and her smile faded into a frown. "Seriously—bubonic plague?" Then she left and closed the door behind her.

Damnit, Quinn! Another fucked-up mess you've gotten me into. Again!

15

B rett glanced through the charts, but the information was only the usual formal notes regarding their brief medical treatment and deaths that soon followed. As Martin had noted, all the blood and sputum cultures were negative. He realized he would have to go down to the Supai village in the canyon and do more investigation. He wanted to talk to the villagers, get a look around the place, and try to get an idea of where to go from here.

Martin came in two hours later and flopped into her office chair. "Did you find any clues or ideas after going through those reports?"

"No, there's not much to go on. I agree this is a mess that we're going to have to try to find answers to. And do it quickly. Have you explained all this to anyone in charge?" he asked.

"I've explained in detail to the IHS director—my immediate boss—then to the BIA director, and finally to Wainz, the Secretary of the Interior. Up the chain of command it goes. They won't even consider my concerns about this. Instead, they are insisting that the Havasupai leave the canyon immediately. To tell the truth, I'm not sure about their motives for this. I'm not convinced they're insisting on it for strictly medical reasons and concern for the Havasupai," she said. "I think it could be something else. I just can't figure out what other ulterior motive they might have."

"Does the federal government have the authority to force the Havasupai to leave their village?"

"Now you're stepping into very murky waters," Martin said. "Sovereign nation status, earlier treaties with the feds and ownership of the land, tribal council law. The short answer is 'no:' the federal government doesn't have the authority to force the tribe out of the canyon. But they're bringing all kinds of pressure to make that happen. Even Chief Jack is on my case to get them out."

"I need to go down to the village," Brett said.

"When would you want to go? You could be exposing yourself to something very deadly."

"I'll be careful. I'd like to go tomorrow morning, and it'd be nice if you could come too, since you know the people and the village."

"Sorry, but I have several patients booked for tomorrow. In two days—Thursday, I'm scheduled to visit the walk-in clinic there for half a day."

"That will be fine. But I still want to go tomorrow morning. Where do I pick up the helicopter?"

She paused. "There's a pad outside, but I'll have to see if the helicopter can be available tomorrow."

"Let's make sure we're clear on something," Brett said. "Whenever I need to go down there to do my work, that should be considered an emergency. We need free, and possibly frequent, access as needed at a moment's notice. If they give you any trouble about that, let me know and I will take care of it."

She nodded, then asked, "Where are you staying?"

"We have a room at The Laredo Inn."

"*We?*" she asked. "Is there someone—"

"No. Just me and Tequila. I'll see you tomorrow."

Brett left, climbed into the Jeep, and sped away.

He would be going down into a canyon tomorrow where at least twelve people had died suddenly, with no possible explanation in sight.

Just great, he thought. What could possibly go wrong?

16

Twelve dead so far, the ghost thought. And all within a period of twelve days. Twelve within twelve. There was a kind of symmetry that made Ghost smile. Quick and easy. And one vial is gone.

He was hiking two miles downstream from the Supai village to his camp. It was practically invisible to hikers and anyone rafting down the Colorado River. And since the trail into the canyon had been closed to the public, the chance of being detected by anyone was nil...well, except for the few canyon wrens that perched on the outcrops above him.

Unfortunately, the canyon blocked any cell signals, so he had to get to the top rim to communicate and to learn if any new instructions had come in.

He couldn't use the switchback trail during daylight hours, since all traffic was forbidden, and also, he couldn't take the chance of being spotted during daylight. The cartel would never stop looking for him. He had to remain diligent every moment of every day. He'd learned that over a thousand Hispanic men and women worked at the South Rim area, working as highway maintenance, groundskeepers, cooks at restaurants, chamber maids, bus drivers, etc. If someone even remotely associated with the cartel happened to spot him just by chance, the cartel would have him within hours. He didn't live in fear. He lived by being virtually invisible. And by being cautious to a fault.

He decided he'd have to hike up the trail to the top mesa tonight to get any new text messages that might have been sent. More than eight miles up the switchbacks in total darkness. Then eight back down again. During the darkness of night was when the aggressive diamondback rattlesnakes and scorpions came out. There was also a rattlesnake called the Grand Canyon rattler and—like the ghost himself—was nearly invisible.

It promised to be a busy and tiring night. Once he arrived at his hidden camp, he crawled inside his well-camouflaged tent to catch up on some sleep before his trip up.

17

The next morning, Brett got up early and went for a long run with Tequila along a trail where he could see the magnificent sunrise glowing in the Grand Canyon. He ran hard over a route that he guessed to be about six miles round trip back to the room. He wanted Tequila to get a good workout since he'd be leaving him in the room for the day while he flew down into the canyon.

He showered, put on clean clothes, and grabbed a quick breakfast. Then he drove his Jeep to the hospital and pulled up beside the waiting helicopter.

Brett tossed his canvas backpack containing his laptop, latex gloves, and surgical masks, along with minor medical supplies, into the helicopter as he climbed in. The pilot turned and handed him a set of headphones. "Morning. I'm Tim Reiser, and I'm going to take you down this morning. Put these on so we can talk. They'll also block out most of the engine noise."

Tim wore a green nylon flight suit, black laced-up boots, and reflective Ray Bans. He looked like he'd just come from the set of *Top Gun*. Brett smiled and gave him a thumbs-up.

They landed in an open area in the Supai village and Brett jumped out. He handed the headset back to Tim and gave him a thumbs-up again to say 'thanks.' He grabbed his backpack and went to the small walk-in clinic, a brown wooden building of log construction, with a green metal roof.

The nurse practitioner, wearing surgical scrubs and a mask, met him at the door. Brett slipped his mask on as well. "Good morning, Dr. Carson. I'm Julie Burkhart, the certified nurse practitioner here at the clinic," she said, as she extended her hand. "Please come in. I'm glad you're here. Would you like some coffee?"

"Sure. Thanks."

He glanced around while she left to get coffee. The clinic had a small waiting room, a medical supply closet, and a combination treatment and examining room. There were no patients waiting.

She returned with two coffees and pointed to a desk, where they both sat down. "Thanks for the coffee, Julie. Tell me what you know so far. Dr. Martin was able to fill me in on quite a bit, but I would like to hear your take on this."

Julie slipped off her mask and sipped her coffee. "As you probably already know, twelve people in the village have died within the past two weeks. The most recent victim—Daniel Ortege—was found unconscious by the river where he was fishing. I ran over and tried to stabilize him while waiting for the helicopter, but he died soon after we got him to the hospital. His girlfriend—his fiancée, actually—was found dead."

"Tell me about Daniel. What did you see when you got to him?"

"He was unconscious, barely breathing, thready pulse, and tachycardia."

"Fever? Sweating? Rash? Bleeding? Anything else visible?"

"It all happened so fast, I didn't even have time to start an IV. We found him facedown by the river, saw his condition, and called immediately for the chopper. When they loaded him into the chopper, I noticed his face seemed flushed."

Brett nodded and thought for a moment. "Did you see any of the others before they died? Did any friends or family members tell you about any symptoms? Coughing, choking, nausea, anything?"

"Sorry, no," Julie said. "It's strange. It's like blam, blam, blam. They look startled, fumble, fall, and soon after, die. Just like that. I have to tell you, I'm scared for everyone in the village. And for myself."

He could see the fear on her face. "That's understandable, Julie. It's very brave of you to stay down here to take care of every-one. Have any dogs or other animals in the village been sick?"

"Not that I know of."

"You've been with several of them when they were actually dying, or already dead."

"Yes..."

"I'm wondering why you haven't gotten sick. Do you wonder how you've dodged this thing?"

"Every day I ask myself, am I going to be the next person to succumb?" She looked down for a moment, then said, "Dr. Martin is in a heck of a jam, trying to decide what to do with the rest of the tribe here in the canyon. She's already issued an emergency cancellation of all tourists, climbers, and any visitors to this part of the canyon owned by the Havasupai."

Brett nodded, then said, "She already told me there haven't been any autopsies. Did you get any blood samples, sputum, or cultures? Anything I can have to get evaluated?"

Julie went to the freezer and pulled out a small tray holding four tubes of blood. "These are the only samples I have. Their names are on the tubes."

"Great. That's a start. I need to ship these to our lab in Atlanta ASAP. And I need to interview everyone who was around or near the victims when they died. I saw on the Grand Canyon map that there is a place called Phantom Ranch. Has it also been restricted and closed off to visitors?"

"No. That's part of the national park system, and we have no control over it. Only this village and the land around it are part of the Havasupai reservation and are not actually a part of the national park."

"Have there been any cases from Phantom Ranch or other areas in the canyon that you know of?"

"None that I've heard of, and even though we are not associated with them, we would have heard of any cases. And they are aware of what we are dealing with. The National Park Service people in charge have chosen not to quarantine any part of the rest of the canyon outside of the reservation." She thought a moment, then added, "If you're going to explore any of the canyon on foot, Bright Angel Pass is twenty-four miles south and relatively easy. But North Kaibab Trail is brutal. Don't even think about it unless you're well prepared."

"My first priority is to get the blood samples back to Atlanta and get a team out here to help me." He knew this had the makings of one hell of a medical and political nightmare. Julie called for the helicopter to take him back up.

"Thanks for the coffee and your help here, Julie. I'll be back tomorrow with Dr. Martin. Be careful and let us know if anything happens before we get back."

"No problem. As you can see, the clinic is deserted for now. No one wants to come here, and there are none of the tourists that usually fill the place, since we are essentially under lockdown."

"I understand that the chief of the tribe also thinks everybody should be moved out of the village and up to the mesa."

"Yes, Chief Jack has also been putting a lot of pressure on Dr. Martin to evacuate the village."

"I'd like to talk to the chief. Can you arrange for him to meet me down here tomorrow?"

"That won't be possible. He's in Washington on business."

"What kind of business does he have in Washington?"

"You'll have to ask him when you see him. Whenever he gets back."

Brett nodded. He carefully packed the blood samples and went to meet the copter.

18

Stewart Lee Udall Building
Department of the Interior
Washington, DC

Secretary Wainz stared across his desk at the man sitting in a chair on the other side. "Chief, I'm really concerned about the safety of your people in the canyon. We need to get them out of there."

"How are you going to do that?"

"We need to put more pressure on the tribal council. They have to know we're concerned about the safety of their people. And that's where you come in. I need your help with this."

Chief Jack wasn't buying that for a moment. It also didn't explain the push by the Department of the Interior to also try and get a mining lease permit from the Havasupai. No—there was something else going on. He just couldn't figure out what.

"I've talked to the public health doctor," the chief said, "but she still refuses to move them. There's a doctor from the CDC there now. Maybe he'll convince her to move the tribe up to the mesa."

Wainz's face stiffened. "The CDC? How did they get involved in this?"

"I don't know. You'll have to ask them."

Wainz looked out the window, collecting his thoughts. He turned and looked at the chief. "Chief, I need you to try harder to convince the tribal council. This is an urgent matter. I'll contact the CDC and find out why the hell they're involved."

"You sound upset. We are glad that the CDC got involved and are out there to help our tribe." The chief paused a moment, then asked, "What's more important to you? Moving our tribe out of the canyon or getting the lease signed?"

The question caught Wainz off guard. He stared back at the chief without answering.

"That's what I thought." Chief Jack nodded, slowly stood up, and left the office.

Wainz picked up his private phone and texted the ghost.

> There is a doctor from the CDC there in the canyon.

> Find out everything you can about him

> Let me know what he's doing there

Wainz put the phone back in a drawer and locked it. Things were moving too slowly and creating the possibility that it could spiral out of control. He couldn't let that happen. The White House was on his ass as it was. The last thing he needed was more outside interference.

He punched a button on his desk. "Karen, get the director of the CDC on the phone."

———

Brett collected the few samples of spinal fluid, blood, and sputum cultures that Martin had collected on the victims at the hospital and packaged those along with the blood samples from Julie. The pilot assured Brett that he would get them packed with dry ice, then send them by express to the CDC labs.

"Thanks for taking care of this, Tim. How can I reach you when I need you?"

"Just tell Dr. Martin. She knows how to contact me. I'm already scheduled to take both of you back down tomorrow, same time."

Brett put his headphones back in the chopper and gave Tim a thumbs-up.

With the loud beating of its rotors increasing in tempo, the helicopter took off toward the airport in Flagstaff. Its prop wash sent dust and tumbleweeds blowing in all directions. Brett watched it until it was just a speck and silence returned.

He had several important phone calls to make. He jumped in the Jeep and drove back to The Laredo Inn. He first had to deal with Tequila, who'd need a good run and some play time after being cooped up all day.

He pulled up to the front door of the inn, went to his room, unlocked the door, and went in. Tequila came barreling out past him, ran down the hall, out the front door, and jumped up into the back seat. Brett caught up and grabbed Tequila by the furry neck and wrestled with him for a few minutes, then climbed in and drove to a nearby park in the center of Parker. Huge cotton-woods lined a small stream that ran through the park.

He pulled under the shade of a tall cottonwood. The large, leathery leaves rustled in the breeze, while some floated down in spirals. Tequila jumped down and ran over to greet a golden retriever, who at first seemed intimidated by Tequila's size. After a few minutes, they ran off together to play in the grass.

Brett's first call was to the CDC's Bio-4 lab.

"You've reached the Biological Secure Laboratory. How may I direct your call?"

"Hi, Denise. This is Brett Carson. Would you put me through to Janet Boggs in Bio-4?"

"Hi, Dr. Carson. Sure, just a minute."

Janet Boggs, MD, oversaw Bio-4. She was a brilliant medical investigator, part geneticist, part detective. She had a PhD in microbiology, a medical degree from Stanford, and was board certified in infectious diseases. She was the most experienced and knowledgeable person in Bio-4. In short, she was a whiz and able to find answers that seemed to elude everyone else, and far faster than anyone thought possible.

"So," she said, "I hear you're out west on vacation in the Grand Canyon, huh? Must be nice."

Brett smiled at her witty comments. Just being around her or hearing her voice always made him smile. "Sure, it's great, as long as I don't die."

"Don't you remember the song 'Only the Good Die Young?' You're not that good, and you're not that young, so don't worry. You won't die. At least for a while."

After a good laugh, he explained the full situation to her about the unexplained deaths in the canyon. "I've sent you blood, CSF fluid, and sputum samples from a few of the victims. The Arizona State Lab was unable to turn up anything."

"What's your best guess?" she asked.

"I doubt it's poison or toxin, but I can't rule that out yet. Best guess is that it's a virus. There's something very strange about this—I just can't figure out what it is yet."

"We'll get on it as soon as we get the samples. And Brett—"

"Yeah?"

"Take care of yourself."

Tequila had returned from romping around the park with the retriever, drank a full pan of water, found a spot in the shade beside Brett, and stretched out. Brett looked at his phone. One call down, two more to go. He punched in the next number.

"Quinn here."

"Mitch, you've got to work on your phone etiquette. You sound more like a city editor rather than the director of EIS."

"Nice talking to you too, Brett. How's it going out there?"

"It's a hell of a mess here. I need a team out here as soon as possible to help me. And make sure Ross Solt is part of the team." He went on to explain the situation to Quinn and told him of the conundrum of whether to move the tribe out of the canyon. "The Arizona State Health Department worked for a week on this, but they couldn't come up with any answers. I've sent a few samples to Boggs in Bio-4. Maybe she can come up with some answers."

"I can probably get a team out there in the next couple of days. They'll either fly into Vegas or Flagstaff, depending on flight availability. Be careful on this one, Brett. Where are you staying?"

"At The Laredo Inn near Parker, Arizona."

"Good. I'll get rooms there for everyone. Anything else?"

"No, not at this point."

Brett hung up. His next phone call would be his hardest. He punched in her number and braced himself.

"Brett, I'm so glad you called. Are you back from Arizona? How did it go?"

"I'm still in Arizona. We have a real mess out here. Quinn is sending a team out here to help me." He could hear her sighing on the other end.

"Is Ross with you?" she asked.

"No, a team is coming out in a couple of days, and Ross should be with them. The bottom line is, I won't be able to see you this weekend or next week."

"Yeah, I'd already figured that out. That's the third time in a row that your trip here has been canceled."

"You know how much I want to see you and be with you. Unfortunately, my job—"

"Yes, your *job* keeps getting in the way. I'm starting to think it will always be like this, won't it? Both of us are trying to find time in our jobs so we can be together. So far, I'd say we're not too successful at it. It seems like we're destined to just be close friends with incredible benefits."

He could hear the disappointment in her voice. "Kari, after this assignment, I'm coming to see you. Period. I'll quit before I let them stick me with another job before I get to see you. Just hearing your voice makes me miss you that much more. Please understand, I don't want it to be like this. We'll figure something out."

"George has already offered to take me out for my birthday next weekend in case something like this happened. So, I'll be fine. In fact, he's taking me out to dinner tonight."

"George?"

"George Pettit. I've mentioned him to you before."

"The rock man. You've been seeing a lot of him."

"Geologist. He's an associate professor of geology. And I've known him since junior high. He's great company to share dinner with."

Brett was silent for a moment.

"What—are you jealous or something?" she asked.

"No, just mad as hell and disappointed that I won't be able to be there for your birthday. I'll try to make it up to you." After a moment, he said, "Okay, maybe I'm a little jealous."

She laughed. "Oh—he's here now. Sorry, I gotta run. Call me whenever you get the chance. I love you, Brett. Take care of yourself."

The rock man? Did he actually say that? He realized he'd

sounded and acted like a stupid, insecure, jealous high school kid. Which, at the moment, pretty much described him.

———

After he left the park, he grabbed a pizza and a six-pack of Blue Moon on the way back to the room. After a refreshing shower and a change of clothes, he ate the entire pizza, drank two beers, and stretched out on the bed. His mind was swirling with thoughts of Kari with the geologist, of the dead Havasupai, of the work that faced him and the team in the coming days...but mostly how much he missed Kari. And worried that he might have to choose between his work and the woman he loved.

He had to get out of the room. Brett grabbed his guitar, signaled for Tequila to follow him, and they both left the inn and climbed into the Jeep. He drove to a small parking lot and walked out to a ledge on the South Rim, onto a large, flat rock overlooking the vast network of cliffs and deep canyons. The sun hanging low in the sky, just over the horizon, bathed the landscape in brilliant orange. A cool breeze rustled dry leaves and weeds, but the wide, expansive area was otherwise silent. The scent of ponderosa pine and mesquite was carried in the breeze. Looking out over the vast rock layers and empty deep canyons, he felt a deep loneliness, even with his dog beside him.

He held his guitar and began to play. Soothing, classic guitar music floated over the canyons. He played song after song as the sun sank lower, the orange light began to fade, shadows grew longer, and the breeze grew colder. After an hour, he stopped, ruffled Tequila's fur, and stood up. He turned around and saw a large group of people silently watching him. Then they spontaneously broke into a loud applause.

"Fantastic."

"Beautiful."

"How incredible to watch the sunset to such wonderful music."

"Thank you."

The accolades from the gathering crowd continued.

Brett smiled at them, waved a 'thank you,' and climbed into his Jeep.

A few people walked over and asked if he was going to be playing every evening. He thanked them but explained that he felt especially melancholy tonight and just needed to play. "I'll probably play again sometime, just don't know when," he said. "I'm glad you enjoyed it."

The children were at first leery of Tequila due to his size, but in a few minutes, they knew they'd found a friend. They ran around and chased Tequila and each other to a background of happy squeals and barking. After a few minutes, Brett gave a sharp whistle and Tequila immediately went to the Jeep and jumped in. Brett started the bullet-ridden Jeep, waved to everyone again, and drove off back to the inn.

What a day....

19

The following morning, Brett met Jo Martin at the hospital, and they went out to catch the helicopter. While they were waiting, Brett turned to Martin and asked, "Why is Chief Jack pressuring you to evacuate the village and relocate everyone up here?"

"I don't know. You'll have to ask him."

"And why is he in Washington? What kind of business does he have there?"

Martin glanced up at the helicopter as it flew over the town and prepared to land. "The chief is an interesting man. Most of the time, he's an okay guy. But yeah, recently he's been a real pain in the ass regarding evacuating the village. And I have no idea why he's in Washington."

The helicopter landed, and the pilot handed them headphones as they climbed in. Fifteen minutes later, the copter rotated and then landed smoothly. Before Brett took off his headphones, he said, "Thanks again, Tim. See you later this afternoon." Then he climbed out and gave a thumbs-up. The blades accelerated to a high rate along with a deafening thump-thump-thump as the copter rose, turned, and flew away.

They met Julie in the clinic building and planned their day over fresh coffee. They met with dozens of families and friends of victims and questioned them extensively about what happened, any symptoms they noticed, any different foods they may have eaten, etc. Brett questioned people about pets, livestock, or any dead wildlife they may have found. Brett also asked if any of them had seen any hikers or climbers that seemed sick. So far, everything they inquired about only returned negative responses. They had learned nothing of interest or importance during the entire day. That didn't mean that it was a wasted day. Brett now had some ideas about what they might be dealing with.

"Are there any cases other than here in Supai Village?" Brett asked.

"No," Martin said. "I checked, and there haven't been any reported. There are a few dozen campsites in the canyon, as well as Phantom Ranch and three ranger stations, and none have reported any sickness or deaths. Just here in this village. I'm starting to question my judgment about having the villagers remain down here. Apparently, only those down here are at risk, and nowhere else in the entire national park."

He'd already formed an opinion that whatever the cause, it wasn't contagious. That fact was somewhat comforting to him regarding his own safety and that of the staff and villagers, but he still didn't know the etiology.

"Whatever is killing them, it doesn't seem to be contagious. When the team gets here tomorrow, they'll start testing water, soil, animals, and insects, looking for toxins, poisons, whatever, in addition to infectious agents. Thanks to all the help from both of you, we did a thorough initial evaluation of the situation." Brett turned to Martin. "Maybe I'll hear something about the samples I sent back to our CDC lab. Let's catch the helicopter and go home."

The four-person team, which included Solt, arrived the following afternoon in Parker. They had flown from Atlanta to Phoenix, then caught another plane to Flagstaff, and finally drove over the mountains to the Grand Canyon. After everyone got settled into their rooms, they went down to the dining room to meet Dr. Martin. Brett introduced her to everyone.

"Thanks, everybody, for coming here to help us," Martin said. "And please call me Jo."

After everyone had eaten and finished their desserts and coffee, Brett addressed them. "Dr. Martin—Jo—has a decision to make here regarding whether or not to recommend moving the tribe out of the canyon. From the information we've learned so far, whatever is killing victims doesn't seem to be contagious, not spread person-to-person. It could be something ingested by the victim and, therefore, doesn't spread from person to person. Or it could be carried by a vector such as mosquitos, or like the hantavirus—carried in the dust from mouse droppings. Of course, that's just a theory at this point based on the information we've gathered so far.

"We need to still be very cautious when we're down there. There's no cell phone service in the canyon. A helicopter will take us down and bring us back up each day. Jo contacted the Phantom Ranch, several ranger stations, and campsites. But the only deaths reported so far have all been restricted to the Supai village.

"As usual, we need food, plants, and water supplies tested. We need air samples for testing. All livestock and any wildlife we capture must be examined and cultured. It's my opinion that there is no reason at this point to recommend that the Havasupai move out of the canyon. I think Jo's first instincts were correct. Jo, do you have anything to add?" he asked as he turned to her.

"First of all, as I said earlier, we are grateful to have all of you here to help us. If my staff and I can be of any help to you, or if you need anything, please let me know."

Brett, along with the rest of the team, went into the lounge area for a round of drinks after a long day of travel. He and Solt found a table and sat down with their drinks.

"So, what are we dealing with here?" Solt asked.

"Not sure. From what I've been able to learn so far, all twelve victims appeared to have died within twelve to twenty-four hours of their first symptoms. Of course, there haven't been any autopsies, so events like intracranial hemorrhage, heart attacks, or pulmonary emboli can't be ruled out. But none of the physical findings or lab tests suggest any of those. Other than some type of poison or deadly toxin, what else could kill so quickly? Things just don't add up, and we better figure out what's going on before we have more deaths to deal with."

———

Late that night, Ghost scrambled up the trail to the South Rim, well after midnight. He settled down behind a large bush and turned on his phone. As expected, there was a text from Wainz:

> What have you learned about the CDC doctor out there?

Ghost was surprised the Secretary apparently didn't know that a team of four others had arrived yesterday. Ghost quickly typed out a text and hit send:

> His name is Carson

> Team of 4 others from CDC also arrived today

> One vial gone, two vials left

Twelve dead

Advise

Ghost waited to make sure his message was sent. He didn't expect a reply, but would wait an hour to make sure.

Back in Washington, after two glasses of scotch, Wainz was sleepy. He yawned and rubbed his eyes as he read the text. Suddenly, he was wide awake. A team of four had also arrived. What did that mean? He feared that things could quickly get out of hand.

He immediately texted back to the ghost:

Stay close to Carson.

Tell me what he does, who he contacts.

Everything.

Keep me informed.

Ghost turned off his phone. Before heading back down, he slipped into a large public restroom by a large parking lot. He charged his phone while freshening up and using the facilities. The latest text was troubling. This had turned into a different kind of assignment, one that was outside his skill set, and he didn't like it. He wasn't some kind of intelligence-gathering spy—he was a killer, plain and simple. He made people disappear. He would have to think about this and consider his next move. He needed a plan. The problem was, nothing came to mind.

He knew he couldn't continue climbing up to the top every night, then all the way back down. The trail was too risky at night and took too long. He needed a place halfway down, some place he could get to either the bottom or back to the top in short order. If he were to shadow Carson, that meant he had to be able to move more quickly, either at the top or down at the bottom of the canyon.

After his phone was fully charged, he picked up sandwiches and beer at an all-night convenience store in Parker, then started back down. Halfway down the trail, he stopped to eat one of the sandwiches and down a beer. The night air was cold. A great horned owl called somewhere off in the distance, and stars dotted the otherwise black sky.

Ghost was comfortable in the wild and knew how to take care of himself. But he had to admit that scrambling up the trail with a vertical height of over a mile had taken its toll on him. He'd have to come up with a better plan. Once down, he finally crawled into his hidden spot and immediately fell asleep.

20

Brett and the rest of the team spent the next week doing extensive testing of everyone in the village, getting samples of water, air, every plant and animal, collecting blood and saliva samples, and sending dozens of tubes back express each night to the CDC labs. Now all they could do was wait for answers—if any were forthcoming. After a full week of collecting samples from everything and everyone, they were finishing up for the day and waiting for the helicopter to take them back up when Martin and a man he had never seen before walked up.

"Brett, I'd like you to meet Chief Jack."

Brett shook his hand. "Chief, it's an honor to meet you. Thanks for taking the time to help us with some questions." He guessed the man to be in his early seventies with long silver hair pulled back in a ponytail and stood ramrod straight. Deep furrows crisscrossed his face, etched by the western sun and wind. He wore jeans, boots, and a suede fringed jacket. A necklace made of a thin leather strand and wooden carved tokens hung from his neck. He could have passed for a model for the Indian nickel. He was, Brett thought, exactly what he thought an Indian chief would look like.

"My name is *Jacq-teh Kwa-ki*, meaning 'the Path of the Bear.' But since most people outside the tribe can't pronounce it, they just call me Chief Jack," he said with a big smile. "And I thank you and your team for coming to help our people. It's sad that twelve have already died so far. I fear for our tribe if they stay in the village, but the tribal council refuses to listen. They can't risk losing their land here forever."

"Dr. Martin explained to us the problem if they leave the canyon," Brett said. "I hope we can get some answers soon to figure out what's going on. Can I ask, why were you in Washington? I presume it had something to do with the crisis here?"

"My presence was requested there, and yes, the meeting was about the problem here. They want me to convince the tribal council to move our people out of the canyon."

"Who exactly are *they*?" Brett asked.

"The Department of the Interior," the chief said. "The BIA oversees the various tribes, but the Interior oversees them. Department of the Interior is ultimately in charge. They also want a mineral lease signed, but the tribal council refuses that, too."

"A lease for what? Does that have anything to do with the situation out here?"

"That's all I know currently. If I learn anything that will help you, I'll let you know."

The loud beating of the helicopter grew in the distance.

"Chief Jack, it was nice meeting you."

The man seemed as if he had the weight of the world on his shoulders as he walked away.

"I like him," Brett said to Martin. "But I get the impression something else is bothering him."

"That's stating the obvious. He's got a lot on his mind right now with everything that's going on," she said.

"Yeah, probably," Brett said. But he thought there was more to it.

Tim landed the copter, everyone climbed in, and they flew back up to the Laredo for some downtime.

———

Two hours later, Brett and the rest of the team were in the restaurant at The Laredo Inn, finishing their meals and having drinks after completing a full week's work. He was sitting at a table by a window with his best friend Solt.

"So now what?" Solt asked. "Any out-of-the-box ideas this time?" He was referring to the fact that Brett had solved the devastating situation in Nova Scotia.

"Nope," Brett said. "No ideas yet. It doesn't add up. Twelve sudden unexplained deaths over a short period of time. Then none since we showed up. Why do you think that is? I feel like I'm missing something obvious, I just can't figure out what it is. And what was that thing about a lease that Chief Jack mentioned?"

"I don't know, but I can't see how that has anything to do with whatever is killing the Havasupai."

"And there's another thing that doesn't make sense," Brett said. "Nobody other than the Havasupai has been even sick, let alone die. That includes Julie at the clinic, Dr. Martin, scores of hikers, and guests at Phantom Ranch or anywhere else in the canyon. Whatever it is obviously doesn't seem to spread person-to-person."

"So that leaves the question, what is the vector?" Solt added. "I still think it could be a variant of the hantavirus carried in mouse turds."

A waitress walked over to their table.

"Dr. Carson, there's a phone call for you. She said it's urgent."

21

Brett realized he'd forgotten to turn his cell phone back on after coming back from the canyon. He hoped it was Kari, and he raced over to the bar and picked up the receiver. "Hello?"

"Brett—you have to get back here. You're not going to believe what I uncovered."

He knew the voice on the other end. "Boggs, what are you talking about? Can't you just tell me and save me a trip?"

After a brief pause, she answered, "Not over the phone."

"What did you find that you can't just tell me?"

Silence.

"Seriously?" Brett asked. "You really need me back there? The team is here and I can't just leave."

Her answer was abrupt. "How soon can you get here?"

After letting out a deep breath and thinking for a moment, he said, "Okay, I'll try to get a red-eye flight back tonight, if I can arrange it. I should be back sometime early tomorrow."

"Meet me at my office. I'll be there by six tomorrow morning. Don't mention this to anyone else. See you tomorrow morning."

The line went dead.

What had she discovered that could be so damned important? And why was she being so secretive about it? He paused to compose himself as he returned to the table and sat down. He leaned over to Solt and spoke softly. "Ross, I've got to fly back to Atlanta right away. I should only be gone for a day or two, maybe even back by tomorrow night."

"What's up? Everything okay?"

"Don't know yet. That's why I'm flying back. I'll fill you in as soon as I learn more."

Solt, obviously curious, said, "So at least give me a hint about what's going on."

"I think Boggs may have uncovered something. It sounds complicated. I'm leaving tonight if I can arrange a red-eye. I have a large suite upstairs. Use my room while I'm gone, and you can take care of Tequila."

He dropped his extra room key on the table and walked away.

———

At fifteen minutes past midnight, Brett watched out the window of Southwest Airlines flight 225 as it raced down the tarmac and rose into the dark sky. The lights of Flagstaff receded below. He was exhausted after a full day of questioning and examining almost everyone in the Supai village. He'd been looking forward to a full night's sleep after dinner and drinks with the team. Instead, he'd spent two frantic hours packing, getting a ticket to Atlanta, turning Tequila over to Solt, and driving his Jeep through the mountains at night to get to Flagstaff Pulliam Airport in time for the red-eye to Atlanta. This flight would take more than five hours, with a plane change in Phoenix. He planned to get some much-needed sleep.

He turned off the overhead light, put his seatback down, and closed his eyes. The cabin lights were dimmed and most of the passengers appeared to be dozing, some with blankets pulled up. But sleep eluded him. His mind kept going through all the possibilities of what Janet Boggs might have discovered. Actually, she hadn't said what she'd discovered, but rather what she had *uncovered*. What could that mean? Why was it so secret? He'd already decided that he was going to stop in Chicago on his return trip and have an overnight with Kari before heading back to Arizona.

Eventually, the drone of the engines, combined with fatigue, won out, and he fell into a deep sleep.

———

ATLANTA

After landing at Atlanta's Hartsfield-Jackson International Airport at five thirty in the morning, he took a cab to his condo, handed money to the driver, and asked him to wait twenty minutes for him. The condo was dark, quiet, and seemed empty without Tequila's presence. He took a hot shower, put on clean clothes, and went back out to the waiting cab.

The cab dropped him off, and he grabbed a cup of coffee and a chocolate-filled croissant at the coffee shop across from the Centers for Disease Control and Prevention campus and walked to the Davis building that housed the Biological Level Four Research Laboratory—known simply as 'Bio-4' to those who worked there. Other countries had their own biological level four high-risk medical laboratories, but the one on the CDC campus was the largest non-military research laboratory. It dealt with diseases and infections from all over the world.

Conversely, four countries—the United States, England, Russia, and China—had among them the four largest biological level four high-risk military research laboratories. The research they did was focused on biological weaponry uses. Places like the

Plum Island Military Research Facility in New York, and the US Army Combat Capabilities Development Command (DEVCOM) Army Research Laboratory. But here in Atlanta, they were trying to save lives, not figure out ways to end them.

Trees lining the sidewalks threw spindly shadows from the streetlights as early dawn orange appeared on the horizon. Leaves crunched under his feet. With an uneasy feeling, he kept glancing around at the predawn empty sidewalks as he finished off his croissant.

He swiped his card, punched in the code, and pressed his hand against the biometrics pad to open the main door to the Davis building, then went inside. The building was empty and the sound of his shoes on the marble floor echoed in the large hall-way. He went to the elevator, took it up to the top floor, then walked to Janet Boggs's office. She opened the door before he knocked, pulled him inside, and locked the door behind them.

Boggs was wearing scrubs. Her eyes were dark, and she looked like she hadn't slept in days. "Janet, what the hell is going on? What's so secre—"

"You've got a virus out there," she said. "Just as you suspected. And it's not an ordinary virus."

"You've already identified it?"

"Yes. And here's the real kicker. This virus came from the DSTL lab in England."

"How could you possibly know that?" he asked.

"Because the DNA virtually matches a virus we know they were studying. But this one has been altered, probably CRISPR genome editing to create and modify this virus." She was referring to Clustered Regularly Interspaced Short Palindromic Repeats—a newly discovered technique in molecular biology that was a method for taking apart a virus and giving any property to the virus that was desired. That discovery had earned two researchers the Nobel Prize.

"It's been biologically engineered with a gain-of-function to become a lethal killer," she added.

Brett stood there for a moment, digesting the news. Then he said, "If you are right about its origin, maybe the virus accidentally escaped from the lab and—"

"Yeah, then somehow made its way from the lab in England to Indians living at the bottom of the Grand Canyon. You *do* realize how crazy that sounds, don't you?"

She unlocked a cabinet, pulled out a folder, then sat down at her desk and pointed to a chair for him. "I've checked the DNA three times, and there is no doubt this virus came from the UK's lab. It's definitely from the DSTL. And that opens an entirely new set of problems and questions."

She opened the folder and pointed to a printout showing matching DNA printouts.

"Go on," he said.

She slid the folder across the desk to him. "First, the obvious, as you already mentioned. How does a manufactured virus get from a secret military biological laboratory in England to Indians in the Grand Canyon?" she asked. "The possibilities for that are both numerous and absolutely frightening."

"Why would anyone want to get the virus from the DSTL lab and take it to the Grand Canyon?" Brett asked. "For what possible purpose?"

Boggs looked at him for a long minute, then she said quietly, "More important than 'why' is the question of *who*? Who could be involved? An individual? Terrorists? Or even possibly some secret government agency? Do you see where I'm going with this?"

"And why specifically did it spread to the Havasupai Indians?" he pondered. "Were they being used as a collective test tube since they are isolated in the canyon? But if that were the case, why not use people isolated on any number of small islands closer to the UK?"

"Or why not try it out in a prison where it's a controlled and isolated environment?" Boggs wondered. "Why go all the way to Arizona?"

"If you're right about this," he said, "it means we're talking about the mass murder of at least twelve people that we know of. Why do you think they would even try to make a killer virus like this in the first place?"

"That part is easy," Boggs said as she stood to get the coffee pot to refill their cups. "If you are an invading army and want to take over a city, you can shell it and bomb it. But that leaves buildings in ruins and the infrastructure destroyed. No electricity or running water. The city has to be rebuilt. But if you can just kill the people, the city is still there instead of a pile of rubble. And if the virus doesn't spread from person to person, there is no danger of creating an uncontained epidemic."

"The perfect weapon," Brett said. "That introduces another very big complication. Whoever did this will probably do anything to keep it secret. And if a government agency is somehow involved, they would have lots of resources available to them to make sure it stays a secret."

"Exactly the conclusion I've already made," Boggs said. "That's why I wanted to keep this quiet until we can figure out what's going on. Whoever is involved will probably do whatever is necessary to cover this up. Could be some foreign government."

They stood staring at each other as they considered what was happening.

"Maybe even be our own?" she asked softly.

"Whoever's involved, this means we could be in serious danger when they find out we know about it," Brett stated. "Have you discussed this with anyone else?"

"Nobody. Only you and I know about it at this point," she said quietly, while glancing at her locked office door. "I isolated the virus and did the DNA testing myself. When the rest of the staff in

Bio-4 asked what was happening with the samples you sent, I made light of it and shrugged it off. And I deleted all the information on this from the computers. I have copies of all the tests locked in my office here."

"You are absolutely certain—"

"One hundred percent," she said, anticipating his question. "All the test results are there in the folder. So, where do we go from here?"

"Your job is done for now. Just keep it quiet and deny any knowledge of the virus. For now, I will tell the team in Arizona that we are still looking and considering everything. But my next move is to go to England and see if I can learn something there."

"England? Are you out of your effing mind? As soon as you start asking questions, whoever is involved will soon figure out that we've found something. And then we could really be in trouble."

"For now, nobody has to know that you are involved or have any knowledge of this. I will take all the responsibility for now. And I will hedge and tell them we suspect something but have no definite proof at this point. Hopefully, that will buy us some time to sort this out. We don't know for certain that we are in any danger, but we have to assume we could be, so be extra cautious."

"You're really going to England? You know you're crazy, don't you?" she asked.

"That's what they tell me."

"Take care of yourself, Brett."

"Don't I always?"

"No, you don't," she said as she watched one of her best friends walk away.

22

B rett needed to talk to Quinn, but it was still early, and he probably wouldn't be in his office yet. The morning sun had already burned off the early morning chill as he walked across the quadrangle to his office. He turned on his computer and researched any information he could find on the UK's Defense Science and Technology Laboratories, known as the DSTL.

It was located in Wiltshire, England, just northeast of the village of Porton, near Salisbury. It was southwest of London, and a hundred kilometers from the English Channel. Other than the fact that it was reported to be a CBRN facility—the military acronym for Chemical, Biological, Radioactive, and Nuclear Weapons research facility—not much else was available to him. A plan began to form in his mind. First, he had to clear up a few things.

It was too early to call Solt, who was in the mountain time zone and two hours earlier than Atlanta. Besides, waking Solt up this early would not be a pretty sight—kind of like poking a bear in hibernation. That call would definitely have to wait. Kari was on central time in Chicago and so it was also too early to call her. He dialed Quinn's office.

Quinn's phone rang several times, but there was no answer. Brett knew where he would probably find him, so he left his office and walked to C Building. He punched in his code, and the frosted glass doors slid open to reveal a large rectangular room the size of a gymnasium filled with electronic communications equipment. The CDC's Emergency Operations Center, known simply as the EOC, was a highly sophisticated medical intelligence war room filled with rows of computers, fax machines, and dozens of phones, all focused on the most current diseases around the world. Huge flat-panel monitors filled the wall along the front of the massive room, some displaying various detailed maps, some displaying hot spots of diseases around the globe with updates as they arrived.

More than seventy personnel staffed the center. The intelligence nerve center was tied directly to the Department of Defense and its bioterrorism division. It also tapped into every state health department and the World Health Organization.

The people in the command center had been tracking mad cow disease, SARS, West Nile, bubonic plague, avian flu virus, the resurgence of Ebola, swine flu, and a particularly virulent strain of tuberculosis. He noticed that the outbreak among the Havasupai in Arizona had been moved to the top of the priority list.

Brett saw Quinn sitting at a monitor, talking to one of the technicians assigned there. Quinn turned with a surprised look on his face when he saw Brett walking toward him. "What the...? This is never a good sign," Quinn said. "Why aren't you in Arizona? I sent a team as you requested, and now you're back here. Care to tell me what's going on?"

Brett stooped over and spoke quietly into Quinn's ear. "I've got some sensitive things to tell you. Let's go someplace private where we can talk."

Quinn looked at him for a moment, then picked up his coffee and stood. "C'mon, follow me."

They left the EOC and went out to the courtyard. Quinn pointed to a bench. "Have a seat," he said. "Before you say anything, I got a call from Secretary Wainz wanting to know what we're doing out at that Indian reservation in Arizona."

"Wainz? Isn't he Secretary of...?"

"Secretary of the Interior."

"What did he want?" Brett asked.

"He seemed bent out of shape because the CDC was on the reservation. I filled him in on the situation out there, which, of course, he already knew about. I assured him that we were doing everything possible to find the cause of the deaths and to protect the Indians. This is the part of the conversation I'm still trying to figure out. He wanted to know who'd given us permission to get involved. I told him we don't need permission from anyone—including him or the Department of the Interior—to get involved when our help is needed."

"It sounds like he isn't pleased that we're out there trying to solve their problem," Brett said. "What's his concern?"

"That's what I'd like to know. He then said that I'll be hearing from the director of the CDC. So, that's what I've been dealing with. Now, what the hell's going on that you need to talk about?"

"I need to go to England."

23

"England? Well, this ought to be good," Quinn said. "Go ahead, fill me in."

Brett explained everything that Boggs had uncovered about the virus and its origin from the DSTL in the UK. "I need to go there and find out more about this. How could the virus make its way from England to the Grand Canyon? And there is the bigger question of who is involved. And why?"

"Are you and Boggs absolutely certain of this?" Quinn asked. "There couldn't possibly have been a mix-up of some kind in the lab?"

"I asked Janet the same question. She assured me that she ran the DNA tests three times. No mistakes. She stated that her findings are one hundred percent accurate."

"And what do you hope to find by going to England?" Quinn asked.

"I won't know until I get there and ask some questions. There is one other thing we need to be aware of."

"Oh? What's that?" Quinn asked.

"If we're right about this, then how the hell did the virus get from their lab all the way to the Grand Canyon? And for what purpose? It had to be deliberate, and whoever is behind this will definitely *not* want this information getting out. They will probably do anything to cover their tracks. What I'm saying is, we could be in serious danger until this is cleared up. So far, only the three of us know about this."

"Hmm...I wonder if we should call in the FBI," Quinn said. "This is beyond the scope of what we do here."

"No, we definitely do *not* do that," Brett said firmly.

"And why not?"'

"Because we don't know who, or what organization, could be involved. It seems unlikely, but could our own government be involved? Or possibly some foreign government? Terrorists? Or even some wacko nut-job group? In short, we don't know who we can trust. So, we can't contact the FBI or anyone else. Not yet. Not until we know more."

"What the hell kind of situation are we involved in here?" Quinn asked. "Anything else?" he frowned.

"Yes. It seems far-fetched, but this seems like an international scheme that involves the deaths of at least twelve innocent Native Americans. When I start looking around and asking questions in the UK, somebody will learn that the secret is out. And whoever is involved will probably do everything possible to shut us up. You've got to take every precaution you can to stay safe and keep out of sight as much as possible."

"You're scaring me," Quinn said, looking around the quadrangle.

"Yeah, well I'm scared too."

———

Brett went back to his office and sat down to read through all the test results. There were graphs, charts, and multiple DNA sequencing photos to review. There was no question that Boggs had done an incredible job in a very short time, first isolating, then identifying the virus, and finally tracing it back to the UK. He made copies of the ones he wanted to take with him. Then he locked the rest of the charts and graphs in his desk. Not very secure, but the best he could do for the time being. He collected the papers that he needed and took an Uber back to his condo. He had to schedule a flight and pack for the trip to England, but first, he had another important phone call to make.

Kari answered on the second ring. "Good morning, Brett. You caught me just before my first class starts. Are you still coming—"

"I'm on my way to the airport to catch a flight to England," he said, interrupting her. "I don't expect to stay more than one or two days at the most."

After a long silence, Kari asked, "England? What's going on in England? I thought you and Ross were tied up in Arizona."

"Yes, we are. And that situation has become very complicated. My trip to England is just to clear up a few things. I just wanted to say 'hi' and hear your voice before I have to catch a plane." He didn't want to tell her the possible danger he faced.

"Brett—George has proposed to me."

"Wh—what do you mean 'proposed' to you?"

"Just what it sounds like. He asked me to marry him."

Brett was speechless, and his knees felt weak. His breath caught in his throat, and his heart pounded.

After a long silence, she finally said, "Brett? Are you still there?"

"Yeah, still here."

"I don't want to spend the rest of my life alone," she said. "Coming home every night to an empty, cold house, not having anyone to share things with. After my father was killed, I had no one. I just can't do it anymore. I don't want to eat every meal alone the rest of my life."

"I thought we were—"

"We were what, Brett? Friends? Part-time lovers? I only get to see you briefly between your assignments. We are seven hundred miles apart. What future could we have? You are the most incredible, exciting person I've ever met, and I will always love you. But at this time in my life, I want something more than just passionate weekends whenever you can manage to see me."

And there it was. Solt was right. She needed more. She needed a commitment. The status quo was not enough going forward, and things were about to change.

"Can you wait a bit before you give him an answer?"

"Wait for what? For life to pass us by?"

"We are like pieces of a puzzle. We fit, we're a—"

"You're right," she said. "We're like pieces of a puzzle. And like everything in life, we are changing. But we are each changing. Separately. We don't fit together like we used to."

He didn't know what to say. He had never really been ready to commit to anyone, but now he was at a loss. He wanted nothing more than to keep her. He wanted stability, but he wasn't sure he was ready for any significant change. Since meeting her, his life had finally seemed complete. He had his dog, Tequila, and he thought he had Kari, whatever that meant.

Finally, he said, "Are you asking me to quit my job and—"

"I'm not asking you to do anything. I love you. And I'm eternally grateful to you for saving my life in Guatemala."

He couldn't think of anything to say. "Look, I have to run. I have a plane to catch."

"Brett, know that I will always love you. Please take care of yourself."

Brett closed his phone, slipped it into his jacket, and blew out a deep sigh. His heart was breaking. He felt a chill deep inside him.

Could his life possibly get any more fucked up than it was now?

24

THE UNIVERSITY OF CHICAGO
COBB HALL

Kari managed to struggle through her first class, then went to her office and closed the door. Her hands were trembling, and tears were running down her face. She hadn't meant to say it like that. What the heck had she been thinking? She should have given it more thought instead of just blurting it out. Had she possibly just lost the love of her life after telling him that she might be marrying someone else? Had she chosen her career and the university over a life with the man she dearly loved?

She sat alone at her desk and sobbed uncontrollably with her head buried in her hands until she finally ran out of tears. She wiped her eyes, sat up, and looked out the window of her office. She had cried herself out and was left feeling both physically and emotionally drained. Had she made a serious mistake, or had she finally made the decision she had been avoiding for a while?

She would be thirty in two weeks and was staring middle age in the face. What did she really want in life? Where did she see herself ten years from now? Where would she be in twenty years? Thirty years? A lonely old woman teaching kids about other cultures, about previous generations and their lives and families?

Time was moving on, but her life seemed stagnant. The rest of the world seemed to be where they were meant to be, doing what most people do. Families, dinners out, weekends together, and sharing their lives.

Could she give up her profession to marry Brett? If she decided to do that, there was just one big barrier to overcome first. *He hadn't asked her to marry him.*

She was madly in love with him. But how long could passionate, romantic weekends together every few months be enough? That still left her alone the other sixty or seventy days.

She liked George Pettit. She even loved him—but like a brother, not romantically. She enjoyed his company and was grateful to have someone to go to dinner with. He was like comfort food. Easy to be with, good company, always funny, and he made her laugh. George had early on made his intentions known to her. He let her know he wanted to have a more serious relationship. And now he had finally asked her to marry him.

But as she sat there thinking of all the things she and Brett had done together, she realized she missed him more than she had ever wanted to admit. She had been chased by the Guatemalan secret police, captured by guerrilla rebels, nearly raped by a gang that killed her father, and made a daring last-minute escape from the jungle. She remembered their harrowing experience at the monastery in New Mexico that had nearly cost them their lives.

With Brett, she had faced the most life-threatening danger she'd ever faced, and it was the most thrilling, exciting, romantic, carefree time she had ever experienced. In their short time together, they had shared more adventure, danger, and sorrow—the feeling of being alive and living life on the edge—more than most people even dream of experiencing.

Nobody could possibly understand the emptiness she felt now.

Had she just made the biggest mistake of her life?

25

"England?" Wainz yelled into the phone. "Why the hell would he be going to England?" He was furious. Why *would* Carson be going to England—unless he had learned something about the DSTL and the vials? That didn't seem likely, but he had to be certain. It seemed too much of a coincidence to ignore.

Ghost sat on top of the South Rim. He had just sent a message to Wainz, informing him that Carson had flown back to Atlanta. And according to the CDC information desk, Carson was now on his way to England.

Ghost was so shocked at hearing a voice on the phone that he didn't answer.

"Follow him!" Wainz snapped. "We can't let this get out of hand." Wainz knew he could not let anyone find out what he had done—ordering the deaths of twelve innocent Native Americans. Even though he considered it a small cost, considering the incredible implications it meant for the future of the country. If what he had done somehow leaked out, his life as he knew it would be over. No, he could never let that happen.

"Do you want me to take care of him?" Ghost asked.

"Eventually, but not yet. Not until we know everything he knows and what he is doing and why he's over there. There'll be a private jet waiting for you in Flagstaff."

Ghost hung up. He had a long trip to plan. He had left the last two vials at the camp below. He hoped nobody would find them. But there was nothing he could do about that now.

It seemed he, too, was on his way back to England.

———

Heathrow Airport
London

After the nine-hour flight from Atlanta to Heathrow, Brett cleared customs and headed to the rental counter to get the car he'd rented. He grabbed his carry-on duffle and went outside to find his vehicle. The young woman at the rental counter had assigned him a small Fiat equipped with GPS, which, she assured him, would be perfect for the narrow English roads.

He found the car, tossed his bag in the back seat, climbed in, and entered the address for Porton Down outside of Salisbury, a short distance from the English Channel. The GPS showed the 129-kilometer trip would take approximately two hours, considering the traffic.

He'd tried to doze during the flight, but there were too many things on his mind to sleep, and now he was struggling to remain alert. Except for a short doze on the flight to Atlanta, he'd not had a full night's sleep since leaving Flagstaff two days ago. As he steered the car out of the airport and into traffic, he needed to stay focused. Driving on the left side of the road at any time of the day was challenging, but it was even more daunting in early morning rush-hour traffic. He finally broke free of the London traffic and headed toward Salisbury and the town of Porton Down.

There were two ways to get to Porton Down from London, and he chose the one that looked the most direct. He stopped to grab a cup of coffee and a scone, then followed the A-303 highway for over an hour. He sipped his coffee and tried to concentrate on the road, which was narrow and seemed backward for him since he wasn't used to driving in the left lane. Sunrise was still an hour away, and a thick fog muted what little light there was.

He needed to focus on his reason for being in England, but he couldn't get Kari out of his mind. Did she actually intend to marry that dufus professor? Had Solt been right? Was he going to lose her? She'd never complained about their relationship, never asked him for more. When he was with her, he felt...what? He felt complete, a part of something—he felt happy.

He suddenly had to swerve to take a sharp turn, and he refocused his attention on the narrow, winding road and the dense, foggy conditions. His personal concerns would have to wait. There were more immediate problems—like staying on the road. And, of course, the unknown that lay ahead.

He swung onto the A-338 and drove to the city of Salisbury. He pulled into a diner for a quick breakfast and more coffee. After leaving Salisbury, he turned onto Porton Road, a challengingly narrow road with many curves. At the end of this dark maze, he hoped he could get answers to the situation they were facing in Arizona.

Finally, a large compound emerged through the morning mist. A tall security fence ran the perimeter, topped with coiled razor-sharp concertina wire. Large stone buildings hovered in the gloom beyond it. It was a menacing scene. He turned into the entrance and stopped in front of a large steel gate manned by two armed guards. The sign on the gate read:

DEFENSE, SCIENCE, & TECHNOLOGY LABORATORIES

NATIONAL INSTITUTE FOR BIOLOGICAL RESEARCH

RESTRICTED SECURE AREA

This was the UK's most secretive and controversial military research and bioweapons lab. The compound spread over seven thousand acres of manicured lawn. Brett rolled down his window and showed his ID and papers to one of the guards. The steel gate remained closed. The other guard made a phone call. Finally, the gate opened.

"Off you go," the guard said, handing back his papers. "Follow the road signs marked B. You'll be looking for Building 5. Park outside and someone will escort you in."

As he entered, a chill skimmed up his back. He was no longer at a medical research complex. Rather, he'd just entered one of the big four military research facilities. Kind of like going from a bakery that served people to a bomb factory to blow them up. It was an impressive compound. Six tall cement buildings arranged in a rectangular pattern were surrounded by hundreds of acres of manicured lawn inside the fences. A large courtyard filled the center of the buildings with multiple crisscrossing brick sidewalks connecting them. Three military Jeeps were parked off to the side, and a few armed soldiers strolled between buildings.

He found the building marked *5* and parked. Uncoiling

himself from the small Fiat, he stretched and yawned, trying to feel alert. *Sleep—he needed sleep.* But now it was time to focus. He needed answers. A man in a tweed suit walked up to him and extended his hand. "Dr. Carson, I'm Dr. Young. Welcome to our facility."

"Thank you. It's nice to meet you." The two men shook hands.

"We got advance notice of your visit, but we're a bit confused. What exactly is it we can help you with?"

"Are you the director of the DSTL?"

"No. I'm only responsible for Building 5, which houses our Biological Level Four High-Risk Research Laboratory on level three. This is a military facility. General Schulte is the director of DSTL and oversees this entire facility and research areas."

"Is there somewhere we can go to talk?" asked Brett.

"Yes, of course, my office." He led the way into Building 5, through security, which involved a scanner, then down a hall, and into a clean, open office with leather furniture, bookshelves, and a large desk holding three computer screens. "Would you care for some tea or coffee?"

"Coffee, please. Black."

Young poured and handed him a cup, then poured tea for himself and sat down.

Brett took a large swallow of coffee, then began. "The CDC has been asked to help solve a cluster of fatal infections that we believe might have been caused by an unidentified virus. Currently, we have more questions than answers."

Young nodded his head sympathetically. "Most unfortunate. But how does that involve the DSTL?"

Brett stared over his cup. "The evidence suggests the virus we isolated may have come from this laboratory."

Young stiffened. "That's preposterous. I'm sure you know that most viruses are ubiquitous and appear almost anywhere on the planet. It's absurd that you believe you've identified our lab as the origin of your virus of concern."

"That's not the case with this virus. Our own Bio-4 lab at the CDC discovered that this is a unique virus, unlike any other we've encountered. We were able to trace its DNA here to the DSTL. We suspect that it may have been engineered, then modified for a specific gain-of-function. As far as we know, it doesn't exist anywhere else on the planet. That is, until the outbreak in the American Southwest less than four weeks ago."

Young's eyes narrowed. "No. You must be mistaken. It's not possible. Who told you it was the identical virus? One that we may have created?"

"Our research staff at the CDC stated unequivocally that the DNA mapping shows it's the exact same virus. We presume you used CRISPR genome editing to create and then modify this virus."

The muscles in Young's jaw twitched, but he said nothing.

"What we want to know is how a virus created here ended up in America."

"It's simply not possible that it's our viruses," Young said again, more determined and agitated than before. "Look around you. We have security here second to no other military biological level four research laboratory in the world. There is no possible way a virus could have escaped from our labs. And it most definitely couldn't show up in America."

Brett put his cup down and stood. "Can we visit your Bio-4 lab?"

Young looked at him for several seconds, then said, "Currently we have three different genetically engineered virus strains we're working on, and they are stored along with all the other usual lethal viruses in our biological level four high-security area. One of the three strains has been shown to be extremely lethal. Dr. Theodore Bell, who is our lead research viral geneticist, is in charge of our lab. I will have him take you into Bio-4 on level three. However, I won't be accompanying you into the lab."

Brett stopped and turned to Young. "When I'm finished talking to Dr. Bell and looking around in Bio-4, I would like to see all the information you have on that particular virus, including animal studies, as well as any other testing that was performed."

"That won't be possible. That information is highly classified."

Brett had run out of patience and glared at Young. "Well, since we also have cultures of the virus—it's not really classified anymore, is it? I'm sure neither of us wants it to become common knowledge that the virus killing American Indians was created and genetically engineered here in your laboratory. And that it somehow escaped your lab. And finally, that your country refuses to cooperate. I understand that it is sensitive information and your need for security. But we need that material so we can figure out how we can prevent any more deaths at this point."

Young turned red and the muscles of his jaw twitched. "I will need to get a release approved and have the material made available to you. That will take a week or more to get cleared by the Ministry of Military Documents, located in London."

"Today. I will need everything when I get back from visiting Bio-4." Brett was bluffing. He had no authority to demand anything. But, he had to try everything possible to get some kind of answer. He wouldn't be coming back and wouldn't get another chance. It was now or never.

Young led Brett up to floor level three, unlocked the door to the floor, and held it open. Brett walked through and down the hall to the restricted security Biological Level Four Research Laboratory entrance, where another man waited for him.

Brett extended his hand. "Hello, I'm Brett Carson. I'm with the American CDC. Thanks for taking the time to show me around your Bio-4 lab."

"I'm Dr. Theodore Bell. Nice to meet you. Let's go through decontamination and get suited up, then I'll show you around."

All biological level four restricted laboratories were virtually identical. A sealed door opened into a decontamination section, then another sealed door led into the main laboratory. They went into the decontamination chamber where they went through a phenol shower and then changed into full-body airtight PPPS—positive pressure personnel suits. The suits were hooked to air hoses so that they breathed reverse air that had passed through flame burners, triple-filtered. No new organisms in, and definitely *no* infectious agents out.

Brett was familiar with the process, having gone into their own Bio-4 many times. But he still was uncomfortable every time he went through the procedure. After fully protected and isolated from the outside world, he entered the near-freezing lab, an air-locked isolated room that held some of the world's most lethal viruses known. How the hell Boggs could spend her life inside a similar place, he'd never understand.

Bell then opened the sealed door to the sterile secured working laboratory of Bio-4. It was like every other Bio-4 lab Brett had been in. Brilliant blue-white light illuminated the room, and the temperature was notably much cooler. Brett spotted several live-feed cameras at the corners of the room. More than a dozen technicians and researchers were working throughout the massive room.

A woman in similar gear walked over to Brett. He held out his gloved hand. "I'm Brett Car—"

"I know who you are, Dr. Carson," she said. Her eyes through the plexiglass revealed she was smiling. "I'm very glad to meet you. I read about your exploits in Guatemala and the 'Mayan' virus in the *Journal of Virology*. How can we help you?"

"Could you show me where you store your recently engineered viruses? I'm interested in the most virulent strain that Dr.

Young mentioned." Of course, Young hadn't mentioned any such thing, but he hoped his casual ruse would work.

She turned to Bell as if to ask permission, and he nodded approval to her. "That would be the TSV-9LG virus. It's stored over here in freezer H." She went over to a locked freezer built into the wall and punched in a code, then pulled open the door as frozen vapor curled out. There were multiple trays, each tray containing dozens of various frozen samples. "We keep the super dangerous babies in here, frozen with liquid nitrogen coolant, same as probably in your lab. In addition to the new TSV-9LG, this freezer also holds Ebola, Marburg hemorrhagic virus, smallpox, along with a few others, including even a culture of your MEH-130 Mayan virus."

She slid out a tray containing two dozen tubes. Using tongs, she pulled one out, read the label carefully, then placed it on a soft, insulated pad and stepped back to let Brett examine it.

"When was the last time you had this tube out?"

"We do a monthly inventory and check to make sure every tube and culture can be accounted for, and that there has been no damage, leakage, or broken tubes. The record showed that this tray was last checked and inventoried twenty-eight days ago."

Brett looked at the frozen tube, and using his gloved hand, he rubbed frost off the label. "Who labels these tubes?"

"Only two of us. Theodore or I handle the highly dangerous material here in locker H. The fewer people involved, the better."

Brett held up the tube. "Is this your printing or Dr. Bell's?"

The frown on her face was evident, even through the plexiglass shield. She held the vial up and examined it more closely, then gasped. "Something's wrong here. That's not even our label!"

Brett stared at her. "Could the real tube be missing and have been replaced with this one?"

"I—I don't see how that could be possible," she stammered.

"Would you mind putting a droplet of this under the electron microscope and let's see what's in it?"

A few minutes after bringing the frozen tube to a chilled room temperature, they examined a sealed micro-droplet under the electron microscope.

She looked up, and the color drained from her face.

26

Theodore Bell had been watching and walked over to her. "What's the problem?"

"There's nothing in it," she said. "Not a single virus particle."

"What? Are you sure?" Bell blurted out.

She merely nodded.

"Just as I suspected," Brett said. "Probably just water or a saline solution. Your tube has been replaced with this one. Has there been anything unusual here at DSTL recently? Anything out of place, any security breaches or break-ins?"

Bell grew incensed. "Security breaches? Break-ins? Seriously? Have you seen our security? This facility has got to be the most secure area in the entire UK. The Queen herself doesn't have this kind of protection."

"He's right," she said. "It takes me more than ten minutes every day just to work my way through security to get up here."

Brett thought for a minute, then asked, "Has there been any change in personnel, either among the professional staff or secondary supportive staff?"

"No, I'm not aware of any..." She paused, then said, "One of our night security guards was found dead three weeks ago. Right outside Bio-4 here on floor level three. At the time we wondered why he was on level three, but nothing came of it."

"His autopsy suggested he died of a heart attack," Bell hastened to add.

Brett nodded, then reached to shake her gloved hand. "You've been a great help. You can put the tube and tray back and lock it. Then, can we have a look around on this floor?"

Twenty minutes later, after going through the decontamination procedure and changing back into their clothes, they went out the outer door to Bio-4, and the thick sealed door closed and locked with a hiss as air was forced out.

Dr. Young rushed up to join them outside Bio-4 after he'd been informed that a tube containing the TSV-9LG virus was missing. Sweat trickled down his face and neck and his voice trembled. "Are we sure the tube is missing, and not just misplaced?" he asked Bell.

"Actually," Brett said, "they discovered that three tubes of your virus are missing, and fake duplicate tubes were put in their place. Can we review the security camera tapes from both inside Bio-4 and on this floor?"

"You're welcome to review them. They're on a seventy-two-hour loop, and then they get recorded over. If anything happened more than seventy-two hours ago, it won't be of any help to you. They aren't intended to monitor for break-ins because of all our security measures throughout DSTL. They're used to confirm daily procedures and ensure the safety of personnel working with dangerous cultures."

"Actually," Brett said, "you might have a security leak on the inside."

Young grew more agitated and distressed by the minute. "Why would you jump to that conclusion?"

"Simple logic. How else could anyone who broke into the lab

have known the security code to the Bio-4 door? And once inside, how would they know to look in locker H for the virus?"

They continued walking down the corridor of level three, with Brett taking in everything and trying to put the pieces together. Midday sunlight pouring through the windows created bright rectangle patterns on the marble floor. In the hallway, Brett glanced down at the floor and stopped. He stared at a sunlit window pattern on the floor. He had spotted a thin—nearly imperceptible—strip of sunlight brighter than the rest of the sunlit pattern of the window on the floor.

"Is there something wrong?" Price asked, looking down at the sunlight on the marble and seeing nothing.

Brett walked over to one of the windows and pointed to what looked like a slit that had been cut from the bottom pane.

"I wonder if this could be the entry point into your building," Brett said, pointing to the barely noticeable cut in the bottom of the windowpane. By now they had been joined by both General Schulte, the director of DSTL, and a man introduced as the head of security.

Turning to the director, Brett said, "I think you've had a break-in. It looks like someone may have cut a thin slit in the window to unlock it and gained access to this floor. Then they somehow managed to get into both Bio-4 and locker H and switched vials on you. Three vials of your TSV-9LG virus are missing and have been replaced with replicas. You may want to contact Scotland Yard. This could be an international crime, not something the local authorities would be able to handle."

Schulte turned to the head of security and nodded. "I'll get right on it, sir," the security man said.

"You may want them to review the autopsy findings on the security agent again more carefully," Brett said.

"Why would that be necessary? What could it possibly reveal?" Schulte asked.

"Because he may not have died of a heart attack. Maybe he was killed after getting caught in the middle of a serious security breach. They should look for subtle findings of possible suffocation or even the presence of a drug."

The general said, "Let's not jump to conclusions. It's not possible that there could have been an unauthorized incursion into this facility. There has to be some other explanation. Let's go down to Young's office and wait for Scotland Yard."

They went downstairs and waited in the office. Young came into the room and handed Brett a note, along with a metal briefcase that was locked. "Here is the combination of the case and all the information you requested. It is important to remember that these documents are top secret, very sensitive military documents and should be kept within a very small circle of need-to-know personnel only."

Brett thanked him and assured everyone that he and the CDC would respect their concerns and keep it under tight security.

More than two hours later, Inspector Mark James from Scotland Yard arrived, accompanied by a young officer. Brett, along with Dr. Young, Theodore Bell, General Schulte, and the head of security, were all gathered in Young's office.

Schulte told the inspector about the stolen vials from the Bio-4 lab and about the death of a security guard around the same time as the vial was stolen. "We can't stress enough how important it is to find those vials," the general said.

The head of security answered his phone, and then told them that a possible breach under the main fence at a far corner had just been discovered.

"And there has been a slit cut into a window to level three," Brett said, "suggesting that the window might have been the point of entry into the building."

Inspector James nodded in agreement, then asked, "The question is, how did they manage to get up to level three, which is actually the fourth floor? That's at least twelve meters up—or nearly forty feet to you Yanks," he said, looking at Brett.

"I doubt they went up to get in through the window," Brett said. "It would seem more logical that they came down from the roof."

The security man stood and said, "I will send someone up to check the roof for any clues." Then he turned and left the room, along with the other officer.

"I think you have to consider that this could be an inside job," Brett said again. Young and Schulte both looked uncomfortable.

Schulte, obviously angered at that suggestion, said, "To the contrary, everything seems to show that someone broke in from the outside, first under the fence, then through a window to level three."

"I agree," Inspector James said. "Why should we consider it to be an inside job in view of the apparent evidence?"

"How did they get through the security lock door to your Bio-4, and then into locker H?" Brett asked. "And how did they know which vials to look for, or even that they were in locker H?"

"All very good points," Inspector James said. "We'll need to find out if anyone inside the DSTL gave the information to outsiders—and why." He turned to Director Schulte. "If there's been a security leak, this is quite serious. I'm going to need a complete list of all personnel working here at the DSTL. We're going to have to do background checks, review financial records, and try to learn everything about them. We will also need to check all phone calls from here over the past month, and I will need the logbook of any visitors during that period."

"I'm afraid we can't do that, Inspector," General Schulte said. "We will do our own investigation. This is a military facility, and we need to keep everything contained. What goes on here is much too sensitive to allow outside involvement."

"I totally agree with the general," Dr. Bell chimed in. "What we do here is much too sensitive to allow that. Our military investigators should handle it from here on."

"While I understand your concern," the Inspector said, "it appears that this involves more than just this facility. This seems like an international conspiracy of some sort. So, no, General. Scotland Yard will continue to investigate this for now."

It was obvious that the people at the DSTL were not at all comfortable with Scotland Yard's involvement. Brett wondered why there was resistance to having Scotland Yard getting involved. He decided that wasn't his problem for now. He had his own issues to deal with.

The younger man who had accompanied Inspector James entered the room. "Sir, we found what appear to be fresh scrapes along the roof edge, which could have been caused by a grappling hook."

Inspector James let out a sigh, then turned to Brett. "You're a Yank from America, right? So how are you involved in this? Why are you over here, and how do you happen to be at this facility?"

"Yes, I'm a 'Yank.' I'm here to find out why and how a virus from here could get from here to America."

James turned to Schulte and said, "Is that so?"

"That's only conjecture at this point," Young hastened to say, "but we are all looking into it. It seems extremely unlikely that could be the case."

"Not really that unlikely," Brett countered, "since we know for certain there's been a break-in here and three vials of a virus are now missing."

General Schulte glared at him, obviously displeased with the turn of events.

Inspector James sat down, took out a notebook, and said, "Okay, let's start at the beginning of this bloody mess and tell me everything. We need to know what we're dealing with, so we know what to investigate."

"Twelve Native American Indians died from a virus that appears to have originated at this facility. We want to know how that happened." After Brett explained everything he knew so far about the situation, he glanced at his watch, then stood and said, "I've got to go now if I'm going to catch my flight back. We'll keep you informed of any new information we turn up on our end. And I will make sure we keep these documents under the strictest security and get them back to you as soon as possible."

Inspector James stood and shook Brett's hand. "Dr. Carson, it is we who should be thanking you for everything you've done for us today. You not only discovered that three lethal vials are missing from our lab here, but may have also discovered how the invaders may have gained access into our facility."

"But we still don't know how or why the virus apparently showed up in America," Brett said. "There's still a lot that we still don't know about at this point. Please let us know if your investigation turns up anything on this end." After shaking hands all around, he headed out to the Fiat, armed with a thick folder locked inside the metal case. Two military men approached him before he got in.

"What's in the metal case, sir?"

"I'm afraid I can't reveal that to you. Above your pay scale," he said, smiling.

He immediately realized that was obviously the wrong approach. "Stay where you are and place the case on the ground," one soldier demanded.

Fortunately, General Schulte had noted the commotion from his office window and stepped outside to wave the soldiers off. "Stand down, Sargent. It's okay, he's clear to go."

With that, Brett climbed into the Fiat and started it up. He was anxious to get back to Heathrow before dark. Starving and exhausted, he planned to eat a meal and sleep on the flight back to Atlanta. Driving through the gate, he noted that the fog had grown thicker.

He turned and headed back toward Porton Down, his headlights barely able to penetrate the thick gray mist. He had a long, tiring trip ahead of him.

It didn't occur to him to check behind him to see if he was being followed.

27

Ross Solt stood outside the Parker Health Center, talking with the other four members of the team, discussing their possible next plan of action. A police car with NAVAJO NATION POLICE in bold letters on the door pulled in beside them and came to a stop. An officer, obviously a Native American and presumably Navajo, stepped out and approached them.

"Dr. Carson?" he asked.

"No," Solt said, "he's not here at the moment." He wasn't ready to give up too much information yet until he figured out what was going on.

"Do you know where he is, or when he might be back?"

"Afraid not. He didn't say. Can I help you with something, officer?"

"Your group here is with the CDC, correct?"

"Yes, we arrived over a week ago."

"The BIA wants to know how long you plan on staying here on the reservation. The National Park Service is pushing to have the quarantine lifted so tourists can return to the canyon for hiking and camping."

"We can't say. We aren't finished yet with our work here. We don't have time restrictions. It doesn't work like that. And as far as I know, this doesn't even involve the national parks."

"Actually," the officer said, "the BIA, which oversees the Indian Health Service, has requested that you leave the reservation by the end of the week. This is, strictly speaking, Havasupai sovereign nation land. We thank you for your help. But the IHS and the Arizona Health Service have been asked to take over now."

"What authority does the Navajo police have over the Havasupai reservation?" Solt asked.

"There are over eleven tribal nations in this area. The Navajo Nation is by far the biggest, while the Havasupai is one of the smallest. We provide police service to several adjacent tribes because we have the largest police force."

"Well, we were requested to come here to help with a health crisis that I'm sure you're aware of. We can't leave yet since our work here isn't finished."

"The Havasupai didn't actually send for you," the officer said. "It was Dr. Martin, the American IHS doctor who sent for you, and she has no authority to do that. Nor does that give you permission to remain here."

The young Navajo officer was starting to piss Solt off. He walked up to the officer, face-to-face, and said in an even voice, "Have the BIA or the IHS contact us. Until then, we aren't going anywhere. Tell them our work here isn't finished. I'm sure they wouldn't want any more Native Americans to die."

The officer raised his voice. "As I already told you, this isn't federal land. So, you have no authority here."

Just then, Chief Jack walked up.

"*Ya'at'ee*, Samuel," he said to the officer.

"*Ya'at'ee abini*, Chief Jack," he said.

"What's the problem?"

"I've just asked these men to leave the reservation at the request of the BIA. They decided that the IHS and the Arizona Health Service should take over from here on."

"Humph," the chief said. Then he turned to Solt and asked, "Are your people finished with their work here?"

"Not yet," Solt said. "We still have a lot of work ahead of us."

The chief nodded and turned back to the officer. "*Nijaa' dooga'a'l, nidi noodah*," the chief said. "Now I'm officially asking them to stay."

The officer's face turned red, then he walked away, got back in his car, and drove off.

"What did you say to him, Chief?" Solt asked.

"An old Indian saying. Essentially, I told him his ears would rot and fall off listening to such garbage." The chief watched the car disappear down the street. "Samuel's a good man. He means well. I know his father, Daniel Red Feather, who's on the Navajo tribal council. His grandfather *Sha-nut'ah* was one of the 'code talkers' during the war."

"We appreciate your help with the police," Solt said. "We're doing everything we can to find out what happened here, but at this point, we don't have any good answers. We know more now than when we started, but we still have a lot of work to do. Whatever we're dealing with doesn't spread person-to-person. It's not contagious. But that still leaves a million questions unanswered. Tell me this—why does the BIA want us to leave now?"

"Humph. I will try to find out more about this if I can. Let me know if there is any more trouble about you being here," the chief said. "Be sure to keep me up to date on any new information you find."

Solt smiled and nodded. But the question filling his mind was why had the Bureau of Indian Affairs suddenly wanted them to leave the area? And why had no more deaths occurred since they had arrived? Why had Brett taken off in the night without warning? And what had he discovered?

So far only more questions and no answers.

He felt certain there was something else going on here beyond the obvious, something as yet unknown, just below the surface. He stared out across the land.

What other secrets did the great canyon hold?

28

PORTON DOWN
REGION OF WILTSHIRE, ENGLAND

Thick fog blew in off the channel, and visibility on the tortuous, narrow road was limited, made worse by headlights reflecting from the thick mist. Thankfully, so far Brett had seen only two or three cars coming toward him, their lights blurred and disorienting in the fog. He concentrated on not hitting them.

After one sharp turn, he glanced in his rearview mirror and spotted headlights behind him. He ignored the car and focused on staying on the road and not hitting anyone head-on. After observing it for more than fifteen minutes staying behind him, he wondered if he was being followed or just being paranoid. It was just as likely that someone else was headed the same way and didn't dare pass him in this blanketing fog.

The GPS showed an intersection coming up. Maybe he could find out if his mind was working overtime or if his suspicions were well founded. He approached the intersection and turned sharply to the right, directly in front of a bus. Tires screeched, horns blared, and headlights bounced in all directions in the fog. During a moment of panic, he'd forgotten the rules and drove reflexively into the wrong lane and had nearly been killed in the process. He swerved back into the correct lane, narrowly missing a collision. With all the lights and confusion in the fog, he'd lost track of which set of headlights he wanted to follow.

He was left shaking, feeling stupid, and suddenly lacking confidence in himself. There was no way to know if he had been followed, but for now, that didn't matter. His heart was racing and pounding against his sternum. Near death scenarios like he had just experienced caused that response with the body's massive surge of adrenaline to survive.

Until yesterday, he would have felt that worrying about anyone following him was a silly notion. But after what Boggs had learned and what he discovered at the DSTL, the fact that someone could be following him was no longer a far-fetched idea. And that realization put a cold fear in him. Because he seemed to be on the verge of finding answers, had he just become a target for whoever arranged the murder of twelve innocent people? And probably also a night guard? By comparison, his death would seem a trivial matter to them.

As he approached London and moved through heavy traffic, there was no way to isolate a particular set of headlights. Once in the airport, he left the rental car, practically ran into the terminal, and found the Delta gate where his flight would depart from. Instead of sitting in the area of his flight, he walked a short distance to another gate and sat down, positioned so he could watch the crowds.

Nobody stood out or looked menacing as he watched people coming and going. He closed his eyes and tried to remember or play back what it was he thought he saw. Then, he resumed watching people while something kept nibbling at his mind. He couldn't get a grasp on what bothered him...

Brett suddenly sat upright. A leather flight jacket, light brown suede. Not something anyone would notice. The dusty leather coat wasn't flashy, didn't stand out in a crowd, didn't say *money*. He merely noticed it because it was *unique*. He felt certain he'd seen that jacket—or one exactly like it—before. The problem was, he couldn't remember where he'd seen it. He again racked his brain trying to remember. Where had he seen that jacket?

Then the hairs on his neck stood up. He'd seen that jacket—or one exactly like it—outside the waiting room at the Parker Health Center on the reservation. Coincidence? Was he in fact being followed? The locked metal case by his side suddenly felt like a neon sign saying, '*Here I am, come and get me.*' He didn't stare at the jacket, but out of the corner of his eyes, he kept it in sight.

His flight was announced, but he didn't move. Everyone in the seating area got up and formed a line to board the plane. He still didn't move. When everyone was on board and they announced final boarding for Delta flight 672, he stood and practically ran to the gate just before they closed it. He boarded and started down the aisle, glancing around but couldn't spot the jacket. Maybe the man wasn't on this flight. Or, if he had taken off the jacket, he could be any one of the other passengers.

At this point, there was no way he could be sure.

Everyone on board watched the last passenger walk down the aisle carrying a locked metal case. He found his seat, sat down, slid the case under his feet, and buckled up. He closed his eyes and let out a deep breath. What had he gotten himself into? What the hell did he think he was doing? He wasn't James *fucking* Bond! He was a physician, but somewhere along the way, his life seemed to have gotten off track. And he'd probably lost the love of his life in the process…

He was tired, depressed, paranoid, and now fearing for his life.

Not that he felt that he had much of a life without Kari.

With the background noise of the plane, he slipped into a much-needed deep sleep.

29

Wainz's phone gave notice of the incoming new text. He looked at the phone. The message from the ghost was short but devastating.

Carson went to DSTL

He left with metal case

Advise

What the hell? Why had Carson gone directly to the DSTL? What could the CDC possibly have discovered? It didn't seem possible they could have learned what had happened this soon. Hopefully, they were just fishing for answers they didn't have the means to confirm. They *did* know enough to go to the British lab for god's sake! Wainz had to know what documents were in that metal case.

It was time to stop this immediately. He quickly texted back to the ghost.

> Find out who he's been in contact with at the CDC

> Need to know who knows what

> Get the documents

> Urgent

He went to his cabinet and poured himself three fingers of Macallan's. The amount of scotch in the bottle was disappearing faster than usual, but the extra liquor didn't help anymore. He had to move quickly, somehow get the lease signed, and put this tangled mess behind him. There were others in Washington depending on him to get it done.

The question remained: how did he intend to do that?

ATLANTA

Brett called Janet Boggs from the taxi while on his way back to the CDC.

"Brett," she answered. "You're back from England already? What'd you find out?"

"I'll meet you in your office. I should be there in twenty minutes at the latest."

He paid the cab driver, grabbed his small travel bag along with the metal case, and headed to the Davis building. He glanced around every few seconds to see if anyone was following him. He swiped his card, punched in a code, and breathed a sigh of relief as he went inside, the door closing safely and locking behind him. He took the stairs two at a time to the third floor and knocked on the door to Boggs's office.

The door swung open, and he went in. She glanced down the

hall in both directions, then closed and locked her door. "I've been scared of my own shadow ever since we talked. What'd you find out? Are we way off base, or do we need to be scared out of our minds?"

"No and yes," Brett said. "No, we are not off base. Your suspicions were spot on. So, yes, we need to be extra cautious."

He proceeded to tell her about the missing vials of the virus, about the break-in at the DSTL, and finally about the questionable death of a night guard just outside their Bio-4 lab. He put the metal case on her desk and opened it.

"These are supposedly all the documents regarding the virus that was stolen. We need to make copies of everything, then lock it up. At this point, we can't tell anyone about this, not until we know how far this reaches. Who knows what? And why?"

"Coffee?" she asked, reaching for a few papers to glance over.

"Yes. Black and strong. Thanks. There's more," he said. "I thought I might have been followed while I was in England."

She put fresh coffee in the filter, turned on the coffee pot and leaned back against the cabinet holding cream, sugar, cups, tea bags and assorted snacks. "So, here's what you've told me so far," she said. "Someone broke into the DSTL—a feat that in itself that seems improbable—then somehow the virus shows up in Arizona. And now someone knows that you've learned about the engineered virus. Does that about sum it up?"

"That's about it. And as I mentioned, I thought someone might have been following me, but I'm not sure. Could be just my imagination since my mind is working overtime. At this point, I don't know if anyone knows you are involved, and we need to keep it that way. I don't want you also being a target."

"What do we do with this information, and where do you go from here?" she asked as she poured two cups of coffee.

"I've got to talk to Solt and decide on a plan of action," he said.

"The first thing I want to do is send the team that's out there back here before they're involved and get into any kind of danger."

They sat quietly, sipping their coffee while they considered their possible courses of action.

He finished his coffee, then took the case and all the papers over to her copy machine. "I'm going to make two copies of everything, one for you and one for me. I'll keep the originals locked in this case and keep it locked up. The fewer people that know about this, the better."

She put her cup down and helped him feed papers in and sort them into two stacks as they copied. They worked without speaking; the weight of what they were facing and its implications were overpowering.

When they finished, he reached for the metal case, intending to return the originals to it. Boggs grabbed his hand. "Wait. I have a better plan." She took a thick stack of discarded old, copied papers from the trash can and put them in the metal case. "I will put the originals in my large safe here. If anyone wants to see or steal these documents, that case is the first thing they will go after. Keep this in your office, and if someone happens to steal the case, they won't get what they're wanting. I will go through my copies, make notes, then lock them up along with the originals."

"Brilliant. That's why I always come to you first," he said, smiling. "I wish I could stick a bomb in it."

"Yeah, wouldn't that be nice? Wait!" Janet said. She went over to the counter, opened a porcelain rack, and pulled out three sealed vials filled with liquid. "Stick these in there. That'll scare the shit out of them."

"What's in them?"

"Sterile saline," she said, grinning ear to ear.

"Brilliant. I'm glad you're on my side. I'm going to my office and go over my copies. For god's sake, watch your back; stay inside either your office or inside Bio-4 as much as you can for your own safety."

He opened the door to leave.

"Brett," she said, "I'm scared. And I don't want anything to happen to you."

"Don't you remember? Only the good die young? And—as you said—I'm neither." He smiled at her and carried the metal case that held discarded old useless papers and three vials back to his office, along with his own copies of the research files.

Once back at his office, he locked his door and sat down to plow through all the data on the lethal, mysterious TSV-9LG virus. In the silence of his office, he realized he missed Tequila, and he especially missed Kari.

He had just flipped through the first few pages when his phone rang.

30

"You aren't going to believe this," Quinn said on the other end. "Come to my office. I don't want to discuss this over the phone."

What now? What could Quinn have possibly learned while Carson was gone? He carefully locked all the copied papers in his metal filing case, then put the metal case on the floor beside his desk. He locked the door to his office and walked across the quad to the building where Quinn had his office. There were several people walking in different directions around the quad, so he felt relatively safe here.

He went to the eighth floor, knocked on Quinn's door, then opened it and went in without being invited.

"I see you made it back from England. I don't know what you've done, but now I'm left with these!" He held up a dozen phone messages. "These are complaints and inquiries from Washington to Arizona to England. What the hell is going on? What kind of mess have you gotten us into now?"

Quinn went over to the counter and refilled his coffee cup, then sat back down at his desk. He had that look on his face that he occasionally got just before he exploded about something. The muscles on his face twitched and the veins on his forehead stood out. After taking a drink from his cup, he continued.

"Why is it," Quinn asked, "that when you go out on assignment to investigate some disease, you always seem to find other problems to deal with? When we sent you to Guatemala, you managed to get involved with Mayan artifact smuggling while somehow getting get both the rebel forces and the Guatemalan government after you. To top it off, you also succeeded in closing a two hundred and fifty-year-old historic monastery in New Mexico."

Brett sat quietly while Quinn ranted. He knew Quinn was proud of the work he and the team had done, but he needed to vent. He suspected Quinn was worried about his agents' safety while they were on assignments.

"And this time..." Quinn paused to pour cream into his coffee, picked up his pen, and stirred it. "And this time," he tapped cream off his pen and dropped it on his desk, "this time you've managed to somehow get the Havasupai and Navajo tribes mad at each other. The county sheriff and Navajo police are involved, and the Secretary of the Interior is telling us to fold up and leave."

"Navajo?" Brett asked. "What do the Navajo have to do with it?"

"How would I know?"

"And what's going on with the Department of the Interior?"

"How would I know?" Quinn repeated. "To top it off, this morning I got a fax from Scotland Yard. They need to talk to you. Scotland Yard, for god's sake! You haven't killed anyone, have you?"

"No. But it's still early," Brett grinned.

"What do you have to say?"

"Actually, it's so much more than that. As I told you earlier before I left, Boggs learned that the virus that infected the Havasupai tribe originated at the DSTL facility in England. It's a genetically engineered virus made by them using CRISPR. And I might add, apparently with a 'gain-of-function' to kill within twenty-four hours or fewer. Why would anyone even think about creating something as dangerous as that? God knows what they intended to do with it. How and why that virus made its way from England to the Havasupai is the mystery of the century. We were able to—"

"*We?*" Quinn interrupted.

"When I went to England to track the origins of the new virus, I was able to show them that there had been a break-in at the DSTL and confirm that the virus in question was missing and presumed stolen."

Quinn shook his head, smiled, and put his coffee down. "I don't know how you do it. I swear I don't. You're a doctor and the best damned EIS agent I have. But somehow you seem to stir up more trouble besides whatever disease you're chasing down."

Brett took a sip and looked at him.

"You and Boggs have done a bang-up job so far at getting to the bottom of this," Quinn said. "Don't worry about that pompous-ass secretary of state. I'll give you whatever support you need from here. I can't do anything about the county sheriff or the Navajo police. Or with Scotland Yard. You're on your own with all that. Just two things before you leave."

"And what's that?"

"First, I want you to keep me informed of everything that's going on. I don't want to learn about Scotland Yard involvement from a damned fax."

"Okay. What else?"

"Don't get yourself killed. I'm not sure what, but there's something big going on, and now we somehow find ourselves in the middle of it."

"What do you want to do about our team out there?" Brett

asked. "They're no longer looking for the cause of the deaths in the canyon, since we apparently already know the answer to that."

"You're right," Quinn said. "I'll make arrangements to get everyone back here. And I want to know what you find in those documents you brought back."

After a moment of thinking about the situation, Brett said, "No, don't recall the team yet. Leave them there for a few days, then recall them. If you hear any more from either the Navajo Police or the Department of the Interior, you can tell them you're recalling the team, which will be mostly true. That will buy us some time. Ross and I will stay and try to find out more about what is going on there. I'll have the team stay up on the South Rim at the Parker Health Center to keep them out of danger or at risk of becoming a target."

"Good idea, as long as they're kept safely out of the way. I don't want any of my people to start dying. I'll send them back at the end of the week." Quinn handed him a piece of paper. "Here's the fax from Scotland Yard. Give them a call. And for god's sake, be careful."

"Why should you worry? Just like you said earlier—*'it'll just be a couple of days out there to assess the situation.'* Remember?" He decided not to tell Quinn how he thought he might have been followed while he was in England. Quinn seemed spooked enough as it was.

"Smart-ass. Just be sure to watch your back," Quinn said. "I'm not sure what we find ourselves mixed up in, but whatever it is, it isn't good."

Brett stood, collected the fax from Scotland Yard, let out a sigh, left Quinn's office, and headed back to his own.

———

Brett looked at the note with the phone number, then had to figure out what time it was in London. It would be late afternoon there, and he might not be able to reach anyone at this hour. What could Scotland Yard want to talk to him about? Had they already found out something about the missing vials? He dialed the number and waited.

"Scotland Yard Metropolitan Headquarters. May I help you?"

"I'm Dr. Carson returning Inspector James's call."

"One moment, please, while I connect you."

"Dr. Carson? Inspector James here. Thank you for returning my call. I wanted to tell you where we are so far in the investigation. We reviewed the records of all the personnel at the DSTL, including financial records. One file stood out from the rest. We discovered that Susan Wagner, a thirty-eight-year-old lab technician, recently moved into a new apartment. She also purchased a new Mini Cooper convertible. Based on her salary, that seemed suspicious enough to dig further. Also, she hadn't been at work for the past week. So, we went to have a talk with her."

"It looks like you may have found the inside security leak. What did she have to say?"

"Nothing," James said. "We found her dead. Suffocated. A very professional hit. No prints, no clues. We're checking deeper into her background and looking at her phone calls, emails, and bank records—anything that might help, but so far, we've turned up nothing. Her past has essentially been scrubbed."

"Do you know if she would have had access to the security codes for the Bio-4 lab?"

"That's the first thing we asked Dr. Bell. She was not authorized to have the codes, but according to him, since she worked inside Bio-4, she could have easily learned the codes. We presume she was paid to pass the stolen codes on to someone else. That allowed for the break-in and stealing the vials. We are early in our investigation, and we have many unanswered questions. We still don't know who was involved or why they wanted those vials."

"Thank you for letting me know," Brett said.

"There's more," the inspector said. "At your suggestion, the medical examiner went through all the postmortem photographs and autopsy findings again of the night guard and decided that McRury probably suffocated—not physically strangled, mind you —but suffocated, much like the manner in which Miss Wagner was murdered. The medical examiner did a very thorough examination of the guard and discovered a tiny prick on the back of his neck, previously not noted. We suspect he was also given some type of drug, but nothing showed up in his blood toxicology report. Their murders were possibly committed by the same person, but there were no trace clues left behind. Nothing. Do you have new information on your end?"

"Unfortunately," Brett said, "we have nothing new to report. We've just started to go through all the research material, and that will take a while to digest."

"Be careful, Dr. Carson. This whole situation is quite troubling."

"Thank you for keeping us up to date, Inspector. Good night."

What the hell was going on? Whatever it was, it involved more than a stolen virus. What was their underlying goal? What was the end purpose, the master plan? Who? Why?

Nothing was adding up. A dead night guard and a lab technician at the DSTL? Why was the Department of the Interior concerned about CDC's presence in Arizona? How did the Navajo get involved? Nothing was connecting or making sense. The most important part of the puzzle was still missing.

He just had to figure out exactly what the hell it was!

31

Brett collected his copies of the DSTL report, locked the office, and headed back to his condo. The sun had set, and an autumn moon oozed its way above the horizon, casting moonlight mixed with streetlights on the leaf-covered sidewalks. Thankfully, he was too deep in thought to be concerned about his own safety as his mind sorted through all the questions still unanswered.

Arriving at home, he turned on lights and ordered a double pepperoni pizza. Yeah, nothing like good old home-cooked meals. He was both too wired and too tired to think about cooking. He grabbed an Amstel Light from the fridge, slipped a moody Diana Krall CD into his player, then fell into his favorite chair and started through the research papers. But as he tried to read and concentrate, something was bothering him. Something he'd missed, something in the back of his mind that he couldn't quite...

The metal briefcase!

How had he missed that until now? When he'd returned from Quinn's office, the case in his office was gone. It had been stolen in the short time he'd been gone. How had they gotten in? The office had still been locked when he came back. He stood up immediately and checked that all the doors and windows were locked. He wished Tequila were with him. For safety and because he missed his dog. He did manage to smile when he remembered the three fake vials in the case.

Somebody was in for a surprise.

He picked up his phone and called Kari. There was no answer. She was probably out to dinner again with that rock guy. Her fiancé. He still couldn't believe it. Then he remembered.

Damnit!

It was her *birthday!* He'd missed her thirtieth birthday, and she was probably out celebrating with someone else. He was angry, depressed, lonely, and mad at himself, all at the same time. The doorbell rang and he jumped.

He didn't have a gun or any other kind of weapon with him. He went to the window and peeked out.

"Pizza delivery," the boy shouted.

Brett unlocked the door, opened it, and took the pizza, then paid the boy with an additional twenty-dollar tip. "G'night," he said to the boy, who still couldn't believe his good luck as he stuck the money in his pocket.

Brett locked the door again and sat back down with the pizza beside him. He ate a slice and washed it down with cold beer, then reached for the phone again.

"Thought you'd decided to leave for good," Solt said on the other end. "Where've you been for the past four days, anyway?"

"To hell and back," Brett said. "I think we've solved one important part of the puzzle, but there's still too much we don't know yet."

"*We?* We haven't solved anything. What's going on?"

"Not over the phone. I'll be there tomorrow. I've got lots to tell you. Be careful and stay safe until I get there."

"You got her a lovely Navajo skirt and tall suede leather boots."

"Her who?"

"Kari. It's her thirtieth birthday and I didn't want you to miss it."

Silence. Brett sat stunned that his friend had remembered, but he had forgotten in time to do anything about it.

"A simple thank you would—"

"Thank you. I can't believe I missed it."

"You didn't. And she loved the gifts."

"Can I ever make it up to you, Ross?"

"You probably can't, but I'll keep it in mind."

"Just be sure you watch your back and stay safe."

"You sound like we're in some kind of horror movie. What the hell's got you so spooked?" Solt asked. "Is there something I should know?"

"I'll see you tomorrow. Thanks again." He hung up and let out a deep breath. How could he deal with both losing Kari and hiding from killers hunting him at the same time? He wanted to call Kari and wish her a happy birthday. But wasn't it kind of late for that? He'd missed it and she was probably aware of that, despite the Navajo gifts that were supposedly from him.

He wondered what the rock man had given her for her birthday. What the hell was he thinking? Of course—the rock man would have given her a real rock. A diamond.

He put the papers aside and grabbed another slice of pizza.

Well, shit. What a twisted pile of crap everything had become.

32

After breaking into Carson's office, Ghost spotted the metal case almost immediately. He slipped it into a large canvas shoulder bag so it couldn't be seen. He drove back to the motel room he had rented for the night, took out the metal case, and put it on the small table against the wall. In less than a minute, he'd picked the lock and opened the case.

Three vials of fluid rolled to the edge of the case.

He leaped back in sheer terror!

What the hell? He'd been caught completely off guard, not expecting to find anything other than papers. He glanced at the door, trying to determine if he needed to get out. He couldn't have been more scared if he'd seen a snake strike at him. He stared at the vials for a moment while his heart rate began to slow down after pounding at a dangerously high rate. After collecting himself, he looked across the room at them. The vials hadn't fallen, hadn't broken, and seemed to be intact. Was any of the material in the case contaminated? The papers under the vials were dry, with no evidence of any leakage.

He carefully closed the case, put it in the trunk of the rental car outside, and drove to a Walgreens three blocks away. He came back out with sterile gloves, masks, 95% isopropyl alcohol, and an empty spray bottle to sterilize the case and its contents.

He drove behind the drugstore and pulled up beside three large dumpsters, out of sight from the street and parking area. After putting on gloves and a surgical mask, he carefully removed the three sealed tubes, placed them in a plastic bag, sealed it, and placed it gently into one of the dumpsters. The last thing he wanted was to break one of the vials. He then pulled off his gloves, tossed them away, and washed his hands with the isopropyl.

Next, he put on a new pair of gloves and poured isopropyl into the empty spray bottle, then proceeded to spray the inside of the case and its contents with a generous amount of alcohol. After waiting more than twenty minutes for the alcohol to sterilize the case, he cautiously lifted out papers and looked through them.

It didn't make any sense. All he saw were printouts of old emails, reports of tests, old work schedules...basically discarded scrap! He'd been tricked.

He had to admit it was clever. Whoever it was had achieved their goal—that of scaring the living hell out of him.

It would be the last time he would let that happen.

———

STEWART LEE UDALL BUILDING

DEPARTMENT OF THE INTERIOR

C STREET

WASHINGTON, DC

"Did you get the metal case?"

"Yes, that part was easy," Ghost replied.

"Well," Wainz asked impatiently, "what was in it?"

"Nothing."

"Nothing? You're saying it was empty?"

"No, not empty. It was filled with scrap papers. And three vials."

"Vials? What the...? What was in the vials? Any labels on them?"

"No labels. I have no idea what's in them."

"He knows we're onto him, and he's playing with us," Wainz was disgusted at the way things were going. "I think we're soon going to have to get rid of that bastard. But not yet. Not until we know exactly what he knows and who he's talked to before he meets with some kind of accident. You screwed up with that geologist by killing him before he could tell us what he knows. That was a big mistake on your part."

"No, that wasn't a mistake," Ghost said.

"The hell it wasn't!" Wainz yelled. "Now we have no idea where to look for the mineral."

"He didn't know exactly where he found it. He didn't know."

"How can you be certain of that? He could have been stalling, or just plain refused to tell you."

"Believe me, if he'd known, he would have told me."

"What makes you so damned sure of that?"

"When you are hanging upside down two hundred feet above a canyon floor, with the threat of dying, already bruised and battered, you don't choose that time to bluff or stall. I know it was somewhere in the Black Canyon. That's all he knew. He said he'd need time to try to find it again, but didn't even know where to start. He was obviously stalling. The Black Canyon is narrow, steep, and a little more than three miles long. He said we'd never find it without him. That was the last thing he'd said."

Not exactly true. The last thing he uttered was a loud, terror-filled scream that lasted during his entire four-second fall to the jagged rocks below.

There was a pause while Wainz pondered that, then he said, "For now, just find out what Carson knows."

"What about the other people from the CDC?"

"Don't worry about them for now. When Carson is dead, the rest of them will leave." What a fucked-up mess it had turned into. Three successfully stolen vials of a deadly virus, fourteen deaths—make that fifteen, if you included the geologist—and they still didn't know the exact location of the mineral.

Then, an idea came to him. Chief Jack just might have the answer he was looking for.

———

ARIZONA

Brett shifted down into second as he drove up the mountain pass. It felt good to be back behind the wheel of his Jeep. He loved it, despite its many quirks. He and the Jeep had a long history. This morning, he'd caught an early flight back to Flagstaff and was now headed to The Laredo Inn to join the rest of the team. He'd purposefully taken the earliest flight possible. He hadn't seen any sign of a dusty leather coat during his trip. But he still kept glancing in his rearview mirror.

This morning he'd finished the last few slices of the pizza from last night along with coffee, but that was over five hours ago. He was hungry and wanted to have lunch with Solt at the Laredo. He pulled into the parking lot and went up to his suite. When he opened the door, he was knocked down by one hundred and forty pounds of one excited furry monster. Tequila was all over him, and Brett rolled on the carpet and wrestled with the dog before he finally stood up.

"I guess he missed you," Solt laughed. "You're a welcome sight for sore eyes for us, as well as the dog. Care to fill me in on what you've been doing the past week?"

Brett closed the door and proceeded to tell Solt how Boggs had isolated a virus, then discovered its origin from the DSTL in England. He also told how he went to England and discovered that there had been a break-in at their Bio-4 lab, resulting in three missing vials of the virus.

"England?" Solt asked. "How does a virus get from England to here? That doesn't make any sense."

"You've just asked the million-dollar question. There's more good news. Whoever is behind all this is ruthless and dangerous. In addition to the twelve people murdered here, a night guard and a lab technologist at the DSTL facility were also killed. I have no idea who is involved or why they did this. I'm almost certain they don't want anyone to know what they've done."

"Obviously, this is out of our hands," Solt said. "We're done here. We need to call in the FBI or state police to handle it now."

"That's what Quinn also recommended. But I explained that until we know exactly who is behind this, we don't know whom we can trust. Could this have been done by terrorists? Or by some foreign government agency? Or even—and I hate to even suggest it—by someone in our own government?"

"I don't care if it was done by the *Dirty Dozen*," Solt said, "it's not something we're prepared for or trained to handle."

"Well, yes and no," Brett countered. "We know we're dealing with an extremely lethal virus, and no one else is better equipped to handle this than the team we have here. Neither the FBI nor the state police would have the foggiest idea how to proceed from here as far as the virus is concerned. But at least we know what we are up against. We know the virus is deadly but not contagious. It seems it was deliberately used to kill twelve people. And we know that one or two vials might still be out there unaccounted for."

"What do you suggest we do?"

"Let's go have lunch. I'm starving," Brett said.

———

After a lunch of southwest fajitas, guacamole, spicy salsa with chips, and cold beer, they were back in Brett's suite, trying to decide what their next move should be.

"Are you going to fill our team in on what is going on? I think they have a right to know what's happened and the danger they may be in."

"Of course. Quinn suggested he should send the team back to Atlanta, but I talked him out of it. He's going to let us wait until the end of the week. We'll have them stay at the inn here or at the medical clinic for their own safety."

"What about Dr. Martin? How much are you going to tell her? Or Chief Jack?"

"I'll figure that out later. Ross, for now, you can organize the team's return home for when we're done here. Have someone back in Atlanta arrange for their tickets and make sure they fly out of Phoenix. I'm going to find Chief Jack," Brett said. "There're too many damned loose ends here, and we need to get some answers soon before someone else gets killed."

"Should we be armed?"

"Probably," Brett said. "But who are we going to shoot? Maybe you should move and get a room on this floor, next to mine, where it'll be safer for both of us. I'm going to go talk to the chief. I've got some questions for him."

Brett opened the door and left, with Tequila trotting along beside him.

33

Brett drove to the Parker Hospital to ask Dr. Martin to contact Chief Jack. He needed to ask the chief some questions. When he pulled his Jeep into the parking area, the chief was standing there talking to someone in a police car marked NAVAJO POLICE. As Brett approached them, the police car backed up and drove away.

"Hello, Dr. Carson. I'm glad to see you're back. Do you have any new information concerning the deaths in the village?" the chief asked.

Brett debated how much to tell the chief, because, at this point, he didn't know much he could trust him. "Well, we found out it's caused by a virus, and it's not contagious. That means you can't catch the disease from someone else."

"Then how did twelve of our people get the virus and die?"

"That's the problem. What we don't know is how they came into contact with the virus. That's what we still have to find out," Brett said. "It could be something in the environment, like the hantavirus that was found to be spread in mice droppings." That obviously wasn't the case this time, but he didn't want to go into details. At least not yet. He looked in the direction the police car had gone. "Why do the Navajo want the CDC off the reservation?" Brett asked.

"There are many reasons. History is not on our side as far as the government helping Indians. You don't understand our people," the chief replied. "Our people have lived in the canyon for more than eight hundred years, and the federal government has been trying to take the land away from us for the last two hundred years. We are the only full-time occupants down in the canyon. This is our land, our home. The Navajo Nation is many times bigger than ours, so they look out for us. Their police keep an eye out for us."

"Chief, who do you meet with in Washington?"

"The Department of the Interior wants us to leave the canyon, but you already know we can't do that. They also want us to sign a mining lease. And we also will never do that."

"That's the second time I've heard about some lease. What's that all about? Does it have anything to do with coal, oil, uranium, gold...anything like that?"

"I don't know what the lease is about. They've never told me."

"Why are they pressuring you to leave the canyon? I assumed they want you to leave for your own safety." Even as Brett asked the question, it hit him. Could they be using the deaths to force the Havasupai to leave the canyon, which would cause them to forfeit their land back to the federal government? If that happened, then there wouldn't be a need for a lease—the land would automatically revert back to the government. As the thoughts raced through his mind, a chill went up his spine. Would his own government go so far as to kill twelve innocent people to obtain a mining lease?

"Who exactly do you meet with?" Brett asked.

"Secretary Wainz."

And there it was. The pieces were starting to fit together, but many unanswered questions remained. Why were they so desperate to get a mining lease? What were they after that could be so valuable that they would go these lengths?

"What's going to happen next?" the chief asked. "Are you planning to have everyone vaccinated?"

"No, Chief, we won't be vaccinating anyone. It could take several weeks to develop a vaccine that could prevent infection from the virus. As for a vaccine to treat someone already infected, it would take at least a few days or even a week for a vaccine to attenuate any symptoms. With this particular virus, you'd be dead long before a vaccine could take effect. Have you met with anyone else in Washington?"

"No. Just Secretary Wainz," the chief said. "Follow me. I want to show you something."

They walked over to where they had a spectacular view of the Grand Canyon that stretched in front of them for more than two hundred and seventy miles. The chief spread his arms out wide. "See all that land and all those canyons? It's all federal land—as far as you can see." He turned his head. "And most of the land behind us up here on the mesa is made up of several Indian reservations."

The chief turned and looked at him. "The guy in the White House is not our president. He doesn't govern us. It's the Secretary of the Interior. He controls all of it. That is why I go there when they tell me to. So, tell me—what are my people supposed to do at this point?"

"I wish I knew, Chief. I wish I knew."

"Humph. Let me know if I can help in any way, and please keep me up to date on any information you find." His sunburned, craggy Indian nickel face looked sad as he walked away.

It's said you can tell a lot by looking at a person's face. But the chief's face was a busy map of crisscrossing deep wrinkles. Like a confusing map, Brett had no idea what his face was saying. But what he was certain of—the old Chief was holding back and hadn't told him everything.

The question was, what possible secret was he hiding?

34

I *don't think you understand our people.*

Chief Jack's words echoed in Brett's mind. The chief was right—maybe he didn't understand the native culture very well. But he knew someone who did. He picked up his phone and dialed.

Why had he recently found it so difficult to call Kari? He knew the reason. It was because he was always canceling any plans they'd made to be together. Of course, even worse since she'd gotten engaged. *Engaged?* He didn't even dare think about it. He couldn't imagine life without her.

"Hi, Brett. Haven't heard from you for a while."

"I'm sorry I haven't called sooner. I've been busy," but he knew the words rang hollow even as he said it. He didn't mean to be short with her, but he was both hurt and angry that she was engaged.

"That always seems to be the case these days," she said. "You're a busy man, and I know you're doing good out there."

After a painful pause, he said, "I need you to come to Arizona to help with an Indian problem. I don't know where else to turn, but I know you can help."

"I've heard a million different pickup lines, but that one's out there in left field," she said. "I don't see how I could be of any help. If it's a medical problem, then I'm the last person you should call. It feels ridiculous to even have to say that. Are you serious, or are you just trying to get me away from George? Which is it?"

"Which is what?"

"Why do you really want me to come out there? Do you need me, or do you just want information?"

"Both," he said, his voice barely above a whisper. "I would love to see you, and we really need your expertise to help deal with the Navajo and Havasupai tribes."

"For the life of me, I can't see how my being there can help with any problems involving Indians. I will say, your come-ons have become more and more provocative."

"I miss you. The other reason is real and very serious. Twelve people on the Havasupai reservation in the canyon have died so far, and we're trying to prevent more deaths. I need your help."

"Are you actually saying that if I don't drop everything and come out there, then I might be responsible for people dying?"

"Not directly. But as ridiculous as that sounds—yes, possibly."

She didn't respond, so after a long pause, he continued.

"I think the chief of the Havasupai tribe knows something that may provide the answers we need, but he doesn't trust us. I thought if you talked to him..."

"The blue-green people," she said.

"What are you talking about?"

"The Havasupai are the 'blue-green people.'"

"What? Why in the world are they called blue-green people?"

"Have you seen the Havasu River? It's a blue-green or turquoise color. The word *havasu* means blue-green, and *pai* means people. *Havasu Pai* means people of the blue-green water. And before you ask, it's that color because of a combination of high levels of calcium carbonate and magnesium in the water."

"See, that's exactly just what I'm talking about. You know more about the people here than probably anyone else. I really need your help."

"I've got three classes every day, it's the middle of the semester, and I'm an adviser for two graduate students who are preparing to defend their theses. I don't see how I can possibly get away."

Silence. He didn't know what to say. He'd made his pitch, but it seemed it wasn't going to work.

Finally, she said, "Look, I'll see what I can do to come out there for a couple of days. I can't promise anything, but I'll try to make it happen."

"Thank you. Let me know where you'll be arriving, and I'll arrange to pick you up at the airport. And if you can stay longer—"

"I said I'll *try* to come out for a couple of days, no more than that. I'll see what I can do."

———

Chicago

She'd spent the two days furiously making arrangements to be away for four days. She didn't know what kind of jam Brett had gotten himself into, but four days there should be more than enough to help out. If this was a scam just to get her out there, he was going to be in serious trouble. The entire premise of the reason for her going out there looked ridiculous from the beginning. What had she been thinking to fall for it? At the same time, she was excited to be with Brett again. She also had to admit she was flattered that he had gone to such extremes to try to coax her into coming.

Her flight was scheduled to leave in three hours, and she'd just finished packing when her phone rang. She hoped there weren't any snags from the department about her leaving.

"Hello?"

"I just heard that the academic review committee announced three junior faculty have been granted full professorship with tenure," George said.

"Congratulations, George. You deserve it. You worked—"

"*Me?* What are you talking about? You're the newest—and by the way, also now the *youngest*—full professor at the University of Chicago. I'll tell you all about it over dinner tonight."

Dinner? *Oh my god!* She'd forgotten all about dinner with George.

"And you still haven't answered my question," he said.

What question? Her mind raced. Too much going on all at once in her mind.

"I asked you to marry me, and you said you needed some time to think about it. I was hoping we could celebrate both our engagement and your new title as professor at the same time."

Silence.

Her mind was a quagmire of emotions. She'd told Brett, the man she loved more than life itself, that someone else had proposed to her. And then proceeded to tell him how any kind of serious relationship could never work out due to their jobs and the distance between them. Now, she was about to break George Pettit's heart and maybe lose him as a friend forever.

"George, I won't be able to go to dinner tonight. I have to—"

"I don't want you to feel pressured for an answer. Just tell me you'll consider it."

He'd kissed her after their last dinner out together. A passionate kiss on his part. The problem was, it left her feeling anything but romantic. It felt like kissing her brother on the lips. He'd kissed her on the cheek before, even a quick kiss on her lips once. But this one was different on all levels.

She'd grown up with George. They'd done everything together, like sister and brother. Played pranks on others, skipped school to go to a movie, gone through confusing adolescence together, and now taught at the same university, where their fathers had also taught. By canceling dinner and leaving, would she be severing that close bond forever? She might be losing the two men who meant the most to her in her life.

"There's been an emergency in Arizona, and I need to see if I can help. I'll be back in a few days. We can talk then."

"A few days?" He sounded hurt and more than a little angry.

"Again, I'm sorry about tonight. You're so sweet for under-standing, George, but it's out of my control. They need someone with knowledge of Indian culture to help them through this."

"Indians? What the hell are you talking about?" His voice grew louder and angrier. "It's not about any Indians. It's about Brett. Why can't you just be honest with me?"

"George, I'm—"

"Have a nice trip. Call me when you finally figure out what it is you want."

Click.

Damnit! She'd just managed to piss off her best friend since childhood, battered his ego, and put his marriage proposal on hold. She doubted if he would even still want to marry her after this. She'd always let him know that Brett was number one in her life, and that he would always still be her best friend. Now this.

As for Brett, why had he asked her to come? As far as he knew, she was engaged to be married. She hadn't told him that she'd decided to come after all. She hadn't told him because she felt that at any moment, she might still change her mind and decide not to go. She stuffed the last of her things into her suitcase, left her condo, and went out to the waiting Uber.

She was headed to Arizona.

But why she was going there, she had no idea.

35

Chief Jack had saddled his horse just before dawn, loaded plenty of water and a snack, then headed out of Supai Village. He followed the Havasu River eastward. Thoughts and questions had been swirling around in his head. The more he tried to sort things out in his mind, the more complicated everything seemed to get. He had no idea what he'd expected to find, but he somehow hoped that by making this trip, he'd find answers to something that was bothering him.

Did the federal government want the tribe's land just to a lease to mine a large portion of it? What had they found that they so desperately needed? Where was it? And what was it? Could it in any way be the answer to all this? That didn't seem possible.

Why did twelve people in the village suddenly die? And why

had no one died after the medical team arrived? In the far corners of his consciousness, a thought kept trying to come to the surface. He kept trying to understand what was nagging him, but it remained out of reach.

Why did they need the mining lease? What had they so desperately needed? Where exactly was it? What was it? Maybe—just maybe—the answer lay ahead of him.

He'd been on the trail an hour, and the horse slowed as its footing became more treacherous as it moved into a narrow, steep canyon known by the park service as the Black Canyon—but his people knew it as *kúuchil yéek'joch'e'en,* 'the Valley of Darkness.'

In Indian folklore, there were many tales of the dark canyon. Some thought it was filled with evil spirits. Others thought it was a healer because a beacon of sunlight was said to have been trapped within its walls in the most sacred part of the great canyons—the very thing the chief hoped to find. Could it hold the answer he was searching for?

As the horse carefully made its way along the uneven, rocky train, something caught the chief's attention out of the corner of his eye. He reined in the horse and turned in his saddle as he looked up the narrow cliff wall. He almost missed it. Movement off to his right caught his eye. What appeared to be a blue climbing rope swayed in the wind that blew through the canyon.

Two or three hundred feet up the side of the cliff, a small flat butte projected out from the cliff halfway down the steep side. The rope dangled down toward the butte. The chief dismounted and climbed up the rocks to the floor of the butte. At first, he couldn't understand what he was looking at. Then, with shock, he realized he was looking at a human body—at least what remained of it.

Someone had apparently fallen while climbing and lay crushed on the rocks. Dark, dried blood smeared the rocks under the body. Wild animals in the canyon had left little of the body recognizable as human.

The trip he'd hoped to make had come to an end for today. He looked around for any kind of personal belongings or identification, such as a billfold, but he found nothing.

Something seemed amiss—beyond the obvious of the poor dead person crumpled, broken, and alone on the ground. He looked up at the rope and saw that the rope was more than a hundred feet too short to reach the butte. The climber would not have been able to reach the butte from there. And there didn't appear to be any of the usual climbing items most climbers carried with them. Very strange. The whole scene was eerie.

The chief left out a sigh and headed back to his horse. His trip hadn't answered any questions. It had only generated more. He climbed back up into the saddle, turned the horse around, and headed back to the village. The Valley of Darkness, filled with evil spirits, apparently still lived up to its name.

The chief slumped forward in his saddle, his heart filled with more sorrow.

36

Brett and Solt were sipping cold beers in the dining room at the Laredo while they waited for their buffalo steak dinners to arrive. "How do you figure the chief fits into all this?" Solt asked.

"Not sure," Brett answered. "He's been to Washington and met with Secretary Wainz at the Department of the Interior. And the chief has been pushing Martin to move the Havasupai out of the canyon. But I get the feeling there's something else he's not telling us."

"Such as...?"

"Such as, why the Department of the Interior wants a mining lease from the Havasupai? What are they looking for? What have they discovered or think they might find in the canyon?"

"But the chief won't tell us what it's all about, right?" Solt asked.

"No, he won't. Maybe he doesn't even know what the lease is all about. I was hoping Kari could help us by talking to him. She knows a lot about—"

"You're not serious, are you?" Solt asked, surprised that Brett would even consider such a thing. "You're not thinking of asking her to come out here, are you?"

Brett paused and bit his lower lip. Finally, he said, "I've asked her to come in the hope that we might get more information from Chief Jack. He's holding out on us. I want to know why. And what is it that he doesn't want to tell us?"

Solt stared at him, then said, "We don't know what kind of danger we could all be in here, and you still asked her to come? Are you really willing to risk her life? We still don't know how the virus was delivered to those twelve victims. Every time I take a drink, brush my teeth, or take a bite of food, I wonder if someone has placed some of the virus there. Am I scared? You damned well better believe it."

"Don't worry. I'll keep her out of harm's way," Brett said. "I won't let anything happen to her. No one even has to know that she's with us. As far as they'll know, she'll be just another tourist."

"Uh-huh. Sure. What could go wrong?"

"Don't worry, Ross. She's already said there's no way she'd be able to make it work with her teaching schedule."

Just as their steak dinners arrived, they were aware that several people in the restaurant had turned to look at something. They both turned to see a statuesque, beautiful young woman with long, dark hair make her way to their table. She wore a suede skirt with a slit up the side revealing a long, bare thigh as she walked. A silver and turquoise squash blossom necklace hung around her neck. She looked beyond exquisite. He recognized the necklace as one that her father had given her.

"Kari!" Brett said. He jumped up, grabbed her in his arms, and kissed her.

"You're right," Solt said, "nobody will ever guess she's with us."

She leaned down and gave Solt a quick kiss on his cheek. "Hi, Ross. What did you say?"

"I said welcome to Arizona," Solt said. "Wow, you look awesome. Nice rags."

"Brett got it for me for my birthday." She discreetly winked at Solt and had a smile on her face. "I heard someone was looking for an Indian scout, so here I am. Am I too late for dinner? I haven't eaten since breakfast."

"Not at all," Brett said, with a mile-wide smile on his face. "Come join us. We're having buffalo steaks, au gratin potatoes, and asparagus." He pulled out a chair for her beside him. As soon as she sat down, he leaned over and kissed her again.

That kiss sent a warm sensation through her, and she hungered for more. It was nothing like the bland kiss with George had been. Kissing Brett caused her knees to go weak, her heart to beat faster, and her body wanting him to wrap her in his arms.

"Ah-hem," Solt said, clearing his throat. "Let's just enjoy dinner for now. Kari, we're so surprised—and thrilled—to see you here."

"Thanks. Until the very last second, I still wasn't sure I was actually going to go through with it and come out—not until the plane finally left the ground. But I'm glad I did. It's great seeing both of you."

Solt spoke to the waitress and pointed to her. Then he smiled and said, "I let the kitchen know you were here, and your dinner will be here shortly."

After a great dinner filled with laughter and catching up on old times together, the three of them left the dining room and went up to their rooms.

"G'night, Ross," Kari said.

"Yeah. I'll be right across the hall if you need me."

"Why would I need you?" Kari asked.

Solt looked at Brett, who nodded in response. Then she realized he was talking to Brett, not her.

She knew something was going on between them, but decided this wasn't the time to pursue it.

37

Once in their room, Tequila tackled her just as he had Brett.

"Tequila!" she yelled. She hugged the huge dog while he whined and wagged his tail furiously. Finally, he sat down beside her while she rubbed his fur.

"I think it's safe to say he missed you," Brett said, grinning. After he fed Tequila, they took him outside for a walk. The sun hung low just above the horizon and bathed the hundreds of cliffs and canyons in various shades of orange and deepening shadows. They walked to the edge of the South Rim and stood beside each other with his arm around her.

"It's beautiful," she said. "It seems like it goes forever."

He took her in his arms and kissed her, a long, hunger-filled, wanton kiss. They looked into each other's eyes for a long moment, then he suddenly turned, and they went back to the room. His actions were confusing, holding her and kissing her passionately one moment, then turning and walking away from her the next. She was left bewildered and not sure what had just happened or what she should do.

Back in the room, she was somewhat surprised when Brett

grabbed his guitar and sat on the floor. Something was definitely bothering him, but she didn't have a clue what it could be. Wasn't he glad to see her and anxious to be with her? Leaning back against the wall, he started playing romantic Spanish guitar. She sat down beside him and smiled. The music was beautiful, but she still didn't know what was happening. Any previous time they had been together, he couldn't keep his hands off her.

What was going on? Had he decided they should just be friends?

Tequila stretched out on the floor at their feet. Kari rested her head on Brett's shoulder as he played. Finally, she asked, "Why do you keep staring at my skirt?"

He stopped playing. "I'm not staring at your skirt. I'm staring at that incredible exposed thigh."

She sat up and smiled at him. "Wanna do something about it?"

"Why did you come out here?"

His question came like a sudden slap-in-the face. "What?" she asked, completely devastated. "You asked me to come. You thought I might be able to help." Her eyes started to tear up.

"What did what's-his-name think about that?"

"What's his name? You mean George? He hated the idea of me coming here."

"I've never made out with a married woman, or with someone who's engaged," he said, with just the faintest hint of anger in his voice. "I'm pretty sure your fiancé is going to be upset if we continue."

"My what?"

"Fiancé," he repeated.

She stared at him for a moment. Then she understood, and suddenly all of his previous actions made sense. Relieved, she burst out laughing. "So, that's what this is all about? You think

I'm engaged?" She threw a pillow at him while laughing. "I didn't say I was engaged, you doofus."

"You said—"

"I said George asked me to marry him. I never told him yes."

He put his guitar to the side. "Did you tell him no?"

"I told him I could never marry him. He's like a brother to me. I love him, but not in a romantic way. I told him I was madly in love with someone else."

He stared at her, then reached out and hugged her firmly against him, as if she might fly away. Then he leaned down and kissed her, a long, hungry, passionate kiss, leaving no doubt of his desire.

Finally, she pulled back from him, smiled and pushed him down on the soft carpet, and straddled him. "So how about it?" she asked in a husky voice, unbuttoning her blouse.

He slid his hand up her leg.

"Won't this ruin your skirt?"

"No, because I won't be wearing it." She pulled off her boots, then slid out of her suede skirt and straddled him again.

He pulled her down and kissed her with obvious desire and arousal. He rubbed his thumb over her cheek to wipe away a tear and gently pushed her hair back from her face. They both worked to get his jeans and shirt off in short order, and they fell onto the bed. He started to lean over her, but she pushed him down and straddled him again.

"Now, where were we?" she asked. She felt his firmness against her soft skin. She moved over him and expertly guided him into her. His moan of contentment and arousal sent a surge of heat through her.

He looked up at her and said, "I forgot..."

Moving her body over his, she said, "Evidence to the contrary, it doesn't seem you've forgotten anything."

"Not that..." he said, staring at her. "I forgot how beautiful you are."

A big smile spread across her face, and she bent over and kissed him. In a raspy, aroused voice, she said, "Show me," and she pushed herself against him with increased intensity.

He removed her blouse, pulled her bra off, and ran his hand smoothly over her breast.

"God, I love you," he said breathlessly.

She stopped, her face flushed. "What did you say?"

"I said I love you. But if you stop again, I might retract that."

She smiled, punched him on the shoulder, and proceeded to make sure he didn't retract anything.

Later, lying beside each other on the bed, he said, "I've missed you. I love having our little family together again."

"Our family?"

"Yep. You, me, and Tequila."

"Well, in that little equation, who comes first? Me or Tequila?"

"It was a toss-up until you showed you were able to do things Tequila wasn't capable of." After holding her in his arms, he looked over at her and said, "There's something I've got to tell you. It could be very dangerous for you to be here right now. I've put you in a very risky situation by asking you to come out. Ross thinks you shouldn't have come because he's worried about you."

"What do you think?"

"He's right. It might be too dangerous for you to be here."

"So—then why did you ask me to come out?"

"I hoped you would be able to get more information out of Chief Jack. But mostly..."

"Yes?"

"Mostly, I just wanted to be with you."

She looked over at him, the moonlight casting a pale blue glow to the room. At that moment, everything seemed as it should be. They were together, lying beside each other, just them, Tequila, and the moon. Safe, happy, satisfied, and in love.

She snuggled closer, afraid of what the future might portend. She hadn't told him yet that she'd just been appointed to a full professorship. She feared their lives were going to grow further apart rather than closer together.

What was going to happen to them?

38

The following morning, they went to Solt's door and knocked. Brett was ready to knock again when a young woman finally opened the door. Taken by surprise, Brett started to check the room number again when she said, "Dr. Carson. Good morning."

It took Brett a second to recognize her. She was the young nurse from Nova Scotia. "Sarah, good morning. It's nice to see you again."

She smiled back at him. "Ross is—"

"Morning," Solt said, poking his head around. "I'll meet you down at breakfast in a while."

"Who was that?" Kari asked.

"Tell you later," Brett said.

Kari and Brett found a table in the dining room and looked

over the menu. A short time later, Solt joined them just in time to give the waitress his order.

"Where's Sarah?" Kari asked.

"I made sure Sarah was on the shuttle to the airport. She had to get back to Nova Scotia today. She'd earlier planned on coming to Atlanta for a long weekend, but when she learned I was out here, she decided to change her flight and come out here. She was only able to stay one night."

"She's adorable, Ross," Kari said. "I wish she could have stayed longer."

"Yeah, we were supposed to have time together in Atlanta until someone arranged for me to come to Arizona," he said, looking at Brett with a smirk on his face.

"How are you doing?" Brett asked him. "You look tired. Are you okay?"

"Yeah. Didn't sleep much last night."

"Coffee?" Kari asked as she proceeded to pour for all of them.

"Yeah, thanks." Ross took a drink from the cup, then asked, "Have you heard the news?"

"No. What? Another death?" Brett asked.

"Good guess, but not from any virus. I heard they found a body up in one of the remote canyons. Probably a climbing accident."

"Who found it?" Brett asked.

"Apparently, Chief Jack found it yesterday when he was out for a ride on his horse," Solt said as he tore into his corned beef hash and fried potatoes.

"I would have guessed the chief would somehow be involved," Brett said as he finished the last of his coffee, then put his cup down.

"So, what's the deal here? Is the chief causing a problem?" Kari asked.

"I don't know, actually," Brett said, spreading strawberry jam on his toast. "I'm still trying to figure him out."

"What do we do next?" she asked.

"I'm actually on my way to talk to the chief now about some other issues," Brett said. "I'd like you to come with me. Maybe he can also provide more information about the dead climber."

"Of course I'm going with you," Kari said. "Maybe I can help. Isn't that why you sent for me?"

Solt looked at him. Brett knew what had caused the stern look from his friend. Solt was worried for Kari's safety.

"What?" she asked, as she looked at both men.

"Don't worry, Ross. I'll take good care of her." But he could tell Solt wasn't convinced. "Tequila will be with us the entire time."

"What's going on?" Kari asked. "Is there something I need to know—such as just how safe is it for me to be here?"

"We don't know anything for certain yet. So, for now, we're just always being cautious."

"Am I in any danger here?"

"We don't think so," Brett said.

"Well, that's encouraging. As long as you don't *think* so. What —are you guys my protector now?" she asked.

"Yes," Brett said, then stood to leave. He turned to Ross. "See what information you can dig up about this. We'll be back for lunch. Dinner at the latest."

———

With Kari and Tequila in the Jeep, Brett drove to the hospital. "Dr. Martin said she would try to get the chief to come here to answer some questions," Brett told her as he pulled into the parking lot. With Tequila lying in his usual spot in the Jeep, they went inside to Martin's office.

"Good morning," Martin said. "How is everyone this morning? Anything new to report?"

"Have you heard about the dead climber the chief found yesterday?" Brett asked.

"Yes. That's not as unusual as you might think. We have about a dozen or more deaths each year from a variety of causes such as medical problems, suicide, heat, drowning in the river. In addition, at least a handful of people fall off the rim every summer to their deaths. Accidents, suicides, maybe while trying to get the 'perfect' selfies—who knows? The rangers keep a sharp lookout for stupid people too close to the edge trying for the perfect picture, but they continue to fall every year."

"We heard Chief Jack found the body yesterday," Solt said.

"That's what I understand. He should be here shortly."

No sooner had she said that, than the door opened and the chief walked in. He immediately stopped as both he and Kari stared at each other.

"Chief, *Jacq-teh Kwa-ki,*" Kari said with a big grin on her face. "*Ya'at'eeh,*" she said.

"*Ya'at'eeh,*" the chief repeated as he moved up and hugged her. "I never thought I would see you again. How are you? You look *nizhóní*—beautiful as ever."

Brett asked, "Do you two—"

Kari turned and explained to Brett and Martin that she and Chief Jack had met before, during her nine months living with the Navajo and Hopi people while she was doing her dissertation research on southwestern tribes of the United States. "My father came to spend the summer with me here at the end of my research, and that's when we both met the chief here."

"How is Forrest?" the chief asked.

Her head sagged for a moment, then she looked up at him and said, "My father was killed in Guatemala."

Chief Jack was obviously taken aback. "Oh, no. Was it an accident?"

"The leader of a rebel gang shot him in cold blood."

The old Chief shook his head. "I'm so sorry. Forrest was a good man. We shared many laughs together." Then he asked her, "Are you here with Dr. Carson?"

"Yes. Brett asked me to come and see if I could be of any help. He saved my life, at least three times. I'm here to see if I can return the favor."

"Chief, can I ask you some questions?" Brett asked.

"Of course. I'm glad to help in any way I can."

"I understand you found a body in one of the canyons yesterday," Brett said.

"I can see that news and gossip travel faster than the smoke signals my ancestors used. Yes, I found a dead body yesterday morning."

"How far away was it?"

"About twelve miles up the Black Canyon."

"Isn't that area still restricted to everyone?"

"Yes, but he apparently climbed down, anyway."

"How did you happen to find him?" Brett asked.

"I stumbled on him by accident. Almost missed him. Saw movement out the corner of my eye. A rope swaying in the wind. I went to investigate and found the body, what was left of it. Just briefly glancing over the scene, something didn't add up. Very strange. The victim had no backpack, no water, no climbing harness, no climbing paraphernalia of any kind. And the rope hanging there was at least a hundred feet short of the ground."

"Do they know who the person was? Any identification?"

"I said 'he,' but they still don't know the sex of the victim. The Navajo police and the state police are trying to identify the body, but it was in terrible condition. The fall alone probably crushed every bone in his body. Wolves, foxes, vultures, as well as small rodents, had not left much to identify. The canyon is too narrow in that area to use a helicopter, so they had to bring the body out on horseback."

"Why were you up in that particular canyon? Were you looking for something?"

"Why are you interrogating me? Is something bothering you?"

Kari grabbed his arm to get his attention, but Brett continued. "Yes, as a matter of fact, there is. I'm not sure you've been totally honest with us. You're holding back on something, and I'd like to know what it is. You're the only one talking to the Department of the Interior in Washington, the one who wants to move the tribe out of the canyon. And the one person who may know something about a lease. And you were the one who just happened to find the body yesterday in some remote canyon."

The chief turned and looked at Kari. "It was nice seeing you again, Kari. I'm sorry about your father." Then he opened the door and left.

Kari turned and looked at him. "Just great. Now what?"

"Sorry about that," Brett said, "but I don't trust him. I'm sure he's involved in something here. I just don't know what it is or to what extent. I'll go tell him I'm sorry about that. We're still going to need his help."

Kari gave him a stern look, then said, "Wait here. I'll see what I can do. I might have better luck with him." She turned and hurried after him. Brett watched through the window as they talked.

Ten minutes later, both Kari and Chief Jack returned to Martin's office.

"Chief Jack," Kari said, "Dr. Carson here wants to apologize for what he said, and to ask you for your help."

The chief looked like he was considering her request.

"Chief, I'm sorry I sounded so accusatory before," Brett said. "Things are confusing here, and I'm just trying to figure it all out before someone else dies. Can you take us to where you found the body? Because of some of the questions you raised about what you saw, I'd like to go have another look at it."

"As I said, the Navajo police and the State Patrol are already looking into it. There probably won't be enough evidence left to make it worthwhile."

"Yes, but I'm afraid they might also just chalk it up to just another climbing accident, when, in fact, it could be much more than that."

"Like what?" the chief asked.

"We won't know until we look. We'd be most grateful if you could take us there."

The chief thought a moment, then said, "Yes, I can take you there. It's over a two-hour ride by horse, and the trail is treacherous. First thing tomorrow morning. It's too late to try it today."

Brett extended his hand. "Thank you, Chief. We appreciate your help."

"I'll be down in Supai Village at the corral tomorrow with three horses saddled and ready."

39

After a long, tiring day, Brett and Kari went down to the restaurant with Solt to have a dinner of Mexican corn husk tamales, tortillas filled with guacamole, rice, and red beans. All three of them were sipping margaritas from large-rim glasses.

"How was your day, Ross?" Brett asked, licking salt from his lips.

"Well, I tried to get more information about the body that was found yesterday morning. The state police are hoping their forensic odontologist can identify the body using computerized dental records. I contacted the medical examiner, and he assured me he'll contact me as soon as they have positive identification or anything else to report after the autopsy."

"Tomorrow morning, Chief Jack is taking us by horseback to visit the site," Brett said. "The chief mentioned that some things he noted at the site didn't seem right. I want to go check it out. I want Kari to go with me and the chief."

"Absolutely. I'm looking forward to it," Kari said.

"What did the chief see that didn't seem right?" Solt asked.

"He mentioned some things that didn't fit with a simple climbing accident."

"You mean, maybe—?"

"Yeah, maybe it wasn't an accident."

"Mysteries just keep piling up, don't they?" Solt said.

"Did you bring your father's revolver?" Brett asked Kari.

"No. It's too big. So, I brought this." She slipped her hand into a side pocket and discreetly showed him her new pistol. "It's a 9-millimeter Glock 26. It chambers ten rounds."

"Nice. Always keep it with you while you're out here."

"Looks to me like you guys are playing cowboys and Indians, using real horses and guns," Solt said. "While you're out ridin' the range with the Injun' chief, I'll stay here with Tequila and see what else I can find out."

Just then, Solt's phone rang. He listened, nodded, then asked, "Are you certain about this?" Then, after nodding again, he said, "Thank you for letting me know," and he hung up.

"Well, this just keeps getting better," he said. "That was the forensic pathologist at the medical examiner's office. The victim was a forty-two-year-old geologist from the University of Colorado named Kevin Horton. They estimate the time of death was somewhere between two and a half to three weeks ago. And the chief was right. According to the police, there were things about the site that didn't add up to a simple climbing accident."

"Is that everything?" Kari asked.

"No. Here is the best part. The evidence is minimal, but the ME says it's possible he was beaten and tortured before the fall. Even though the fall onto the rocks did incredible damage, they suspect that a few of his injuries may have occurred before the fall, while he was still alive."

"What the hell?" Brett exclaimed. "So, we have fourteen deaths, three stolen vials of a deadly virus from a lab in England, a mining lease that the Department of the Interior apparently wants for who knows what reason, and a dead geologist in a remote canyon, possibly another murder victim."

"Yeah, that about sums it up," Solt said.

After a few moments, Brett said, "What I'm most worried about is that it's possible there could be one or two vials of the virus still out there somewhere. And if we don't solve this soon, then there might be more deaths in the village."

"And that, boys and girls, is the end of tonight's bedtime story," Solt said after he downed the last of his margarita.

"What bothers me," Brett said, "is how did the virus get into the village? And according to everyone we interviewed, nobody saw anything or anyone suspicious."

"Whoever did it didn't leave a trace. Almost like they were invisible," Solt said.

"Like a ghost," Kari added softly.

"Yeah, well, I don't believe in ghosts," Brett added.

"The simplest answer is that it was someone in the village," Kari added. "Nobody would have noticed anything unusual since they weren't a stranger."

"And they flew to England, then broke into a secure military lab before bringing the virus here?" Brett asked.

"Guess not," she said. "So, someone from outside the village has to be the culprit. But nobody has seen anyone suspicious."

"Yeah, whoever brought the virus here wasn't seen, wasn't heard," Solt said.

"Looks like a ghost is still the best possibility," Kari said, smiling.

They finished their meals and drinks, then said goodnight and returned to their rooms.

At their door, Brett looked at Kari. "I've got too much on my mind to sleep now. Wanna go for a walk?"

"I'd love to."

After feeding Tequila, they walked outside and went to Brett's favorite spot, a large, flat rock on the South Rim. They sat close together as they thought about the day's events.

Tequila sensed something was wrong and kept nudging Brett with his nose and licking his hand.

"I'll be okay, fella," he said as he rubbed his dog's head.

"What are you thinking about?" she asked.

"I'm thinking about the chief. Somehow, he could be the key to the whole mess. I just don't know how or why yet. He's the only one talking to the Secretary of the Interior. He tried to talk the tribal council into moving everyone out of the canyon. He's the person who found the body of the dead geologist. Why was he out in that particular canyon?"

"Chief Jack couldn't kill anyone," Kari said.

"And how exactly do you know that?" He let out a deep sigh as he looked out across the wide expanse. "And we don't know where the vials containing the virus are—or who presumably used the virus to kill twelve people. Or *why*."

They watched the deep reds of an awesome expansive western sunset, with scattered clouds backlit with crimson and yellow. A cold breeze from the deep canyons chilled the night air. An occasional hoot of a great horned owl broke the silence of the night, and somewhere off in the distance, a pack of coyotes yelped at the full moon.

Finally, she looked at him and said, "What's to become of us?"

"We'll be fine. Just be sure to keep the Glock with you."

"No, I mean *us*. What's to become of you and me?"

"I knew what you meant," he said quietly. "I just couldn't give you an answer yet—because I don't know."

She took hold of his arm and laid her head against him. "I'm scared, Brett. Of everything. Of the future. Of us."

He leaned over, pulled her in closer against him, and kissed the top of her head.

"Maybe not today, maybe not tomorrow, but sometime soon,

you'll understand that the problems of two little people don't amount to a hill of beans in this crazy world..." he said, using his best Bogart imitation.

She looked up at him. "You doofus—that's from *Casablanca*, and it's three people, not two. And we're not in a war, fighting Nazis."

Tequila whined and put a paw on her lap.

"How many languages does he understand?" she asked.

"At least two. But he seems to understand best what's actually *not* being spoken."

The sun had long disappeared, and the final faint glow of night had completely faded. Cold wind blew across the mesa, and their breaths blended into a single faint cloud in the cold night air.

The forecast was for a cold night and gusting winds. Just what they didn't need while riding horses in a canyon. They finally stood to leave, and the moon seemed to sense their despondence as it oozed its way slowly up through the scattered mesquite and scrub oaks. Moonlight grew brighter and turned the ground to a silver glow as they walked together back to the Laredo and their room.

———

They each showered, then climbed into bed. She cuddled against him and rested her head on his chest.

He stroked her hair. "You're incredible."

"Flattery will get you nowhere, but don't stop trying."

He rubbed his hand over her stomach, then down to her legs.

"Hmm. It seems like there's something your body is trying to tell you," she whispered as she felt him stiffen against her.

"Well then, I guess I better listen to it."

He leaned over and looked down at her, lying there naked and bathed by faint moonlight coming through the window. He caressed gently over her breast, then kissed it. "You are so…"

"Yes?"

"Perfect." Then he bent down and kissed her on the lips. Soft, gentle, but with a hint of growing desire. Then he moved lower and kissed her stomach, then moved lower. She moaned a deep, guttural sound and wrapped her legs around him. He wouldn't allow himself to rush this time. Slow and sensual, he thought, both of them feeling every movement, no matter how small.

He then leaned over her, moved between her legs, and pushed gently into her, then pulled out.

She raised her head. "What—?"

He answered by pushing into her again, deeper this time. A smile spread across her face, and she closed her eyes and moaned. He was driving her wild with anticipation. Then she wrapped her legs around him and pulled him as deep as he could go—and rocked her pelvis against him.

The hell with going slow. He matched her frantic rhythm, and they moved entangled in the faint moonlight. Afterward, they lay beside each other, satisfied, and spent. At that moment, it felt like they'd never been apart from each other for weeks.

She blew out a deep breath, pushed a damp strand of hair back from her face, looked over at him, and said in a husky voice, "What'cha thinking about?"

After a quiet pause, Brett said, "I think we need to contact the rock man."

"That is certainly the most unexpected pillow talk after sex ever I've ever heard. And for the life of me, I can't imagine what you're talking about."

"I'm serious. We've been here for almost three weeks, and we still seem to have more questions than answers to this mess. And still, the deaths keep adding up. Maybe the rock man can help us."

She punched his arm. "*Rock man?* Just let it go."

"No—I'm serous. He might somehow be able to help us find out what that lease is all about."

After a long pause, she said, "Do you want me to ask him before or after I tell him that I won't marry him?"

"We need his help, so ask before you tell him that. Just as long as the answer is no."

"*No?* What do you mean?"

"Of course, you've got to tell the rock man 'no' that you are not going to marry him. But not until after you've asked for his help."

She let out a long sigh. "What a tangled web we weave."

"Yeah, well, let's hope our tangled web catches the spider for us."

"*Rock man,*" she mumbled as shook her head in disbelief. But she had formed her own idea of what she needed to do.

And in the quiet that followed, she planned to do just that.

40

Immediately after breakfast the following morning, Kari excused herself and left Solt and Brett sitting at the table, finishing their coffee. She went back up to the room so she could talk to George Pettit in private. It was not a call she was looking forward to. Arizona and the Grand Canyon were in the mountain time zone, so back in Chicago it would be an hour later in the day. If she was lucky, she might catch him before his classes started for the day.

She grew queasy as she reached for the phone. After canceling a dinner reservation and having stood him up, she was now going to ask him for help. She tried to tell herself there was no need to get so worked up about this—they'd been best friends forever. Still, she was asking the man to whom she'd turned down a marriage proposal to drop everything in order to help her.

He answered after the first ring. "Hi, Kari. How are you?"

"I'm fine, George, thanks., I'm so sorry about what happened Thursday and for leaving so suddenly. It had nothing to do with you—"

"Look, I knew you wouldn't marry me," he blurted out. "But I had to ask. I couldn't go through life without knowing for sure. There would always be a 'what if.' I couldn't have handled that."

"Thank you. That's why I love you. And I apologize for skipping out of dinner reservations at the last minute."

After a long pause, he said, "It's obvious there's something you want to say—so go ahead and say it."

"Actually, I'm calling to ask for a favor. The situation out here in Arizona has gotten complicated, and we need your help. Two days ago, a body was found in one of the canyons. It was thought to be from a climbing accident. But there are things that suggest it could have been something else."

"By something else, do you mean he might have been killed? Murdered?"

"Possibly."

"Look, I don't know a thing about technical climbing. Even less about forensics."

"There's more," she continued. "The body was identified as Kevin Horton, a forty-five-year-old geologist from the University of Colorado. Also—possibly related—the federal government apparently wants a mining lease on land that belongs to the Havasupai."

"I don't understand. What do you want me to do?"

"It's possible that what he may have found there is important and could be a big part of the puzzle. We want you to find out as much as you can about Kevin Horton and why he was in the canyon. Horton's death may somehow be connected to the lease and whatever it is the government wants to mine there. We need to know more about the lease and why it's so important."

"Well, why didn't you just say so? I thought it might be something really difficult. Seriously, what the hell is going on?"

"I'm not sure. Whatever it is, it's not good. We need your help."

"I can't promise anything, but I'll do what I can. As it turns out, one of my previous grad students is now at the University of Colorado. He almost certainly knew Horton and might be able to provide some information. I'll ask around and see what I can find out."

"Excellent. Also, buy a burner phone and only use it. Send me a text message with its phone number. That way, I can always reach you, and there's no way it can be traced. Just don't use your own phone or credit cards."

"I gotta tell you, after everything you just told me, I'm not really into doing anything like this. I'm a geologist, not a spy."

"You have no idea how much this will help us."

"Okay, I'll get on it. I can't promise you anything. And you have to know I'll also be spending a good amount of my time deciding how you can repay me," he said.

"One more thing—"

"Here it comes..."

"Be careful. Several people have already died because of this, possibly even Professor Horton. This is dangerous, and I don't want anything bad happening to you."

After a long pause, George said, "You might have led with that. How much danger will I be in?"

"I don't know. Probably not too much. Just be very careful."

"How do you suggest I do that?"

"Call me or Brett using the burner phone as soon as you know anything." She gave him Brett's cell phone number and email address. "I love you, George. I'll be mad as hell if anything happens to you."

"Well, that's comforting. And Kari—I love you, always have, always will. Do *not*—and I repeat—do not let anything happen to you."

"Good luck, George." And she hung up quickly as she grabbed Kleenex to muffle her sobbing. She'd just asked her best friend to get involved in a dangerous, possibly deadly, situation.

41

Kari and Brett drove the Jeep to the Medical Clinic to catch the helicopter ride down to Supai Village. A strong, blustery, warm wind blew out of the west, and occasionally the gusts became almost unbearable. Dust blew sideways and stung their faces, and tumbleweeds rolled across the tundra, like giant bowling balls. Tim landed the copter in a swirling cloud of dust, weeds, and flying bits of stones and sticks, and motioned for them to jump in.

"These conditions aren't safe for flying," Tim yelled over the noise of the copter combined with the wind. "Let's get you down there as fast as possible. Then I'm going to head back and tie this bird down for the rest of the day." They scrambled into the plane, which was being buffeted by the wind. The copter lifted off, banked sharply to the left, and dropped into the canyon, which provided noticeable protection from the wind.

It had barely landed when they jumped out. Tim took off again, raced down the canyon with the wind behind him, and disappeared from sight.

Brett looked at her and said, "I'm glad at least you didn't wear that suede skirt to go riding today."

She smiled at him. "You worried that the chief might get ideas?"

"No. Because it would give me ideas, and I wouldn't be able to concentrate on anything else." He thought she was sexy enough wearing tight jeans, her knee-high suede boots, and a dark blue sweatshirt that failed to hide her figure.

"Wow, you really are randy. Maybe you should try harder to get up to see me more often than every two months or so."

The chief walked over, holding the reins to the three horses. "Morning," he said. "I wasn't sure you'd make it down here with the way the wind's blowing today. Do you folks know how to ride?"

"I spent the past several summers with my father riding horses through jungles and over mountains," Kari answered.

"Humph," the chief said, and nodded. Then he turned to Brett. "How about you, Dr. Carson? Can you ride?"

They had never discussed horseback riding, and Kari was curious what his answer would be. "I can handle a horse. I was raised by my aunt and uncle on their ranch in Colorado. I did my fair share of riding through the foothills."

The chief grunted again and handed them each a set of reins to their horses.

"You're right about the wind. Up on the mesa this morning it was unbelievable," Brett said. "We almost didn't make it down because of the blustery gusts. The pilot said the conditions exceeded the safe limits for the helicopter."

"Chinook winds," the chief said. "It's known as the 'snow eater' wind. It might snow during a cold winter day, then the warm chinook blows during the night, and the next morning—poof—no more snow."

"The chinook winds are actually named after the Chinook

tribe along the Columbia River," Kari said. "The same warm, winter-wind pattern occasionally blows down through the Columbia River basin."

"Chief, I like your version better," Brett said, laughing. "Snow eater."

"Humph," the chief said and climbed up onto his horse. That grunt was obviously an important part of his lexicon.

They both climbed onto their mounts and followed him single file along a dirt path leading away from the village. The wind howled through the red-barked ponderosa pine trees and filled the air with the scent of pine and a hint of butterscotch. After riding for over forty minutes, the pines gave way to more barren, rocky terrain.

Ahead of them was the opening to a dark canyon with narrow, steep walls that blocked out the sun, leaving only shadows. It seemed foreboding, and the horses seemed nervous as they carefully made their way along the narrow, rocky trail.

When the canyon widened in a section, the chief reined in his horse and allowed them to come alongside him. "On the map," he said, pointing ahead, "you will see this canyon is labeled the Black Canyon. But to us, it is known as the *kúuchil yéek'joch'e'en*, meaning 'the valley of darkness.'"

"Horton sure picked a hell of a place to go rock climbing by himself. What in the world could he have been thinking?" Brett said.

"Maybe he was looking for something," Kari replied in a soft voice.

Chief Jack looked at both of them, then nudged his mount and led the way into the canyon.

Their eyes soon adjusted to the muted light. The dark shadows were nowhere near total darkness, and scattered ambient light allowed them to see the rocky trail underfoot and the layered, jagged cliffs that rose on each side of them. The gusting chinooks had died down, leaving a steady light breeze blowing through the canyon. After another twenty minutes of traveling up the canyon, it widened, and a small bluff came into view a hundred feet above them. The area of the bluff's flat ground interrupted the otherwise vertical cliff wall that extended up.

"Up there," the chief said and pointed. A frayed blue climbing rope swayed in the breeze.

They dismounted, and after twenty minutes of climbing, they finally stepped onto the bluff. The only pieces of evidence that remained were a blood-stained jagged rock on the ground and a frayed rope, which ended more than seventy feet above them.

"It seems obvious to me that this was no accident," Brett said, staring up at the rope. "There's no way anybody could reach the ground using that rope."

"So, possibly he was murdered," Kari said. "Why would anyone want to kill a geologist by dropping him into a canyon?"

"Maybe he found something in the canyon that someone else desperately wanted," Brett said, glancing around the area. "Did he have information that they wanted? Or maybe he discovered something—something so valuable that they would go to any lengths to get it. Did his secret die with him?"

Brett had noticed that the chief had kept glancing back. "What do you see?"

"Nothing. But someone has been following us for the last hour or so," Chief Jack said matter-of-factly.

They both looked around quickly but saw nothing. "Why didn't you mention it earlier?" Brett asked.

"No reason to. You wanted to see the site of the accident. If I had told you, would you have turned back? Whoever it is doesn't want to be seen."

"How did you know we were being followed?" Kari asked.

"I didn't. The horses did. They smelled or heard something. I could see their ears moving, their occasional hesitation. They are aware of everything, so they won't be surprised by wolves or a mountain lion."

"But it's not an animal, is it?" Brett asked.

"No," the chief said. "If you're done here, let's head back."

They climbed down off the bluff, mounted their horses, and followed the chief back out of the Black Canyon. Brett and Kari both looked around now more intently than before, and both also glanced at their horses during the trip back for any kind of clue.

They finally rode back into Supai Village, went to the corral, and dismounted. They helped the chief remove the saddles and brush down the horses.

"Chief, thank you for taking us there, and arranging for the horses. You've been a big help. Please drop by the Laredo anytime and let us buy dinner for you."

The chief shook his hand and started to walk away. "Did you spot anything on the way back?" Brett asked him.

"Maybe. Couldn't be sure. Whoever it was, they're very good at disappearing."

42

The following morning, the three enjoyed a leisurely breakfast together, trying to decide what they needed to do next while waiting for any information George Pettit might uncover.

"Yesterday, what we saw seemed to confirm what we'd suspected all along. That was no climbing accident," Brett said. "Horton was almost certainly murdered. And Chief Jack thought we were being followed. We don't know that for sure. And if we were being followed, we don't know by whom or why."

"We don't even know if Horton's death had any connection to everything else," Kari said. "There's no reason to assume there is."

"Maybe," Brett said, "but I don't really believe in coincidence. Especially now. It doesn't look like a climbing accident, and it looks like he was injured—possibly tortured—before he died. It must somehow be connected."

"I swear," Solt said, "for every answer we uncover, we seem to somehow come up with more questions. Where do we go from here?"

"That's what we need to figure out. This is different from any other situation we've faced before," Brett said. "This appears to be some kind of complex, man-made scheme resulting in the deaths of several people. And it's even possible our own government could be somehow involved. If Pettit can turn up anything, that may help answer some questions. But it seems for sure that the medical aspect of this is only peripheral to what is really going on."

"Since this seems to be a criminal situation rather than a medical problem, it looks like our work here is over," Solt said. "We need to turn this over to someone else, like maybe the FBI."

"I agree, but I don't think we should do anything until we hear from Pettit. Until then, there's not much more we can do here. Let's hope he calls us soon with new information. In the meantime, make sure the rest of the team is safely back in Atlanta by this weekend."

———

The phone call came the next evening, just before the three of them were headed into the restaurant for dinner.

It was a phone number Brett didn't recognize. "Hello."

"Hi, Brett. It's George Pettit. Kari asked me to see if I could find out anything about the geologist from the University of Colorado and what he might have been involved in. I'm at the Livermore airport in California, waiting for my flight back to Chicago. "

"You're in California? How in the hell did you end up there?"

"The people at the Lawrence Livermore National Laboratory weren't going to give me any information over the phone, so I flew out here to talk to them in person. I wanted to tell you what I've learned before my flight back."

"How is the Lawrence Livermore lab possibly involved? Okay, now you've got my attention."

"This really is a tangled mess," Pettit said. "I hardly know where to begin. One of my previous grad students, who's now at UC, was able to fill me in on some facts regarding Horton. Apparently, he stumbled onto some kind of strange blue rock at the bottom of the Grand Canyon. He was thrilled about his discovery of what he hoped was a new mineral and told anyone who would listen to him. According to the information he provided at the time, he found the stone at the bottom of some narrow, remote canyon. He did every analysis on the rock sample that he could do in his lab at the University of Colorado, then sent it on to the Colorado School of Mines laboratory in Golden for more extensive evaluation. They were unable to provide definite answers, so they, in turn, sent it on to the Lawrence Livermore lab here in California.

"The scientists out here told me that what they'd discovered about the mineral was incredible. But when I asked specifically what they'd learned about it, they said they couldn't discuss it with me. They said the government considered it to be top secret for some reason.

"Then I told them that Horton was dead, possibly murdered because of his discovery. I also said that at least a dozen Native American Indians were also dead because of it." Kari had filled him in on the deaths among the Havasupai. "That got their attention."

"Actually, the death of the Havasupai wasn't directly caused by that mineral," Brett said. "It was because—"

"Yeah, I know, but I had to say something to get them to give me any information. Then I told them that federal agencies were investigating the situation that also involved the deaths of several Native Americans. When I suggested their involvement could have an impact on their future funding and federal grants in the future, they changed their minds. After a short deliberation, they agreed to let me look at the data and reports they had regarding the mineral. I wasn't allowed to copy or take any material out of their facility, and I had to sign a secrecy document."

"That was clever on your part. I can't believe it worked," Brett said.

"So, here's what they discovered. They estimated the stone Horton had found to be over two billion years old. *Two billion!* That means that it's been buried at the bottom of thousands of layers of rock, stacked over a mile high on top of it for millions of years. It seems Horton had unknowingly discovered the element unbiquadium, with an atomic number 124, also called 'eka-uranium.' Until now, it was considered only a purely hypothetical element, thought to have never existed naturally. It couldn't be created in a fusion reactor. What Horton had found is one of the rarest and most valuable discoveries on the planet."

Brett was busy scribbling notes as fast as he could in order to keep up with Pettit. "Okay, why is it so valuable? Why so secretive about a rock?"

Pettit said, "This incredibly heavy element 124 turns out to have a cubed crystal configuration, much like a diamond. It has a hardness of 2400, which is completely off the MOHS scale. That's more than twice the hardness of a diamond.

"Here's what makes it so valuable," he continued. "When even a small electrical current is applied to it, a thermal reaction makes it extremely hot—to over a thousand degrees Fahrenheit. They described it as a controlled near-fission reaction. A very small amount of it could power a nuclear reactor power plant for over a decade. This could be an incredible source of energy for the future. Of course, people in Washington are now all over this."

Brett whistled. "I can see why the government wants to keep it a secret, at least for now. Sadly, that finding also probably cost Horton his life," Brett said, trying to make all the pieces fit as the story unfolded.

"That's not all. Here's the rest of the story," Pettit continued.

"Horton supposedly died from a climbing accident. But it turns out he was deathly afraid of heights, and the last thing he would do was go rock climbing into a steep canyon. Especially by himself. And, as you already know, he wasn't wearing any kind of harness, or carrying any kind of other climbing equipment. No pitons, wedges, carabiners—nothing climbers would always use. People at UC liked Horton and said he loved geology. But even though he was a geologist, he wasn't an adventuresome outdoors person. Camping or climbing was definitely not on his radar."

"George, we can't thank you enough for everything that you were able to uncover for us. Kari has been worried sick about you, and we're all glad you're safe. By the way, did you introduce yourself to the people at Lawrence Livermore, or at the Colorado School of Mines?"

"Of course. Otherwise, they wouldn't have even talked to me. Do you think I'm in any kind of—"

"Is there any way you can take time off?" Brett asked.

"Sure, I can always grab a day off here and there as needed."

After a long quiet pause, Brett finally said, "I want you to take a month off."

"A month? You can't be serious."

"Two weeks at the least—and yes, I'm deadly serious," Brett said.

"What am I supposed to do during that time?"

"Disappear. Go someplace, anyplace, and don't tell a soul where you're going. Stay low and be cautious every single moment. Don't use your credit cards or your phone. In essence, disappear. I don't know what we're dealing with. But apparently, those involved in this want all the information about this blue mineral kept silent. As to who and why, I have no idea."

"Is there anything else?"

"Is there any way you would be able to get access to Horton's office in Colorado? It would be nice to know the names of anyone he may have contacted regarding his discovery. It would be helpful to see any notes, emails, or phone calls he may have made before he died."

"No, I can't do that. You seem to forget. I'm a geologist, not a spy or FBI agent."

"No problem. I understand. You've already done a fantastic job. Just do me and yourself a favor now and disappear totally for at least two weeks. Call us or text us using only your burner phone. And don't let anything happen to you, or Kari will kill me. Literally. She's already furious that we've involved you in this, but you've been an incredible help. Just know you may have saved countless lives."

"Except maybe my own," George mumbled under his breath.

43

They were just finishing their dessert when Brett said, "I need to fly back to Atlanta tomorrow to discuss the situation here with Quinn and find out if the FBI wants to get involved. At this point, I don't know if it's the Navajo police, the Arizona State Police, or the FBI who'd have jurisdiction over this. Maybe it'll be some combination of the three."

"Can't you just discuss it over the phone and save yourself the hassle?" Solt asked.

"Yes, but there are a couple of other things I need to do. For instance, Ross, where do you think the other missing vials could be? There's no place nearby that I know of that handles dry ice. And the virus has to be kept frozen to remain viable. My question is, if the vials have been stored outside someplace, how long can they remain viable?"

"So, you're saying, either somebody found a dry ice storage place to hide the vials, or they are possibly no longer a danger? The hospital labs might have a dry ice compartment for various medications such as snake antivenom, which requires low-temperature freeze-drying. I'll check it out and at the same time be looking to see if those vials could be concealed there."

"Excellent. I'm going to see if Boggs can figure out how long this particular virus can remain viable at outside ambient temperatures. Maybe she's found more information after going through all the research notes I brought back."

He turned to Kari. "You and I can have a couple of days back in Atlanta, a nice dinner out, then fly back."

"Thanks, but I think I'll stay. I'll keep Tequila company," she said. "There's also something I want to check out. There are some questions I want to ask those on the tribal council."

"They don't usually talk to outsiders about tribal affairs, and I'm worried about your safety. I'd prefer that you come with me."

"She's got her six-shooter, Tequila, and me for protection," Solt said. "I'm sure she'll be okay for a day or two until you get back."

Kari laughed. "It's a Glock. My father's .45 revolver is a six-shooter. Brett, we'll be careful and hopefully get more information while you're gone. You're the one we'll be worrying about."

"I'll leave the Jeep for you guys to use, and I'll take a shuttle to Flagstaff. Besides, Tequila thinks the Jeep is his second home."

———

Later that night, while lying in bed in each other's arms, he said, "I'm serious about wanting you to come with me. I'm worried that the more we learn, the more dangerous our situation here is because somebody doesn't want the information to get out."

"That's sweet of you to worry about me, but like I said, I have a gun and Tequila to take care of me. Besides, you wouldn't have asked me to come out here if you really thought I'd be in danger, would you?"

He couldn't tell her the truth. "The point is, things are heating up and I feel like they're getting more frantic—and therefore more dangerous—in an attempt to cover up what they've done. The murder of twelve people, in addition to a geologist and two other people in England, is a scandal of epic proportions. I'm sure whoever is involved will do anything to keep this from becoming public knowledge."

"I'm going to try to talk to a few people from the tribal council and see what they might know," she said. "I'll also spend a little more time with Chief Jack and see if I can persuade him to tell me more about what that lease is all about."

"You've got to promise me you'll be extremely careful," Brett said. "Don't go off anywhere by yourself. I'll try to get back as quickly as I can. We know a hell of a lot more about what's going on than we did earlier, thanks to everything George was able to learn. What we still don't know is who's behind it all. This is no longer a medical issue. Now it's become a criminal issue, and I don't completely trust the chief. Be careful around him. Once we get the proper authorities involved, we can turn this completely over to them."

"I'm not so sure. I'm anxious for that to happen so soon," she whispered.

He turned and looked at her. He brushed a few strands of hair from her face.

She looked at him. "I don't want us to leave yet. Then we'll go back to just seeing each other every few weeks or so, depending on our jobs."

He leaned over and kissed her, tenderly, on the lips. "Well, don't pack your bags yet. We still have a lot to do before we're done out here. And I don't want you to leave either."

She rolled over on her side, facing him, one leg draped outside the sheet.

"And about these legs you keep flashing me," he said in a husky voice.

44

This had turned into the longest, most complicated assignment Ghost had ever been asked to do for the men in Washington who controlled him. Before, it had been limited to simple tasks: arranging a honey trap and photographing the man; threatening a congressman's family before an important vote was taken; or his specialty—making people disappear permanently. But this time it was different. He had flown to England twice, stolen three vials of a deadly virus, killed a dozen Indians, killed a geologist, flown to Washington, DC, and stolen a metal case filled with scrap paper. He was anxious to finish the job, whatever that meant, and finally get a break. He was exhausted from flying all over, climbing up and down cliff faces, and camping out with snakes and scorpions.

Back up on top at the South Rim, Ghost settled under the shade of a mesquite tree and sent a text:

> They identified the geologist, police now involved

> Carson flying back to Atlanta tomorrow.

> Someone visited Lawrence Livermore lab
>
> Things are moving faster now
>
> Advise

Wainz, who was just preparing to leave his office for the day, stared at the text on his private phone. Why had everything started to unravel so quickly? He'd just gotten off the phone with his contact at the White House, demanding that he clean up the mess, get the damned lease signed one way or another, and allow them to start mining. Clean up the mess? Where to start? The problems started when the CDC stuck their noses into it. Therefore, it seemed logical to get them out of the picture one way or another.

It was time for Ghost to do his thing. Wainz sent him a text:

> Time to clean everything up.
>
> Make the woman and the other CDC doctor disappear.
>
> The damned Chief is also a loose end we can't allow that
>
> Find out what Carson is doing in Atlanta then make him disappear.

Ghost read the message, then smiled. He'd been waiting for a green light to go after her. She was the most beautiful woman he'd ever seen. He'd dreamed about her. Now he was going to have her. She didn't have to die immediately. That would be such a waste. No, he would have his time with her. He deserved it. And it wouldn't matter what he did because nobody would ever know. She would have just disappeared. Along with the chief, Carson, and the other CDC doctor.

He crawled out from under the tree and, after making sure

nobody was around to spot him, made his way back down to his camp. He had plans to make. This had to be done just right. As he continued to think about it, a plan began to form in his mind.

———

After breakfast and saying goodbye to Kari and Solt, Brett took the shuttle to the airport in Flagstaff and flew to Atlanta. He first went to his condo in order to freshen up and check his mail. When he unlocked the door and stepped in, something didn't feel right. He couldn't put his finger on what it was that seemed off. He stood perfectly still and listened, but he heard nothing other than the usual light neighborhood traffic. He flipped on a light and looked around. He sniffed the air. The hairs on his neck stood up—something was different, but he couldn't decide what had tripped an alarm in his head.

After going through his condo and finding nothing of concern, he decided that it was the situation in Arizona that was getting to him. Nobody else was in the condo, everything seemed to be in its place, nothing to worry about. He quickly freshened up after his flight, flipped quickly through the backlog of mail, and was ready to head out. That's when he spotted it.

The metal case from the DSTL that had been stolen from his office was now sitting under his desk.

Obviously, whoever had stolen it from him had somehow managed to break into his condo and place it there.

Now the roles were reversed. What had *they* put in the case? A leaky vial of the deadly virus, not just a decoy? A bomb? A warning? But the case was not what had originally caused his alarm, because he hadn't at first spotted it in the dark. The chair by the window had been moved and turned slightly. Whoever had broken in had come through the window and had to move the chair to climb in. He felt both violated and vulnerable. He was unarmed, alone in his condo, and staring at a metal case under his desk containing who knew what.

The first thing he had to do was get out. He grabbed his travel bag, closed the front door, and locked it. After a moment to reconsider, he went back and unlocked the door, then left again. If a bomb squad had to come and check it out, he didn't want them to have to break his door down.

He was about to call and order an Uber, but again changed his mind. Uber drivers represented an unknown. Maybe the person who placed the metal case inside would show up to collect him. He called for a taxi and walked two blocks away to catch it.

When the cab arrived, he climbed in and gave the driver the address of the CDC campus.

"That's the place with all those deadly germs, isn't it?" the cab driver asked.

"That's the place. I'll be sure to be careful," Brett said and smiled into the mirror at the unshaven, blurry-eyed cab driver. He dialed Quinn, who answered almost immediately.

"Quinn here."

"It's Brett. I'm back in Atlanta and I need to see you about the situation in Arizona. And I have an even more immediate pressing problem." He told Quinn about how he and Boggs had filled the metal case with scrap paper and bogus vials, and that it had almost immediately been stolen from his office. Now, someone had somehow broken into his condo and returned the case. It was under his desk.

"I don't know what's in the case. It could be a bomb for all I know. Or even a leaky vial of the deadly virus. I'll be there shortly, but could you call the police and have them check out the case for a possible bomb? And they'll need hazmat protection suits in case there's a live virus in it. Looks like someone wants me dead, one way or another."

"I'm on it," Quinn said. "I'm calling them right now. I know someone on the force who can get to the right people. See you soon."

Next, Brett called Boggs to fill her in on what he wanted her to do.

"Let me guess," she said. "You're sitting on a rocky bluff, staring at an amazing view, with a cold beer in your hand." Boggs always had a way of somehow erasing all the stress brought on by the job and making him feel like a part of the normal world. And this from a brilliant woman who spent her life inside an isolation suit, inside a highest-risk Biological Level Four Laboratory, staring at the world through a plastic face shield.

"No," he answered, "I'm in a taxi heading over to see Quinn. Someone left me a little present while I was gone. The metal case is now in my condo. They may have left a bomb in it. Either that or they left a vial of the virus for me. Either way, it seems they want me dead."

Brett glanced at the cabbie in the mirror and saw a look of horror on his face as he sped up to get him to his destination. Apparently, the cabbie didn't like the sound of the words bomb-virus-dead used all at once. The taxi slid to a stop across the street from the CDC campus, then sped off before Brett could give him a generous tip.

Boggs continued, "I gave six mice an inoculation of the virus last night as you requested. Three were dead this morning, and the other three seem like they'll be dead shortly. So, what are you looking for?" she asked.

"I need to know how long this virus can remain viable if left outside for a few days. Give another batch of mice the virus tonight after the vial has been at room temperature for twenty-four hours, then repeat the same scenario tomorrow night after being at room temp for forty-eight hours."

"How far do you want to go with this?" Boggs asked.

"Until no more mice die. Then I'll assume the virus is no

longer viable. I hope that whoever stole the virus and used it to kill twelve people may have left the rest of the vials outside. If that's the case, I want to know how long the virus remains viable under those conditions. Gotta run, talk to you later," and he hung up.

He knocked on the door and went into Quinn's office.

45

Later that morning, after Brett had left, Kari and Solt drove to the Parker Health Clinic in the Jeep, with Tequila taking his usual place in the back seat. After parking, they both went in. The receptionist in the waiting room recognized them.

"Good morning. Are you here to see Dr. Martin?"

"Yes," Kari said. "Is she available to see us?"

"She's with a patient now, and there are three more waiting. But I know she'll want to see you. Go on into her office and I'll let her know you are here. There's coffee in there if you want some while you wait."

They thanked her and went into the office. Kari poured them both a cup of coffee. Solt grabbed his cup and said, "I'm going down the hall to the lab. I need to see if they have any dry ice compartments or lockers here." Then he left.

Kari was wondering how Brett was doing and thought about calling him when the door opened and Martin walked in.

"Good morning Kari," Martin said. "How are things going? Do you have anything new to report?"

"Actually, there is," Kari said. She proceeded to fill Martin in on the climber's death who'd been identified as a geologist from the University of Colorado. She then gave Martin a shortened version of what the Lawrence Livermore lab had discovered about the blue rock the geologist had found in the canyon.

"Wow, that's a lot to digest," Martin said. "But what does any of that have to do with twelve dead Havasupai? I'm guessing that we don't have two bizarre mysteries going on at the same time. According to the principle of Occam's razor, the simplest answer is the correct one. That means everything—twelve dead people, a dead geologist, and some rare, unidentified rock—is somehow all related."

Kari looked at her and slowly nodded her head to confirm Martin's conclusion. "That might turn out to be the case. At this point, nothing is definite. Still too many loose ends to know for sure."

"Whew," Martin said. "So, what happens now? Are there going to be more deaths? Are any of us in any kind of danger?"

"All good questions; and those are what we are trying to determine. Ross is down at your lab now, checking something out. I'd like to talk to some people who are on the tribal council. Can you help me locate and contact them?"

Martin slipped off her white coat, hung it up. "The tribal council is made up of seven members. Their names are not secret, and I know all of them."

"Would you give me the names of one or two of them that you think might be the most likely to talk to me?"

Martin sat down at her desk, took a pen, and wrote down the names of three people on a notepad. She tore off the paper and handed it to Kari. "These three people would probably be more than willing to help you. Two of them live down in the Supai village. The last one on the list lives up here on the mesa. I would start with the first two names. Julie at our clinic there can direct you to their homes."

Kari thanked her and left the clinic. The helicopter had already made the morning trip down to Supai Village, and she'd missed it. She would take the flight down tomorrow to the village and hopefully interview the names on the list Martin had given her. Meantime, she would try to locate Chief Jack and talk to him. She sent a text to Solt to let him know she was finished at the clinic and would meet him out at the Jeep.

Solt had located two places that used dry ice freezers. From his time as Chief of Internal Medicine at Columbia, Solt knew medicines had to be stored in one of three defined ways depending on the specific drug: room temperature, refrigerated, or frozen. Most liquid medications could not be frozen because that would cause 'clumping' of the proteins mixed with stabilizers and render them ineffective. Only a few select medications and blood factors required freezing for safe storage. Of course, viruses could be safely frozen for storage and remain viable. The Parker Medical Center had a small freezer for storing their snake antivenom, fresh plasma, and certain clotting factors.

Solt wanted to see if any frozen lockers nearby held any of the missing vials. He checked their freezer thoroughly and found no vials that were unaccounted for. Next, he wanted to drive over to the La Paz Hospital in Parker and examine their lab.

He went out to the Jeep, but both Kari and Tequila were gone.

———

Ghost texted Wainz to let him know what had happened so far that morning.

Carson flew back to Atlanta this morning

Solt and the woman are checking
hospital labs

Advise

Instead of texting, Wainz yelled into the phone. "Why the hell is Carson back in Atlanta again? You left the metal case in his apartment like I asked, right? So, we shouldn't have to worry about him much longer. Take care of the woman and the other doctor when they're away on their own. Just make them disappear. Permanently—and not left smashed in the bottom of the canyon for somebody to eventually find, like what happened with the geologist. Text me when it's done."

46

"I contacted the guy I know in the police department," Quinn said. "They're sending over a bomb squad and a hazmat unit to your condo to check out the case. He said they'd let me know as soon as they find out what's in it." Quinn walked over to the cabinet, poured two cups of coffee, and handed one to Brett. After pouring in a packet of Splenda and stirring his coffee with his pen, Quinn sat down and continued. "What in the hell is going on, Brett? How does a simple outbreak of something among some Indians set off such a shitstorm involving a military lab in England, Scotland Yard, Navajo police, the Department of the Interior, and possibly a bomb in your apartment?"

"Yeah. It's what they call a clusterfuck, and I seem to be in the middle of it. And you can add another death to that list." He then told Quinn about the geologist Horton. "I think it might be time to hand this off to the FBI. The problem is, I don't know who we can trust in the federal government."

"All right," Quinn said, "start at the very beginning and bring me up to date with everything so far. Don't leave anything out."

"This all seems to have started when a geologist from the University of Colorado stumbled onto a rock, more technically a mineral deposit of a material never to have known to exist before. According to the Lawrence Livermore National Laboratory, even a small portion of this mineral can power an atomic energy plant for up to ten years. It has incredible implications for this country's future energy needs. The problem is the mineral is at the bottom of some small tributary canyon within the Grand Canyon that happens to be Havasupai tribal land. It's outside of the National Park Service and the government has no rights to it. They couldn't convince the Havasupai to sign a mining lease. It seems like they tried another tactic.

"Three vials of an extremely lethal virus were stolen from the DSTL in England. A night guard and a lab technologist were killed during the break-in and eventual cover-up there. The virus was then brought over here and used to kill twelve Havasupai Indians in the Supai village down in the Grand Canyon in an attempt to make the tribe leave their village under the pretense of doing it to prevent them from getting the disease.

"They apparently tortured then murdered Horton, the geologist who first discovered the mineral, when he couldn't provide them with the exact location of the rock. The Department of the Interior seems somehow be involved. More specifically, I suspect Wainz, the Secretary of the Interior, could be the brain behind all this. But there are possibly others within the federal government who not only want to get the mining lease, but they're also now desperate to cover up all the mess they've created to get the lease.

"I don't know how much danger all of us are in right now, but if I'm right—it's extremely high. This is no longer a medical problem, it's become a criminal situation involving at least one department within the federal government, break-ins, threats, and extortion, and finally—the deaths of at least fifteen people."

Quinn nodded, then took a drink of his coffee while processing everything he'd just heard.

Finally, Quinn said, "Yeah, it's one hell of a mess we're caught up in. And I agree, the medical aspect of this is now secondary. If you're right about all this, it appears this is mostly criminal activity on a large scale, apparently involving corruption within the federal government. And since we're not exactly sure who all's involved, we've got to proceed with extreme caution from here on."

"I don't see how the FBI could in any way be involved in this," Brett said. "It might be safe for us to contact someone—"

"Wait." Quinn scribbled something on a notepad, tore off the sheet, and handed it to Brett. "Call this man and arrange a meeting. I know him, and he's solid. We'll see what he has to say. I'll let him know to be expecting a call from you. Keep me up to date on everything from here on out."

Brett looked at the name on the scribbled note:

Lee Higgins, FBI

Brett nodded, folded the note, and said, "I'm on my way over to Bio-4 lab to see Janet Boggs. I'm hoping she'll have good news for me about the virus."

"We could use some good news," Quinn said as he reached for his phone. "I'm calling Higgins to tell him you will be contacting him. Let me know what he has to say."

47

Kari called Solt to let him know she was going down to Supai Village to try to talk to one or two members of the tribal council. When she asked if he wanted to go with her, he said he wanted to check out a couple more things at the labs. He said he would see her at dinner or sooner, depending on when she returned.

After she coaxed and pleaded with him, Tim agreed to make another trip and fly her down to Supai. After landing, Kari thanked Tim, then went to see Julie at the clinic.

"Good morning, Kari," Julie said. "As you can see, still no patients and there won't be, as long as the restrictions remain in place."

Kari gave the paper with the names of tribal council members that Martin had recommended she contact. "Can you tell me where I could find any of these people?"

"Sure, no problem. Come with me, and I'll show you where they live, and I can introduce you to the first one to get you started."

Kari followed her through the village until they came to a

small brown log cabin house. After knocking on the door, a woman opened it and smiled at them. "Hi, Julie. What can I do for you?"

"Good morning, Linda. This is Kari Wheeler. She's here to help the CDC doctors and would like to talk to you if you have free time this morning."

"Of course, I'd be happy to talk to you," she said to Kari.

"Kari, this is Linda Ortage, a member of the tribal council and a friend of mine. I have to get back to the clinic but let me know if you need any more help." Then she left to head back to the clinic.

"Come in, come in," Linda said. After Kari walked in, Linda stood there a moment, staring at her. "I've seen you before, haven't I?"

"I've been down here in the village a couple of times since I arrived."

"No, I mean a while ago. I know you from four or five years ago."

"Actually, six years ago, Linda. I was here for almost a year while I was doing research for my doctorate. My father came out to be with me the last three months during my last summer."

"Yes, now I remember. How is your father?"

"He died, I'm sorry to say." She didn't feel like going into any details at this time. "What a lovely home you have here." Kari walked over and looked at a rug hanging on the wall. "That's a beautiful Lucachuki storm pattern rug you have on your wall. I have a smaller Lucachuki in my apartment in Chicago. It was a gift to my father when we were here that summer."

"Yes, I know. I'm the one who gave it to Forrest. I'm so sorry for your loss. Forrest was an incredible man."

"Thank you. I want you to know that I will treasure it even more, since I know you gave it to him." The two women hugged briefly before Linda sat down and motioned for Kari to sit.

"Since you are a member of the tribal council, I wonder if you would mind me asking you some questions."

"Of course. What would you like to know?"

"As you know, we are here trying to find out why twelve people from your village died. First, can you tell me why Chief Jack was trying to convince the tribal council to move out of the valley and up to the mesa? Was that because he—"

"No."

"What do you mean?" Kari asked.

"No, Chief Jack didn't try to convince us to move the tribe. Just the opposite. Dr. Martin was trying to decide what would be best for us, whether to leave, or to stay, and maybe prevent spreading whatever was killing us. Chief Jack was adamant that we were not to leave the canyon. He had been in contact with both the BIA—the Bureau of Indian Affairs—as well as the Department of the Interior in Washington. They were putting pressure on the chief to convince us to move, but unbeknownst to them, he did the opposite and told us to stay. Even Dr. Martin didn't know the chief wasn't really trying to get the tribe to move. He suspected that there was some hidden agenda on their part, and until he knew what that was, we weren't to do anything. However, as far as anyone else knew, it would look like the chief was doing the opposite, just as the BIA had wanted."

That took Kari by complete surprise. "So Chief Jack did not try to convince you to leave the canyon...?"

"That's right."

"What do you know about a mining lease the government wants on your reservation? What is that all about?"

"All we know is what Chief Jack was able to find out, which wasn't much. The tribal council agreed with him that under no circumstances would we sign any kind of mining lease. Why they wanted the lease, or what they intended to mine, we didn't know. Chief Jack tried to find out what it was all about, but they wouldn't tell him anything. Just that they intended for him to somehow get it signed."

Kari was trying to process what she was hearing. It seemed they had totally misjudged Chief Jack. She could hardly wait to fill Brett in on what she'd just learned. "I presume you were well acquainted with everyone who died recently, since the village is so small."

"Yes, of course. I knew them all. We are all like family down here. Daniel and his fiancée both died within an hour of each other. He was my nephew and a good man. He was looking forward to being a father..."

"I'm so sorry for your loss. I know this has been hard for you. Did any of them have anything particular in common with each other?"

"What do you mean?"

"Where they somehow related, did they do anything different from others in the village?"

"They were no different from anyone else in Supai. Three of them were cousins, first or second cousins—I can't remember."

"Let me ask you this—during the period that people were dying, did you ever see anyone suspicious in or around Supai?"

"Not that I can remember. As you know, before Dr. Martin placed restrictions on the area, we always had lots of tourists, campers, and climbers coming through our village. But after everything was shut down, I haven't seen any strangers."

"Linda, you've been very helpful. Doctors Carson and Solt are both brilliant men and if anyone can find out what this is all about, they'll do it. We're doing everything we can to solve this and make sure no one else dies."

They stood and hugged again.

"The Lucachuki rug will have an even more special place in my heart every time I look at it. It was so nice to meet you and spend time talking with you."

Once outside, she turned to ask Linda Ortage one more question.

"Do you know where I could find Chief Jack?"'

"Not at the moment. If I see him, I'll let him know you want to see him."

After she left Linda's house, Kari walked past several other homes and came to a house next to the corral. She checked the paper Julie had given her to make sure she had the right place, then knocked on the door.

The door opened and a weathered, wrinkled, leathery-faced man greeted her. "Yes?" His silver-gray hair was pulled back in a ponytail.

"Are you Jay White Horse?" she asked.

The man stood in the doorway and looked at her. The villagers weren't used to strangers knocking at their door, and he wasn't about to invite her in. Before he could shut the door on her, she added, "Dr. Martin and Linda Ortage recommended I come to talk to you. I'm with the people who are here trying to find out what killed people here in your village. I was hoping you could answer some questions for me."

White Horse finally stood aside and opened the door for her. "Come in. I don't know how I can help you, but I will be happy to answer your questions."

He told her that he too was a part of the tribal council, and he confirmed what Linda had already told her—that Chief Jack did not have any specific information regarding a lease the government wanted them to sign. And that the chief had not pushed the council to move the tribe out of the canyon.

"Chief Jack is a good man. He would never give up our land to the government. Never."

After confirming what she'd already been told regarding the chief, Kari asked if he'd noticed any strangers in the village after the closures went into effect. He also had not noticed any strangers since the restrictions were instituted. Kari stood and extended her hand. "Thank you for taking the time to answer my questions. You've been very helpful, and I hope my friends can solve this soon so that your lives here in Supai can get back to normal."

He smiled at her. "Thank you for coming to help us. You are good people."

She didn't know what to say to that. She smiled back, nodded, then turned and left.

———

It was mid-afternoon, and Kari went out to the clearing to wait for Tim and the helicopter to take her back up to the South Rim. Her thoughts turned briefly to Chicago and her classes and how different the frenetic activity on campus compared to the quiet village here down in the canyon. The two places seemed light years apart. One place filled with the sounds of a bustling city of a few million people, sirens, honking horns, and traffic, while this place had only the sound of the wind in the pines, the nearby river flowing over rocks, or the call of a red-tail soaring overhead.

She wondered how Brett was doing and wished she could talk to him. She even dared to hope that he might fly back tonight. She turned and saw Julie walking from the clinic toward her.

"I saw you sitting here waiting for Tim, so I came out to tell you he can't take you up today. There was a medical emergency that he had to respond to, and it would be too late to come down here today."

"What kind of emergency?"

"I think I heard it was a plane crash. Because of the shifting winds and canyons, it's not that uncommon out here. You'll have to spend the night here in the village. You can stay with me tonight. I have an extra bedroom that is almost never used."

"Thank you. I'll take you up on your offer." She smiled and tried to hide her disappointment.

"I have to get back to the clinic, then close up for the day. My house is the third one on the left, near the river. Here's the key," she said, handing it to Kari. "Go on in and relax. I'll cook us a fresh trout on the grill." She smiled, then turned and went back to the clinic.

As the afternoon shadows grew longer, and the wind turned colder, Kari suddenly felt lonely and more than a little afraid. There was something sinister out there somewhere, something dark, dangerous, and possibly waiting to kill again.

———

Ghost sat high on a bluff, looking down on Supai Village and the beautiful dark-haired woman sitting in the afternoon sunlight, alone, vulnerable, the perfect prey. As his mind wandered to dark places and he planned his attack, the clinic nurse came out and talked to her. Finally, the nurse left, and the woman stood and went to one of the houses, unlocked the door, and went in.

Ghost needed her to be alone. He didn't want to also have to deal with the nurse. He'd wait until morning. He figured the woman would give him one of the greatest thrills of his life. He felt a surge of both lust and the thrill of the hunt, both of which would be quenched tomorrow.

48

Brett left Quinn's office and headed to the Bio-4 lab to talk with Boggs. He pulled out his phone and placed a quick call to Kari to see how she was doing, but her phone went to voice mail.

He left a message: "Morning. Just checking in to see how you're doing. I miss you. Talk to you later."

He felt uncomfortable that her phone went to voice mail but shrugged it off for now. Next, he called Solt.

"Morning, Ross. What have you learned so far?"

"I've been to the three labs in the immediate area with frozen medical lockers and checked each one carefully. None of them had any new or unusual vials, nothing that could contain the virus. Whoever took the vials hasn't left them in any frozen locker nearby."

"That's great work. Nice job. I'm on my way now to talk to Boggs to see if I can learn more about the virus. Also, I talked to Quinn, and he agrees we need to pass this off to someone else. I don't want to discuss this over the phone. I'm headed to DC later today and I should have more information for you after my meeting there."

"I assume your meeting is with one of the three-letter alphabet departments."

"Good guess. By the way, where is Kari? I tried to call her, but it went to voice mail."

"Tim flew her down to Supai. She wants to interview some of the tribal council. She hopes to get more information by talking with them. She also wants to talk to Chief Jack again. She'll be up before dinner. I'll tell her you called."

There was a long pause, then Brett said. "I told her not to go off anywhere by herself. If that creep hurts her in any way, I'll kill him."

"Well, that seems a bit of an overkill, if you'll excuse the pun."

"I'm serious. He'd better not harm a hair of her, or he's a dead man."

"Whoa, let's not get carried away," Solt said. "Nobody's going to hurt Kari, and I know you're not going to kill anyone. Give me a call after your meeting in DC."

"Take care, Ross. I'm headed into Bio-4 now. Talk later," and he hung up the phone, punched in the code to the outer sealed door to the lab, placed his hand on the palm pad reader, and entered.

After a phenol shower, he put on a blue PPPS—which everyone called their "space suits"—then attached an air hose from a HEPA filter that had passed through a gas flame sterilizer. He opened the next vacuum-sealed door with a loud hiss and went into the maximal level four bio-containment area. He was immediately greeted by a smiling face inside the plastic face shield of Janet Boggs.

"Well, look at what the damned cat dragged into our clean little place," she said. "Welcome to the far side of the moon."

"Nice to see you too, Boggs. I like what you've done to the place. Charming. I'd like to book a room for the summer."

"What's going on in the outside world?" she asked.

"Things seem to be spiraling out of control and maybe someone or some department in the federal government could be involved. It's become more complicated. And as we get closer to some answers, it's also becoming much more dangerous. You have to be extremely careful going forward."

"And what do you think is going to happen to me in here?" she asked, waving her hand around.

"You're obviously not going to live here. When you leave at the end of the day, try to have someone with you both going home and coming back each day."

"You're serious, aren't you? Now you're scaring me."

"Damned straight I'm serious. I don't want anything to happen to you. Who else is going to live in this monkey suit and do what you do here? Getting back to the business at hand, what have you found out about the virus so far?"

"As I told you, I injected six mice yesterday with a virus after twenty-four hours at room temperature. This morning, three were already dead, and the other three looked ready to die. However, only one of the last three died, the other two look sick, but no worse and may well survive. Tonight, I'll inject another six after the virus has been at room temperature for forty-eight hours."

"Solt didn't find vials stored in any dry ice lockers in the area. If we're lucky, maybe the virus they have is no longer viable, and that threat is over."

"It's a matter of chemistry. If the virus is stored outside, both the warmer temperatures and the UV from the sunlight will cause the protein of the virus to coagulate. For most viruses, temps greater than sixty degrees for more than a few hours is lethal. That disrupts the nucleic acids and usually renders viruses incapable of infecting cells."

"Great. You've answered an important question—"

"Well, don't count on anything yet. Each virus is different. Remember, the hantavirus can live in mouse turds in the environment for up to four days, depending on the ambient temperature. Let's wait until tomorrow. What's your next step?"

"Since this seems to have become a crime of epic proportions rather than a medical problem, it's time to turn it over to some other agency to handle."

Boggs stared at him through her plexiglass. Finally, she said, "Why, Brett Carson, I never thought I'd live to see this day."

"What do you mean?"

"The Brett I know would never, ever turn a case over to someone else before it was finished. That was one of your endearing qualities—you never quit. You always felt responsible for everything that happened, and you assumed it was up to you to solve it. So...now you're just handing this over to someone else?"

"It's not quite as bad as that. We did solve the medical aspect of it. After you identified the virus—thank you for that—we were able to determine how it was stolen from the DSTL in England, and that it was then used to kill twelve people. We think we know why the killings took place. Beyond that, it's out of our scope."

"Just teasing with you," she said. "You've done an incredible job up to this point. And I agree, it's time to bring in someone else at this point. I'll call you first thing tomorrow about this new batch of mice."

"I can't be more serious about this, Janet. Be very cautious until this is over and don't go anywhere alone. If you get yourself killed, that will really piss me off."

"Well, it won't exactly make me feel good either. Bye, Brett. Take care of yourself."

Through her plexiglass mask, he detected a tear running down her face. They hugged through their suits, then he left.

After leaving the sterile section, he took off his blue PPPS suit and air hose, took the required dilute phenol shower, and changed back into his own clothes. After leaving Bio-4, he went across the campus to his office. There was something that had been bothering him, something he couldn't crystallize in his mind. Until now. He went to his computer, did a search, and found what he had been missing.

There it was, on his screen. The answer to what had been bothering him. This would change everything.

He printed up the material and immediately called Higgins at the FBI office.

After two rings, the voice at the other end said, "Higgins."

Brett didn't know how he should address him, or his official title. "I'm Brett Carson calling from the CDC about a matter of—"

"Yes. Got it. Mitchell filled me in on some of it and said you'd be calling. Come to my office tomorrow at ten a.m. I can talk to you then."

"No," Brett said.

"No?"

"No, I don't want to meet you at your office. Let's meet for dinner tonight or lunch tomorrow. I'm buying."

After some silence, with no answer from Higgins, Brett continued, "This is far too sensitive to discuss in your office."

"I'll make reservations for tonight at a restaurant in Georgetown. My secretary will call you to learn your flight arrival time so she can arrange for a car to pick you up."

Click.

Brett stared at his phone. That was quick and decisive. Obviously, Higgins didn't waste time with chit-chat or even polite conversation. At least now Brett had someone's ear about the problem, hopefully someone who could get things done.

He called Southwest Airlines and scheduled a flight leaving that afternoon, arriving in DC at 5:45 p.m. He made it a round-trip ticket so he could take a red-eye back to Atlanta and spend the night in his own apartment.

He called Solt to fill him in about his contacting the FBI and flying to DC that afternoon.

"Things are moving along," Solt said. "Maybe they can wrap this up and we can go home."

"I should have more information later tonight or tomorrow, and Boggs will also have an update. By the way, thanks for thinking about the dry ice lockers and for checking them out. Nice work. How'd Kari's interviews with the chief and the tribal council go?"

"Ah...well, I don't know yet. She hasn't come back, and I can't reach her. She's probably still down in Supai Village where there's no cell phone reception. Don't worry. I'm sure she's fine."

But Brett wasn't so sure. "Maybe she is, but we don't know for sure, do we? Have her call me the minute you see her. I have to leave now to catch my flight to DC."

As soon as he hung up, his phone rang. It was Quinn.

"I tried several times to call you, but your line was busy. The police called back to tell me what they'd found in your condo. There was a pressurized nebulizer of trichloromethane—chloroform to most people. The police hazmat unit said that the concentration and volume of the gas would have been fatal. Whoever did this didn't intend to render you unconscious. They wanted you dead."

"Lucky me. I assume they're doing the usual, like looking for fingerprints and checking security cameras in the area."

"Probably. But that's all they told me. Did you talk to Higgins?"

"Yeah, I'm on my way now to catch a flight to DC to meet with him."

"Brett..."

"Yeah?"

"Watch your back."

"Same for you. There's some serious shit going on, and we seem to have been caught in the middle of it."

He didn't tell Quinn what he'd found. He would save that for Higgins. He was also going to take the metal case with the original DSTL documents with him, another gift to Higgins.

49

Brett was nervous about his upcoming meeting with the FBI. He didn't know what to expect from Higgins, a person he'd never met. After he landed, a black Suburban picked him up at Ronald Reagan National Airport.

"Where are we headed?" Brett asked.

"Georgetown," the driver said.

That seemed like a nonspecific answer, but the driver didn't elaborate, and the rest of the trip passed without further comment.

The driver finally pulled to the curb and stopped in front of the Four Seasons Hotel. "Deputy Director Higgins will meet you in the Bourbon Steak restaurant on the second floor."

"Thanks for picking me up," he said, but the only response was a nod from the driver. As soon as Brett climbed out, the driver pulled out into traffic and sped off.

Brett hoped this would be a quick meal and discussion, and he could be on his way back to Atlanta. Checking his phone as he walked into the hotel, he saw a message from Solt telling him he still hadn't heard from Kari. Why hadn't she taken the helicopter back to the top? Why was she still down in Supai Village? He felt a knot forming in his stomach. If anything happened to her…

He located the restaurant and was shown to a table. "Director Higgins?" Brett asked, as he extended his hand. "I'm Brett Carson from the CDC."

Higgins shook his hand. He glanced at the metal case Brett was carrying but said nothing. "Nice to meet you. Have a seat. I'm having a scotch. And I'm not the director," he said. "I work for a living. I'm the Executive Deputy Director of the FBI Intelligence Branch. I'm not involved in all the political bullshit like all the 'directors' above me. They couldn't find their own zipper if they had to piss." He pulled a personal information card from his pocket and handed it to Brett. "Here's my number if you need to reach me."

Higgins was a short man, slightly balding, with penetrating ice-blue eyes that seemed to look right through you. Brett liked him immediately, but at the same time, he felt a little intimidated.

"Order yourself a drink and we can talk," Higgins said.

After Brett ordered himself a scotch, Higgins said, "Mitch asked me to meet with you. So, what can I help you with?"

Higgins apparently was a man of direct action, no casual chit-chat or "tell me about yourself" conversation. "Thank you for meeting me on such short notice. We've got a hell of a mess on our hands in Arizona, and I don't have anyone else to turn to for help. Did Quinn fill you in any details?"

Without answering, Higgins said, "Why don't you tell me?"

Brett proceeded to outline everything that had happened, just as he had done earlier with Quinn. He related the deaths of twelve Havasupai, that the virus had been successfully identified and found to have originated in England, and the break-in at the DSTL and the three missing vials of the same lethal virus.

Higgins just sat looking at him and didn't interrupt or ask questions.

Brett took a sip of scotch and continued. "A geologist from the University of Colorado apparently found a rare, blue mineral in one of the tributary canyons and according to the Lawrence Livermore National Laboratory, the rock turns out to be unbelievably rare, estimated to be over two billion years old—one of the oldest known materials on the planet. The geologist's body was found at the bottom of a cliff, and the state police don't think it was an accident. The Department of the Interior wants the Havasupai to sign a lease allowing the federal government to mine on their land. So far, nobody knows what or where exactly they want to mine.

"It sounds like a far-fetched idea," Brett continued, "but it just might be that they used the virus to force the Havasupai to leave their land under the guise of it being for their own safety, which would revert the land back to the national park system and the federal government. It seems like this is no longer a medical problem, but rather a bizarre criminal case, possibly involving someone or some agency inside the federal government."

Having made his case, Brett sat back and sipped his scotch while he waited for Higgins to respond.

Brett continued. "This could also trigger an international incident of some significance."

"How so?" Higgins asked.

Brett opened his leather portfolio and handed the papers to Higgins. "This virus was engineered specifically to do exactly what it's doing. Killing rapidly but with no risk of pandemic spread or blowback. In short, it is a biological weapon of mass destruction. That is a copy of a treaty called the 'Geneva Protocol' which was adopted worldwide in 1972. It specifically prohibits the use of chemical and biological weapons in international armed conflicts. England is in violation of international law and could face serious consequences because of it. In short, it is illegal for them to even design a virus like this. Their own British government may not even know what was going on at the DSTL."

Higgins put his drink down and leaned forward, his ice-blue eyes seeming to bore through Brett. "Okay, I have a few questions. Exactly who stole the virus from the DSTL?"

"We don't know."

"Who delivered the virus to the Havasupai?"

"We don't know."

"How did they expose the Indians to the virus?"

"We don't know."

"Where specifically was this rare blue rock found?"

"We don't know."

"What proof do you have that someone in our federal government is involved in this? Do you know who specifically?"

"We don't know, and we don't have any proof. We suspect the Department of the Interior is somehow involved. If we knew the answers to those questions, we probably wouldn't have asked for your help." Brett felt like he was a student, telling the teacher he didn't know what happened to his homework. And he was starting to get pissed at the direction this discussion was taking.

"Why did someone have to go all the way to England for this particular virus? And if your theory is correct, why didn't they just use poison or another virus?"

"Well, obviously, using poison wouldn't have the desired effect of moving the Havasupai out of the canyon. It would be too easy to identify the cause. Also, most poisons are not as predictable. Some people may not be as affected and may merely get sick, depending on the dosage they are exposed to. It's my guess that they chose this particular virus because of its very unique properties. It kills within a few hours of exposure. It's not spread person-to-person unless they came into contact with body fluids, so there would be no worries about it causing an out-of-control epidemic. There's no risk of a blowback."

"Blowback?" Higgins asked.

"Yes. The inadvertent spread back to your own country and citizens. Not being able to keep it confined to the country you are targeting, but instead, you end up infecting your own people. That's called a blowback."

Higgins nodded his head while he considered that.

"Who are you suggesting might be responsible in this draconian scenario? You mentioned earlier the Department of the Interior. Do you seriously think that department could do something this foolish—and deadly? What proof do you have?"

"No proof—nothing definite. It seems like the best place to start looking," Brett answered.

Higgins kept staring at him, then finally said, "We get a dozen calls every day from nut jobs that say aliens are in their garage, that China is watching them through their TVs, and spies are hiding in Walmart. I only agreed to talk to you as a courtesy to Mitchell."

"Huh," Brett said, getting more pissed by the minute. "I somehow thought the FBI was the one place we could count on for help. At least fifteen people are dead so far. I'm almost certain the Department of the Interior is somehow involved in this. If I can't convince you to help, then what the hell am I supposed to do? At this point, I'm out of ideas." He tossed his napkin down and started to leave.

"Sit down," Higgins said. "Our dinners are here. I didn't say I don't believe you, and I didn't say that we wouldn't help you. I have to know what the hell it is that we're supposed to do and how to do it."

"I'm a doctor. I track down diseases. I don't have a clue what you're supposed to do. But I do know at this point it's out of our hands, and it seems you have a big case to solve. We will do anything we can to help you. If you want to know more about the mineral that was discovered, call Lawrence Livermore National Laboratory. As for information about the break-in at the DSTL, call Scotland Yard. They've been involved at that end. You might also inform them about the Geneva Protocol."

Higgins glanced down at the metal case.

"Inside are the research documents regarding the creation of the virus," Brett said. "What's in there could be very damaging to the British government if it ever leaked out." Higgins just nodded.

Their aged porterhouse steaks arrived. Higgins poured them each a glass of cabernet. After cutting a piece, stabbing it, and forking it into his mouth, Higgins said, "Mitchell told me the same thing that you just did. But not in quite as much detail. He also told me what an incredible job you've done to uncover everything you have so far. Apparently, he thinks you're some kind of super-star in the EIS division."

Ignoring that last comment, Brett asked, "So, can you help us?"

"I need you to send me a complete report of every scrap of information you have, what you suspect, who you think might be involved—everything. Anything from Lawrence Livermore, the CDC, the DSTL, Scotland Yard, a list of everyone who has died. The simple answer is 'yes,' we'll help you. Get me that report ASAP. I will meet with a few of my top people first thing tomorrow and we'll try to formulate a plan on where we go from here." Higgins smiled at him. "More importantly, at the moment, how's your steak?"

Brett smiled back. "Delicious. Absolutely delicious."

———

After dinner, he told Higgins he would get the necessary information to him as soon as possible. Once outside the hotel, Higgins shook his hand, looked at him long and hard, then said, "Amazing job you've done so far. It was nice meeting you—you're one of a kind. I wish you were working for us. I'll be waiting to hear from you." He shook his hand firmly, then, carrying the metal case, climbed into a waiting black Suburban and sped off.

Brett hailed a taxi and headed to Ronald Reagan National Airport for his flight back to Atlanta. He still had a mountain of work waiting for him tonight if he was going to get everything to Higgins by tomorrow. He also had to check with Boggs tomorrow to see how the latest batch of injected mice was doing. He was frustrated as hell that he couldn't talk to Kari and hoped she was safe.

Was the CDC really done with this? Had someone actually killed fifteen people just to get a mining lease? What were they after? Was the whole tragic event finally coming to an end, and they could all get back to the way things were before the Arizona incident? Then he wondered what that would mean for Kari and him. She'd asked what was going to happen with them. If nothing changed, would she eventually give in and marry George Pettit?

Brett wondered why his life always seemed to involve more than just one big crisis at a time. Why was he now forced to figure out his personal life while he was still trying to deal with a bigger problem involving a medical-criminal-political fucked-up mess in Arizona?

Since he was probably going to be up all night working on a report, he tried to catch a short nap before they arrived back in Atlanta.

50

SUPAI VILLAGE
ARIZONA

Kari was unable to sleep in the unfamiliar bed and cabin. She tossed and turned, thinking about Brett and hoping he was okay. As she stared at the shadows of the ponderosa on the ceiling from the moonlight, she smiled, thinking of lying naked next to him in the same moonlight two nights earlier. She missed him. She didn't want it to go back to—

She suddenly sucked in a breath and held it, not daring to breathe out. A different shadow crossed over the ceiling. Outside, a dark form moved silently beside the cabin. She reached out, grabbed her Glock, and waited, listening. Her heart thumped against her sternum. There was no sound, no footsteps, no rattling of the door. She was frozen with fear. Had Julie locked her doors? After several minutes of waiting, watching, and not seeing or hearing anything unusual again, she started to question herself as to what she'd seen. Had it been mere shadows of the pines in the breezes that looked like a person or possibly a bear or an elk? She'd heard nothing. Had her mind played tricks on her? Or was someone outside the house?

After more than twenty minutes of silent shadows swaying on the ceiling, she felt suddenly exhausted. The adrenaline rush had passed and left her drained, and despite her fears, she slipped into a deep sleep, her hand still gripping the Glock.

———

It was after one thirty in the morning when Brett finally arrived back at his condo. He saw evidence of the police having been there and dusting for fingerprints. After going through his condo carefully and convincing himself that nothing else had been left behind, he took an Amstel lager from the fridge, went to his desk, and opened his laptop. He had to stay alert and awake, but he needed a beer to help him relax after the hectic last twenty-four hours.

He finished his twenty-page detailed report at 6:45, just as the first rays of sunlight started sneaking through his window. He related in detail the deaths of twelve Havasupai, the break-in at the DSTL and the theft of three vials of a deadly virus, the involvement of Scotland Yard, a quick overview of the findings at Lawrence Livermore National Laboratory of the unusual stone that had been found in the Grand Canyon, the probable murder of the geologist Kevin Horton, the fact somebody had followed Brett, files had been stolen from his office, a chloroform nebulizer 'bomb' left in his condo, and finally—the possible involvement of the Department of the Interior.

He emailed the entire file to Higgins. He included the addresses and phone numbers for both Scotland Yard and the Lawrence Livermore National Lab, so Higgins could contact them if he needed more detailed information. Brett stood, staggered to the kitchen, and started a pot of coffee. He took off the clothes he'd worn for the last twenty-four hours and headed to the shower while waiting for the coffee. After a long, hot, soaking shower, he toweled off and wrapped a clean towel around him. He poured a large mug of coffee and sat down. After a sip, he took a deep breath and let out a long sigh.

His mind was a scramble of thoughts, worries, and plans for what he had to do next. He realized he needed more than coffee now. He couldn't keep his eyes open, and his brain was foggy. He needed sleep. Just an hour or so. He could get more sleep on his flight back to Arizona later that day. He pulled back the covers, climbed into his bed, and fell into a deep sleep in less than a minute.

———

Kari woke up to the smell of coffee and frying bacon. After a night of fitful sleep, she wrapped a blanket around her, staggered into the kitchen, and dropped into a chair.

"How'd you sleep?" Julie asked.

"You're kidding, right? I feel like I was up half the night, worried, scared, thinking about the future. But that had nothing to do with you or your home. The bed was great, and I appreciate your hospitality. It was so kind of you to let me stay overnight."

Julie filled a cup with fresh coffee and put it in front of Kari. "Here. Looks like you could use this. Bacon and pancakes will be up in a jiff."

"Do you ever get bears here around the village?"

"Bears? We do get black bears, but only very rarely. Definitely no grizzlies. We get a lot of animals, like mountain lions, bighorn sheep, elk, sometimes buffalo, but the terrain doesn't really support bears. So, while black bears do come into the canyon, they are very rare. Why do you ask?" Julie slid a plate of food in front of her.

"I thought something went past my window. I wondered if it could have been a bear. It was just my mind working overtime. This smells delicious."

Julie was in her scrubs and appeared to be getting ready to leave. "I strongly doubt it was a bear. We've never seen any down here in the village. What are your plans for today? Tim will probably fly down sometime this afternoon, and he can take you back up then."

"That's perfect," Kari said. "I'll clean up the kitchen for you. I hope to talk to Chief Jack sometime today before I leave. I don't know how I can repay you."

"Don't be ridiculous. I enjoyed the company. Please feel free to come and stay anytime." She glanced at her watch. "I'd better go open the clinic, even though there are no tourists. There are practically no patients since the entire area has been restricted. Just lock the door when you leave."

After Julie left, Kari finished her breakfast, washed the dishes, and restored the kitchen to pristine order. She took a quick shower and dressed in the same clothes she'd worn yesterday— jeans, a blouse, and leather boots. She hadn't planned on staying overnight, so she hadn't brought a change of clothes.

After she closed and locked the door, she walked around outside the house and looked at the ground for any kind of print, animal or human. There were depressions in the grass, but it was impossible to identify them. Once again, she wondered if her imagination was working overtime, but still—

"There you are."

She nearly jumped out of her skin at the sound of his voice.

"Sorry, I didn't mean to scare you," he said.

"Oh, good morning, Chief Jack. I was just on my way to find you. I was hoping you could answer some questions for me."

"Of course, I'd be happy to. Come over to my house and we can talk."

Her antenna immediately went up. Alone with the chief in his home? Had Brett been right? Was the chief somehow involved in this whole mess? Did he have anything to do with the deaths?

As if he were reading her mind, he said, "We can sit outside in the shade, and I'll get us coffee to drink."

"That sounds perfect. I'd love that." She had to remind herself that the two people from the tribal council thought Chief Jack was a great man, a man of honor and deserving to be chief of their tribe. She was sure Brett's first impressions of the chief were misjudged.

She walked with the chief to his home and sat at a table with four chairs in the shade of a large ponderosa pine while he went inside to get coffee. She watched two squirrels chase each other through the ponderosa pine needles, heard the squawk of a magpie in the branch overhead, and the sounds of the Havasu River. Outside, everything in nature seemed to be content: creatures doing what they always did, content just to be alive, needing nothing more.

———

What the hell were the old chief and the woman doing? Sitting on a narrow bluff looking down at the village, Ghost stared through the binoculars at the beautiful woman sitting under the tree. Speckles of sunlight through the pines danced across her face. She was the most incredible-looking woman he'd ever seen. Her long, dark hair flowed casually behind her in the breeze. Wearing jeans, a sweater, and tall boots, she was more glamorous than any model in gowns and jewels could ever be. His heart raced, knowing that she would soon be his, at least for a while. He felt a pang of sorrow and guilt that she would have to die.

Someone so beautiful should live forever. Sadly, that was not to be.

He realized he was torn between raw lust and his feelings toward her. At least he would make sure she didn't suffer. That much he could do for her.

————

The sound of his phone jarred Brett awake. He sat up, groggy, disoriented, and not immediately sure of where he was. "Hello," he said in a hoarse voice.

"Well, sleeping late now, are we?"

"Morning, Boggs. It is still morning, isn't it? What kind of news do you have for me?"

"Good news—I think. After forty-eight hours at room temperature, it seems the virus is no longer viable, or at least not infectious. No dead mice this morning."

"That *is* good news. It's what I'd hoped you'd find, but I wanted to be sure. Now we can focus on getting to the bottom of this rather than worrying constantly about being exposed to a deadly virus."

"I heard you went to DC yesterday. Anything new to report?"

"News travels fast. Yes, I finally went there to ask the FBI for help."

"And?"

"And the Deputy Director of Intelligence Service assured me they were going to look into the situation."

After a long moment of silence on the other end, he asked, "Boggs, are you still there?"

"Yeah, I'm here. What the hell does that mean, 'look into it'? Are they going to help you or not?"

"Yes. Quinn knows Higgins, and he recommended that I talk to him. If anybody can figure this out, I think Higgins and his people can do it. I've got to catch a plane back to Arizona later today. Thanks for your help, Janet. You have to be aware that things could start to get crazy as the FBI gets involved, so be extra cautious. Desperate men will do desperate things to cover their tracks."

"I think every man I meet is desperate, but yeah—I hear you. Just be sure to heed your own advice. This is some kind of serious shitstorm you've gotten involved with. It can't possibly end well." And she hung up.

He got dressed, drank coffee that had turned cold, and dropped a bagel into the toaster. His phone rang again.

"Good morning," Higgins said. "I received your report. Looks like you worked all night on it. I read through it, and it seems very thorough. I wanted to bring you up to date on where we stand now. I've already formed a task force and went over everything in detail with the group this morning. We're going to move on this as fast as we can.

"At the same time, we can't get overzealous and make mistakes or overlook something. We're just as anxious as you are to get to the bottom of this. I talked to Scotland Yard this morning, and they basically backed up everything you said. They're continuing their investigation at the DSTL to see where security broke down. We also talked briefly about the Geneva Protocol. That's something they are going to take over from here on. You've got my number. Call me anytime you need to talk."

"Thank you, sir."

"Nothing to thank me for yet. We're just getting started. We don't know who's involved nor what they might try to do next. So be extra cautious and watch your back."

After assuring him that he intended to do just that, he hung up. He spread cream cheese on his toasted bagel, took a bite, and punched in Quinn's number while he chewed.

"Quinn here."

"I met with Higgins last night and sent him an up-to-date, full report this morning. I just got off the phone with him. The FBI has agreed to jump in and take over the criminal investigation. And I learned from Boggs this morning that we probably don't have to worry about the stolen vials of the virus. It seems almost certain that the virus is no longer viable."

"You've been busy. When do you ever sleep?"

"I caught a couple of hours this morning, and I hope to sleep on the flight back to Arizona."

"Listen, Brett—things could turn ugly fast. Cornered, wounded animals are always the most ferocious. The closer the FBI investigation gets to the truth, the more dangerous the situation will be for you. I want you to finish up everything as soon as you can and get back. It seems like you and Solt have done everything you can do for now, so let the FBI do their job. Stay out of it and get back here."

"I've just got a few more things that I—"

"I'm not asking you. I'm telling you. Shut it down and get home."

Click.

51

Chief Jack brought out a wooden tray holding two mugs of coffee and some type of warm cinnamon flatbread rolls. Even though Kari had just had breakfast with Julie, she politely took one of the rolls, along with a steaming mug of coffee.

"Mmm..." Kari managed with a mouthful. "This is delicious. Did your wife bake these?"

"No. She died three years ago. She used to make great cinnamon rolls, better than mine. But this is her recipe." The old chief looked suddenly even older, and his eyes were sad. Then he smiled and said, "She would have been glad you liked her rolls."

After a few minutes, Kari asked, "How many times have you recently been to Washington, Chief?"

"Five," he said. "I've been there five times over the past two to three months."

"Why do you go there?"

"They send for me, always for the same reason."

"What specifically do they want?"

"The Department of the Interior wants our tribe to sign a

mining lease, giving the federal government permission to mine on our land."

"What is it that they want to mine? Oil, uranium, gold—something like that?"

"I don't know. They never tell me what they're after," he said.

"Do you know exactly where they want to mine?"

"They never told me that either."

"Who do you meet with when you're there?"

"Secretary Wainz."

"And?"

"Just him. Nobody else."

She sat sipping her coffee, while trying to decide what to ask next.

The chief spoke first. "As you already know, they also wanted the tribe to vacate the village and go up to the mesa. They said it would be for our own safety after several people in the village died. They keep pressuring me to convince the tribal council. I tell them I tried to convince the council, but the council refuses both to leave and to sign a lease. We will never give permission to mine on our land again, and we will never move out of the village."

"You didn't try to convince the tribal council to sign a lease or leave the canyon, did you? In fact, you did just the opposite. Some of the council told me what you did, how you stuck up for the tribe while fending off the feds."

"More than forty years ago, the government mined for uranium on our land. It turned out that the amount of uranium was far less than they'd hoped for, and mining in the Grand Canyon was more effort than it was worth. So, they just stopped mining and left. The tailings they left behind ruined our river and fishing for more than a decade before the waters ran clear again. They lied to us then. They are lying to us now."

"One last thing. I'm guessing you have a strong suspicion about what this is all about. Am I right?"

The chief stood up. "I have something to show you. Are you up for a horse ride tomorrow? It will take most of the day to get there and back again before dark, so it's too late to go today."

"Where exactly will we be going?"

"To a mission," he said.

She trusted the chief. But still—Brett was convinced the chief was somehow involved in all this. How safe would she be alone all day with him? But after everything he'd said, she had no reason to doubt him. This might be a chance to learn what this whole situation was about. She wanted to call Brett or text Ross to let them know what she was doing, but there was no cell coverage, and besides, her battery was low because she hadn't brought a charger and couldn't charge it last night.

"I need to arrange some things for the trip," he said. "Meet me at the corral tomorrow morning."

Kari went to the clinic to let Julie know she would be spending another night, if that was okay with her. Julie assured her that would be no problem. She welcomed her company.

Kari asked if she could use the clinic landline to call Solt.

"I don't mind, but the line will be down for a couple of days. Since there are no tourists, and the clinic is very quiet for now, the park service decided to use this time to upgrade and replace the landline with new fiberglass cables. So, no service for the next two days."

"So, there's no way to get a message to someone?"

"I'm afraid not. Even the landlines at the ranger stations and lodges in the canyon are going to be out for the next two days. I'm glad you're staying, but why have you decided to stay another day?"

"The chief said either we're going *on* a mission, or *to* a mission. I'm not sure which."

Julie looked at her for a long pause. "He's taking you to the mission?"

"I don't know. Possibly that's what he said. Why? Is that a problem?"

"I'm not sure."

———

The following morning, Linda Ortage walked over to the clinic while she watched Chief Jack and Kari ride out of the village, following the trail up the Havasu River. She went inside and saw Julie storing new dressings and medicines away on the shelves.

"Good morning, Linda. How can I help you? Are you feeling okay?"

"Morning, Julie. I'm fine, thank you. I just saw Kari riding out of the village with the chief. Do you know where they're going?"

"Kari said something about them going either on a mission or to a mission—she wasn't sure which. She was sure they'd be back here tonight."

"That means you'll have a guest for another night."

"I don't mind," Julie said. "I enjoy the company."

"When will we have cable service back again? I can't stand not watching my shows."

"Hopefully in a couple of days. If you get bored, come over tonight and the three of us will make it a party."

"Maybe. It sounds like fun. Talk to you later."

"Linda, did you see or hear anything unusual last night?"

"No. Why—what's going on?"

"Probably nothing. The night before last, Kari thought she might have seen something outside her window. She thought it might have been a bear, but I told her there weren't any bears in the canyon."

"Nope, can't help you. She thought she saw a bear?"

"Some kind of shadow outside," Julie said, "but the wind was blowing the trees and I told her that's probably what she saw. She checked the locks on my doors twice last night before going to bed. This morning, she seemed really frightened and told me she slept with her gun under her pillow."

Linda frowned, nodded, and left. But now she had a new concern.

She thought she had seen a strange shadow outside her place a week ago...

52

STEWART LEE UDALL BUILDING
DEPARTMENT OF THE INTERIOR
WASHINGTON, DC
C STREET

Secretary Wainz had just poured himself a glass of Macallan's and settled back in his desk chair. The scotch didn't calm him like it used to, not since things had begun to unravel. He'd started to drink his scotch more frequently, he had fitful, restless nights, and he was jittery. He thought he could tie up all the loose ends and let everything die out naturally, like they always did in Washington. Any new crisis always wiped out last week's headlines and replaced them. All he had to do was wait.

But he worried that there might be too many loose ends to deal with this time. Lawrence Livermore lab had let the White House know how important the properties of the rare blue stone were. But no one was aware of the lengths to which he had gone to get the lease signed. He jumped when his phone rang. He looked at the caller ID.

Damn! It was the White House.

"Hello."

"We're disappointed in you. We need to start mining as soon as possible. More importantly now—we need to know exactly *where* to mine. You said you could get it done, but so far it seems you've only made a mess of things. This project is the biggest in a century. Some people are even wondering if you could have been somehow involved with the deaths in the Supai village."

"Of course not—don't be ridiculous. As for the delay they're causing, have any of you tried working with the Indians? They're worse than spoiled five-year-olds. The chief can't get the tribal council to move on anything. I've tried everything from bribing them to threatening them. They refuse to budge. If you think you know how to fix this, please let me know." His voice had gotten louder as he felt himself being attacked.

"We're wondering why you wanted the CDC to leave the reservation. They were there to help solve the mystery of the recent deaths on the reservation."

"It wasn't a matter of chasing them off," Wainz explained. "They'd already learned that the deaths were due to a virus of some kind, and it seemed prudent to let the Indian Health Service and the Arizona State Lab take over from here."

There was a painfully long silence on the other end, and Wainz wanted to slam the receiver down on the arrogant assholes.

"We've heard some of what's happened. We don't want any bad press to get out. We've just learned that the FBI is now involved. They've formed a task force to investigate the deaths of the Native Americans. You're aware of that, right?"

Shit! Why had the FBI formed a task force? "I'm well aware of the situation in Arizona," Wainz snapped back. "We take the deaths of the Native Americans very seriously. As I said, we thought it might be more prudent to let the Arizona State Health Department and the Indian Health Service get more involved at this point. Hopefully, they will have answers for us soon. I've heard that the deaths are thought to be due to a small outbreak of a virus. There haven't been any recent deaths, so I assume they have everything there under control.

"As for an FBI task force," Wainz continued, "I've heard nothing about that until now. I can't imagine why they would get involved in a small epidemic that already seems to be limited. Can't you take care of that?" Wainz asked.

"Early on—yes, no problem. But now? Now it would become a cover-up story. We don't want anything to reflect on us. We can't afford bad press with elections coming up."

"I don't see how a minor epidemic could possibly become a problem for anyone, especially the White House."

"Some people here are worried that you may have created a real mess out there trying to get a mining lease. More than ever now, we need to get that lease signed. Top priority at this point. We just hope you haven't gone too far to get it done. And maybe screwed it up royally in your attempt. We're not ready to deal with another scandal at this point. Don't let this get out of hand."

"Don't worry."

"I'm calling because we already *are* worrying. Tread carefully, Mr. Secretary."

Click.

Wainz picked up his glass and took a drink of scotch. Sweat dripped off his face, and the glass in his hand trembled. FBI? A real shitstorm was brewing. It was time to rethink the situation, regroup, and try another approach. It was time for Ghost to tie up all the loose ends involving the CDC people there, along with the worthless chief. That would have to be done with great finesse.

He picked up his phone and sent a text to Ghost:

Urgent

Get rid of the woman, the CDC doctors
and the chief

Make them disappear

Without delay

A drop of sweat ran down his face, which he wiped away with the back of his hand. The White House was pressuring him to get a mining lease, the FBI was sticking its nose into it, and he still didn't know exactly *where* the geologist had found the damned blue stone. He knew that if things went south on this, he'd be the fall guy and left on his own. The White House would deny any involvement. So far, there was nothing tangible that could tie him to the events in Arizona. The more he thought about it, the better he felt. He was starting to relax when Karen, his secretary, buzzed him on the intercom.

"Mr. Secretary, there's an FBI agent on the phone for you. Do you wish to talk to him?"

Why would the FBI be calling him? How could they have possibly connected him to anything so quickly? The last thing he wanted to do was talk to the agent, but it wasn't something he could avoid. "Yes, put him through." He pushed the blinking light on his desk phone. "Hello."

"Mr. Secretary, I'm FBI Special Agent Martin Davis. I want to know when we can schedule a time to discuss a serious matter that has come to our attention."

"What serious matter are you referring to?"

"This has to do with the recent deaths of several Native Americans in Arizona. I'm sure you're aware of that situation out there. There are some things that have come to our attention that I would like to discuss with you as soon as possible."

"I would be more than willing to answer any questions you

may have. My schedule is full tomorrow. I will see if my secretary can clear my schedule to meet with you next week, if that—"

"Clear your schedule for tomorrow morning. I can be at your office by eight thirty if that works for you."

"Actually, I won't be available until after—"

"Excellent. We will see you tomorrow at eight thirty."

Click.

Wainz pushed the button to his secretary.

"Yes, Mr. Secretary?"

"Karen, clear my schedule for the rest of today, and for the entire morning tomorrow. And have coffee and rolls delivered to my office by eight thirty tomorrow morning."

"How many people will be coming?"

He assumed it would just be one agent, but there could be five. "Not sure, but plan for six. Thanks, Karen."

First the White House, and now the FBI? That seemed like too much of a coincidence. But any connection between them didn't make any sense. The last thing the White House would want would be for the FBI to get involved.

It was time for Ghost to wipe the slate clean and make it all go away.

53

SUPAI VILLAGE

ARIZONA

On that same morning, twenty-four hundred miles further west, Kari and Chief Jack rode out of Supai Village and headed upriver toward the mountains in the distance. Kari's mind was full of questions, worry, and doubt. Where exactly were they going? What did he want to show her? Couldn't he have just told her? Why all the secrecy?

The only sounds were the horses' hooves on the rocks and the river rushing by. One hour turned into two. Kari noticed the ears on her horse twitch occasionally, and the horse seemed nervous.

Finally, after three hours of riding, they stopped and dismounted.

The chief looked at her. "Let's take a break and let the horses rest. How are you doing?"

"Okay. But I'm glad for a break. My legs are a little sore. I haven't ridden for a while. How much further do we have to go?" She took off her hat and wiped her forehead with the back of her hand.

"Not far. Less than an hour. It's up there."

She shielded her eyes with her hands and looked up, but she didn't see anything.

"Chief, are we being followed?"

"Not sure. Maybe. If someone has been following, in a short while, they won't be able to continue without us spotting them." He nodded toward a canyon with steep cliffs.

What did that mean, Kari wondered? Did that mean whoever was following them would have to take the narrow trail they were on and wouldn't be able to hide? Did the chief know who was following them? Was she being led into a trap? She realized she had put herself in harm's way in spite of Brett's appeal for her to be extra cautious.

They drank water, snacked on trail mix, then, after a short rest, mounted their horses again and continued on. They'd entered a narrow canyon, and the trail went halfway up along its side. The trail narrowed considerably as it climbed along the wall of the cliff. It suddenly didn't feel right at any level, but she couldn't turn back now because the horses barely had enough room to walk, let alone turn around.

Her horse pressed its side against the cliff as it climbed, and she moved her leg, which was being pressed between the horse and the sheer wall. She couldn't blame the horse; it was trying to maintain its footing and not fall. To the left of the ribbon-like trail, the canyon wall dropped several hundred feet straight down. She stole a quick glance back over her shoulder but saw nothing suspicious. It was obvious there was no place to hide in this canyon.

That gave her some comfort, but only minimal. She still didn't know where they were going or what they were going to see. Something wasn't right. She just didn't know what it was yet.

———

Ghost watched them through his binoculars. He was certain he hadn't been spotted. He'd kept more than a half-mile back, but he'd still been able to track them. Everything was going better than he could have hoped for. The old chief and the woman were alone, far away from anyone. He wasn't sure anyone even knew where they'd gone. He would get rid of the chief first. That would make her easier to handle. He hadn't been with a woman for months. She'd make up for it.

He watched while they rested, drank water, and snacked. He noted the old chief pointing up ahead, and the girl looking in that direction. They'd been riding for over three hours. Where the hell were they headed? He was sure they hadn't spotted him.

Ghost scanned the cliffs and valleys with binoculars—then spotted something on a bluff up ahead. A thick stand of ponderosas, rocks, and mesquite nearly hid it from view, but he could make out something that could be some kind of structure. He suspected it might be their goal at the end of their trip. Actually, he thought it *would* be the end of their trip. In this remote area, they'd probably never find the chief's body. And Ghost would have all the time he needed with the girl. She was stunning. Long legs, curvy, with a face that was beyond beautiful. He felt his body tense with excitement and desire.

He saw they'd mounted back up and continued their trip. He focused his binocs on them as they worked their way across a narrow cliff-face trail. Riding horseback, they would have to follow the trail with a few cutbacks to the thickly forested bluff halfway up the cliff. He scanned over the area carefully, taking in the entire terrain. He saw that if he climbed cross-country on foot rather than following the cutbacks, he could get there before them.

This just kept getting better and better. If she screamed, nobody would hear her. If she fought him—and he knew she would—he could easily restrain her. There was nothing she could do to stop him.

He jumped off his horse, grabbed his backpack, and scrambled up the rocks toward the bluff.

54

Karen knocked on his door, then opened it without waiting for an answer.

"Mr. Secretary, there are two FBI agents here to see you."

Wainz and two other men were in a large conference room around a large, polished desk. Wainz stood and said, "Good morning, gentlemen, come in." He'd guessed right. They always traveled in twos as a team.

"Mr. Secretary, I spoke to you yesterday. I'm special agent Martin Davis, and this is special agent Joe Lill."

Wainz turned toward the two men who were with him. "I've asked these men to join us today. Let me introduce our counsel, Thomas Shawk, director of Indian Affairs," he said, pointing to a tall, distinguished-looking man with silver hair, "and this is Phillip Fox, the director of the Bureau of Land Management," pointing to a shorter man who was a former marine. They both nodded at the FBI special agents. "Well, now that we're all acquainted, what can we do for you? There's coffee and breakfast rolls. Please help yourself."

Wainz poured his own coffee, grabbed a roll, then sat down at the head of the long, polished conference table. Both agents poured their coffee and sat down.

"We're here to discuss the recent deaths on an Indian reservation," Davis said.

"Yes. Terribly tragic," Wainz said. "But thanks to great medical work, it seems to be under control, and there have been no recent deaths. May I ask, why is the FBI interested in such a minor medical event that seems to have run its course?"

"It's more than the deaths. Our investigation involves a virus that appears to have been stolen from a research lab in England. And it concerns the death of a geologist."

"Just what is it that you want from me and my staff? I don't think we have any more information about that than you already have."

Davis stared at Wainz for a few seconds before continuing. He pulled out a small notepad and flipped it open. "We'd like to ask you some questions. First, have you or any of your staff been in contact with anyone at the DSTL lab in England?"

"Never heard of it. What kind of lab is that?"

Davis stared at him for a moment, then said, "That's the British military Defence Science and Technology Laboratory."

"As I said, never heard of it," Wainz said. "And why in the world would our department have any interest in it?"

"That's what we're trying to determine. You haven't contacted anyone there by email or phone?"

"Me personally? Of course not. Why would I do that?"

Davis bit his lip as he thought, then asked, "Why did your department want the CDC to leave the reservation in the middle of their investigation into the deaths of Native Americans?"

"We heard that the outbreak was caused by a virus. There have been no more deaths since the initial outbreak, so it seems to have run its course. We thought it would be more prudent for the Arizona State Health Service and our own Indian Health Service departments to take over now."

Wainz was growing more confident by the minute. They had nothing definite on him. They were fishing for answers, and nobody was taking the bait.

"Is there anything else we can help you with before you leave?" Wainz asked.

Davis leaned forward in his chair and put his arms on the table. "We will be checking phone calls and emails from this department, and we will be interviewing your staff. Mr. Secretary, we will get to the bottom of this."

"Bottom of what? There was a small outbreak that unfortunately killed a dozen or so people in a small Indian village, but that seems to have been contained."

Shawk, the department's counsel, spoke up. "On what authority do you have to obtain private emails and phone calls from this department? There is no way that you—"

"Higgins, the Director of Investigative Services, obtained a court order which allows us to get those records."

After a moment of hateful stares between Shawk and the agents, Wainz finally said, "We have nothing to hide. Go ahead and review those, but someone from my department must be present when you review them, since some are top security and may not be reviewed or disclosed. Now, is there anything else?"

Davis and Lill stood. "We'll be in contact," Davis said. Then they left.

Wainz ran through everything in his mind. There was no way

they could have anything on him. All his calls were made from his private cell phone that no one else even knew existed. Payments to Ghost were made from a black ops account by someone else. Every text message Ghost had received had come from a burner phone. There was simply no trail for them to follow. No, he was in the clear. Still, it was another problem he didn't need right now, and he had to remain extra vigilant to maintain secrecy.

A sudden thought occurred to him. The department's private plane had flown the ghost to England twice. Those flight plans were now part of permanent records. However, there was no proof that the flights in any way involved the DSTL. He figured that was something he could work around.

Then, he saw another problem that he had to deal with. If two doctors from the CDC disappeared, there would be absolute pandemonium trying to find them, and it would almost certainly stir up a hornet's nest with dozens of people trying to get to the bottom of what happened. He decided he didn't need that kind of additional scrutiny and worry. Left alone, the CDC would prob-ably be leaving the reservation soon, anyway.

He had to contact Ghost and call him off. Let the situation die down and go away on its own. No need to cause more problems.

"Thanks for coming and your support," Wainz said to BLM Director Fox and BIA Director Shawk. "Sorry to rush off, but I've got a lot of work ahead of me." He left, walked across the hall to his office, went to his desk, and pulled out his private phone. He had to contact Ghost—if it wasn't too late already.

Why was everything always so damned complicated?

55

Brett landed at Flagstaff's Pulliam Airport and took a shuttle back to Parker. Once he was on his way, he called Kari, but again, there was no answer. His concern about her increased by the minute. Where was she, and why wasn't she answering her phone? Why hadn't she contacted Ross? It'd been more than two days since anyone had heard from her, and he was frantic.

He called Solt. "I'm on my way back and should be there in an hour or so. Any word on where Kari might be?"

There was a painful, long pause before Solt answered. "I still haven't heard from her."

"So, maybe she's decided to hang out in Supai Village for now."

"Well," Solt said, "nobody in Supai knows where she went.

Julie said she was last seen riding out of the village with Chief Jack. Nobody seems to know where they were headed."

"What? If that son-of-a-bitch even—"

"There's more," Solt said, cutting him off. "Tequila is missing."

Now it was time for Brett to remain silent. Finally, he said, "What?"

"Tequila is missing since this morning. I don't know how he got out of the room. The door to your room was ajar when I came back from breakfast."

Brett's world seemed to suddenly be falling apart. Tequila and Kari both missing, their whereabouts unknown. He had no idea what kind of trouble they might be in, or if they were safe. His head was spinning with the possibilities. Where was the chief taking Kari? And Tequila would never leave on his own. Who had taken him? How could they have even managed to do that? It would take at least a half-dozen men to control an angry Tequila. What the hell was going on? He was in panic mode. Both missing? Not possible.

"There must be somebody who knows where Kari went," Brett said.

"I'll check again and see what I can find out. Julie from the clinic heard something about a mission. Going to a mission or on a mission, she wasn't sure."

"Mission? What mission?"

"Not sure," Solt said. "When I asked around, one or two people mentioned a story handed down about an ancient mission. They couldn't confirm its existence or even its possible location. Using their suggestion, I'm taking the Jeep and heading toward Shadow Mountain."

"Thanks. Keep me up to date," Brett said. Where the hell was Shadow Mountain, he wondered. Why would Solt be going there? Some kind of ancient mission? Really?

Kari sensed they were nearing the end of their trip, and her mind started working overtime. What did she really know about the chief? He was the one who'd found Horton's body in a remote, treacherous canyon where hardly anyone ever ventured. The chief had been the only one going to DC, and that remained somewhat of a mystery. Why was he going? What was he doing there? And to top it off—nobody knew exactly where the two of them were right now. They were just two specks in the massive, two hundred and seventy-plus mile-long matrix of deep valleys and cliffs that constituted the Grand Canyon.

Her hand dropped reflexively to the handle of her Glock for reassurance.

Then, unexpectantly, Chief Jack stopped. He pointed up the trail to a bluff of a moderate-sized thicket of ponderosa and mesquite trees. She thought she could make out some kind of structure well hidden within the thicket.

"What is it?" she asked.

"Come. I'll show you," and he nudged his horse on.

At the edge of the thicket, they dismounted and pushed their way through the branches to a clearing. There in the middle, virtually hidden in shadow and covered by vines, sat a substantial building made of adobe and stone. A small cross sat atop an archway over the front.

Kari stood there, staring at it.

"Amazing, isn't it?" The chief said. "Francis Coronado first came here to the canyons looking for the lost city of gold. He didn't find gold, but he did find something else. Later, the Benedictine monks from Tucson's San Xavier del Bac monastery arrived and built this mission during the late 1600s, in the hope of converting the Navajo to Christianity. Then in the mid-1800s, the

Franciscans took control after the Benedictines gave up and abandoned it."

"It's completely hidden from view unless you're standing right beside it or know just where to look," Kari said.

"It was built that way to keep it hidden from the Apache, Comanche, Blackfoot, and other marauding tribes. Most of the younger people in our tribe don't even know this place exists," the chief said.

He pulled open the weathered oak door and went in.

She followed him inside. The air was stale and musty. *Why did all churches smell the same?* She let her eyes adjust to the darkness. Dried leaves and twigs lay scattered on the floor. The back of the mission was in total darkness, but sunlight spilling through window openings lit the front of the mission in warm light.

Then she saw it.

Sitting on a rock pedestal was a small statue of a woman, carved in the most brilliant blue stone she'd ever seen. Kari guessed it to be at least two feet tall. Bathed in the sunlight that poured through one of the windows, the statue seemed to glow. It took her breath away. She walked up, stared at it, and reached out her hand to touch it. In sunlight, it seemed almost translucent.

"It's beautiful. What is it?" she asked, in a whisper.

"To the Jesuits and Franciscans, she is the Virgin Mary. To our people, she is the *Pilinisesi ʻo e Mmoʻunga*. The sacred of the Mountain."

Kari stood fixed, unable to take her eyes off the beautiful blue figure. "Who carved it?" she asked as she ran her finger delicately over the surface. "Where did this stone come from? What kind of mineral is it?"

"All good questions, and all without answers," the chief said. "That is the mystery. Nobody knows where the stone came from or even who carved it. It is so hard, nothing can even scratch it, so who could have possibly carved it? I suspect that this might be what all the fuss has been about regarding a lease. Not the statue —which they wouldn't even know about—but probably for the source of the stone."

"How many people know about this?" she asked.

"Look at this." The chief pulled a folded parchment from his pocket with painted symbols on it and handed it to her.

"Where did you get this? It looks like some kind of ancient map."

"This is the secret of the—"

Just then, there was a faint shuffle and a crunch of leaves in the darkness at the back of the mission. Kari turned and for a brief moment thought she saw the shadow of a figure in the darkness.

"Kari—!" the chief yelled out just as a deafening gunshot rang out and he fell to the ground.

A tiny chip of stone stung her cheek from a bullet that ricocheted off the wall beside her. Somebody back in the shadow had fired at them! Kari dropped to her knees behind the stone stand, spun, and drew her Glock in one quick, fluid motion. Who was shooting? What was going on? She fired two rounds in quick succession into the darkness at the back of the mission. She heard a grunt, then shuffling at the back.

"Who's there?" she yelled. "Chief!" she screamed. Silence. "Chief! Are you okay?" she yelled again, but there was no reply. Who'd fired at them? Had the chief been shot? Then she became aware of a stabbing pain in her abdomen. What—had she been shot? She began shaking uncontrollably as the pain in her side became unbearable. "Who's there?" she yelled out again. How many were back there? What happened to Chief Jack? She crouched down and tried to locate the chief. In the dark, she could just make out his crumpled form on the floor, unmoving. Had they killed him? Was he wounded and possibly needed her help?

This was a deadly situation. How many people were back there? Did they intend to kill her? She had no way of defending herself from where she crouched. She had to get out of there. Now! She raised the Glock and fired two more shots into the darkness, then stumbled out through the door.

Once outside, she staggered toward the trees and their horses. She didn't know where to go, but she knew she had to get away. Back to Supai, back to Brett. Her hand went to her side to ease the pain, but it came back covered in blood. She pressed her hand against her side but couldn't slow the bleeding. There was too much blood. She stumbled forward a few steps.

Her face, pale and sweating, grimaced in pain. Blood everywhere. Soaked. Then everything went dark, and she fell face down into the dirt and pine needles.

<h1 style="text-align:center">56</h1>

Since he didn't know how long a trip was ahead of him, Solt stopped at a gas station to top off the Jeep's gas tank. While he was at the pump, Tequila came running down the road and jumped into the Jeep. The dog was covered with bits of weeds, leaves, and dust. He was panting, his tongue out, and he seemed exhausted. Solt did a quick examination of the dog and determined that there were no injuries and nothing serious had happened to him. He filled a bowl with water, and Tequila drank all of it, then lay down. Solt had no idea where the dog had gone, or what had happened to him. He assumed Tequila had been out searching for Brett and Kari.

Thank God Tequila was back. Now he had to find Kari.

He climbed in the Jeep and raced toward Shadow Mountain, which loomed ahead. He didn't know what to do when he got there. He'd try to figure it out as he went. He followed a rough dirt road for a while, then headed cross-country across the flat mesa tundra when the road turned a different direction, while avoiding larger rocks and the occasional cactus.

After fighting the terrain with the Jeep, Solt suddenly

slammed on the brakes and skidded to a halt, throwing a cloud of dust in the air. He'd heard a loud crack that echoed—gunfire! He heard a man's voice shout something, and he would have sworn he'd heard him yell Kari's name. In short order, Solt heard three more rapid gunshots, then more shouting that he couldn't understand. Then another two shots.

What the hell had just happened? He drove the Jeep to the edge of the mesa where the sounds came from. Tequila leaped from the Jeep and ran to the edge of the cliff while barking a deep, baleful bark. He ran back and forth along the edge of the cliff, barking wildly, the hair on the back of his neck standing up. Solt heard Kari's voice yell out, followed by two more gunshots, and Tequila suddenly turned and ran down through the brush at the edge of the cliff while still barking wildly.

Solt looked over the cliff. It was at least five hundred feet or more to the bluff below. There was no good way to get there from the top. He ran along the edge of the cliff until he saw a possible— if not life-threatening—way down. He grabbed at roots and vines as he started down the cliff, sliding and crashing through the brush while risking life and limb. He gathered speed as he shot down the cliff. Grabbing at anything to slow his fall didn't seem to help. He finally crashed to the ground.

Sore and bruised, he lay there a minute as he recovered from the impact before struggling to his feet. He spotted a figure through the trees crumpled on the ground. He knew immediately it was Kari. Tequila, who had somehow made his way down the cliff, now kept up a frantic chorus of barking and whining while licking her face as if to make her get up.

Solt stiffly made his way over to Kari, who was lying face down with a pool of blood spreading out below her in the dirt. She was deathly white since she'd already nearly bled out.

"Oh god! No! No!" he cried out. He carefully rolled her over onto her back to assess her injuries and hopefully improve her breathing. She was so pale she seemed already dead. She was breathing, but he could barely find a thready pulse. She had massive hemorrhaging, and he couldn't imagine her lasting much longer.

She opened her eyes for a brief moment. "Chief," she whispered before she blacked out.

He pulled out his cell phone and checked for service. There was only one bar. It had to work. With his fingers trembling, he called Brett.

"Hey, Ross what's—"

"Kari's been shot. She's hemorrhaging and has nearly bled out. I don't think she's going to make it. She's in shock. Better get here as quickly as you can if you want to—"

"No!" Brett yelled. "She's not going to die. Where are you exactly?"

"Almost to Shadow Mountain. The Jeep's parked near the edge of the cliff. We're below it, down on a bluff."

"You know what to do," Brett yelled at his friend. "Use pressure at the wound site. Don't let her die. I'm coming."

"Brett, I don't think—"

But Brett had already hung up.

———

Damnit. She'd had a gun and had somehow managed to shoot him in the thigh. Ghost's pant leg was soaked in blood, and it stung with searing pain. He'd seen enough gunshot wounds to know it wasn't arterial. If she'd managed to hit his femoral artery, he'd have bled out in short order. It still hemorrhaged freely, and still hurt like crazy, but it wasn't fatal. He wasn't going to die, but he still needed to tend to his wound and stop the bleeding. She was somewhere outside and still had a gun. He'd managed to slide through a window and limp away.

The old chief's warning threw everything off. He hadn't intended to shoot her. She was supposed to be his for the taking, his prize for everything he'd gone through for this stupid assignment. He needed her—he wanted her. He didn't want her to die, at least not yet.

In addition to the woman, he wanted that statue. He'd never seen anything so beautiful or unusual. It had to be worth a fortune. He'd have to come back for it later. He guessed that it probably weighed at least a couple of hundred pounds. Whatever it weighed was more than he could handle by himself. The good news was, he knew exactly where to find both of them and the statue. The bad news was he didn't know the condition of either the old chief or the woman.

He didn't know how badly she'd been injured, but he didn't dare go back now to assess the situation. She was armed and obviously not afraid to shoot. He'd come back and check on her and the chief later. His goal now was to get back to his camp and treat his wound. Then he could decide what to do next. For now, they were alone out here and wouldn't be going anywhere soon— if ever.

———

Brett called Tim Reiser and shouted into the phone. "Kari's been shot and is dying. I need you to pick me up *now!* I'll be at the Parker Hospital by the time you get there. Just land long enough for me to jump in and be off again immediately. Not a second to lose!"

He ran into the emergency treatment room and grabbed bandages and several QuikClot Combat Gauze pads for hemorrhaging. He also grabbed a surgical pack from the trauma room, bottles of Ringer's lactate and Plasma-Lyte, then ran outside to meet the copter.

He was racing against time, racing against death. He couldn't let the woman he loved die.

No! Please God, no!

Tim had barely touched down when Brett jumped in with all his equipment. "Go! Go!" he yelled.

"Care to tell me where we're going?" Tim asked.

"Toward Shadow Mountain. Keep low to the ground and look for my Jeep. When we land, stay ready to take off again and get her to the hospital."

The copter raced over the ground, staying just high enough to avoid the occasional mesquite tree or cactus. Within minutes, Tim said, "There's your Jeep up ahead." The copter spun around and landed in one swift motion.

Brett leaped out, grabbed his equipment, and raced to the edge of the cliff. Tequila raced up to meet him, but instead of his friendly greeting, the dog barked wildly, then raced back down the side. Tears blurred his vision, but he blinked them away as he tore over the side of the cliff, a mixture of sliding and falling, knocking rocks loose as he fell. He finally slammed to the ground. Stunned for a moment, he stood up slowly, then made his way over to Solt and Kari. He had to make it before she died. He had to tell her he loved her. Solt had turned her over, and she was lying on her back, covered in blood.

Solt looked up at his friend and shook his head, his eyes moist.

"It's bad, Brett. I don't think she's going to make it." He checked her again. "I can't find a pulse. I think she's—"

"No!" Brett screamed. "Not yet." He tore open a packet, took out an angiocath, and inserted it into her arm. He turned to Solt. "Attach both the Ringers and the Plasma-Lyte and force the fluids."

Next, he tore open her blouse to expose a wound on her left side that was bleeding profusely. He snapped on sterile gloves, grabbed a scalpel, and opened the wound even further. "With this much blood loss, her splenic artery's probably been severed. It has to be clamped off."

"Brett, you'll lose her before she gets to the hospital."

"She's not going to the hospital, at least not yet. I'm going to clamp it right now," he said. "It's her only chance."

Solt just looked at his friend, but said nothing. He realized Brett couldn't yet accept the fact that Kari was dying in front of them. He concentrated on forcing fluids into her through the angiocath while Brett frantically worked on her.

Brett unwrapped a sterile, curved hemostat forcep and inserted it blindly into her abdomen. He had no chance of visualizing the splenic artery with the small bullet wound and massive blood in her abdomen obscuring everything, but it was a procedure he had done blindly dozens of times in the animal lab during his surgical residency. Fresh blood quickly covered his gloves and ran freely from the wound. He closed his eyes and gently moved the hemostat deeper while feeling the tip as it moved. He grew more anxious by the second. She didn't have much time left. Fear that he was about to lose her nearly paralyzed him, but he fought through his fear. Sweat soaked his face and dripped off his nose.

Then he felt it, a thready pulse against the clamp. He opened the hemostat and carefully clamped off what he knew would be the torn splenic artery. Then he packed two QuikClot hemostasis gauze pads into her abdomen.

"Let's go!" he yelled. "We need to get her up to the copter."

"We can't move her," Solt said, "and we have no chance of getting her up that cliff. She'll die while we're struggling to get her up."

As if anticipating the urgency of the situation, Tim, showing incredible skill, dropped the copter down into the small clearing. The blades were longer than the clearing, and shredded bits of small limbs and leaves were thrown around. Dirt and pine needles blew everywhere in the prop wash. Brett and Solt picked Kari up and slid her into the copter, then Brett jumped in.

Solt grabbed his friend's arm. "Kari managed one faint word —'*Chief.*'"

Brett stared at him for a second, then turned his attention back to Kari.

"I'll bring the Jeep and Tequila and meet you at the hospital," Solt yelled, then gave Tim the signal to leave. The copter rose, turned, and raced toward the hospital.

Brett put on a helmet so he could communicate with Tim. "Call the hospital," Brett yelled into his mic. "Get me Martin."

Martin came on the phone over the headset. "Brett? I can hardly hear you. What's all the noise?"

"I'm in a helicopter and we're headed to you. Get an anesthesiologist and a surgeon ready immediately. Set up an OR and have four units of O-negative ready." He held her head in his lap while he pushed more Ringer's lactate and Plasma-Lyte into her vein. Her breathing was shallow and her skin chalky white. She was in shock. Only a prayer could save her.

"It will be at least twenty minutes before the surgeon on call can get here, and there might not be an anesthesiologist for even longer than that."

"We can't wait. Get all the lidocaine you have. We are going straight into surgery. Get yourself or someone scrubbed now and be ready to assist. Every second counts."

57

Back at his campsite, Ghost pulled down his trousers to dress his wound. The pant leg was soaked in blood, but the wound wasn't actively bleeding. He'd been an assassin for the cartel and had seen dozens of bullet wounds, and he knew his injury wasn't fatal or even serious. The bullet had gone through muscle and had almost certainly severed a vein. But it hadn't hit a bone or an artery. It was painful, bloody, and just another thing he had to deal with.

He pulled off his trousers, and using water from his canteen, washed the wound, taped the bullet hole, and pulled on a clean pair of cargo pants. Just as he finished, he heard a helicopter fly low overhead and land on the flat mesa above the mission.

What the hell? A helicopter? How had they responded so quickly? Who had the copter picked up? Was the chief dead? Was the girl still there?

This had been the shittiest, most dangerous, exhausting, and demanding assignment he'd ever had. He was a trained killer, an assassin, first for a cartel, now for a few powerful men in Washington. He'd killed many men, occasionally women, but never children —at least until this time. He wasn't comfortable with the random killing of innocent people, especially women and young girls. Before, his targets were known threats to the safety and well-being of the cartel and its operations. But as far as he could tell, the recent murders were nothing of the sort. He didn't know why the kill order this time had been given, but he'd obeyed and carried out his task. With the arrival and quick departure of the copter, the situation had quickly gotten out of control and turned into a fucked-up mess.

He was exhausted, and the blood loss left him weak. He needed to rest. He drank the last of the water in his canteen, lay down in the shade of a mesquite bush, and was soon sound asleep.

———

Two miles further east toward Shadow Mountain, Solt picked up the Glock that Kari had dropped and carefully made his way into the mission. Tequila ran ahead of him, barking wildly. Solt spotted a body lying on the ground. Was this the person who shot Kari? Was he still armed? The light inside the mission was dim, but Solt could see that it was the chief, and there was a lot of blood coming from a head wound.

Keeping a grip on the Glock, Solt checked his pulse, which was strong. He carefully turned the chief over onto his back. There was a nasty large gash over the chief's eye that accounted for all the bleeding. A quick exam did not reveal any other significant injury. He didn't spot any other weapon nearby. Now, his main concern was whether or not the chief had a significant, possibly life-threatening, internal head injury.

"Chief!" Solt yelled. "Can you hear me?"

The chief opened his eyes and said, "Jesus—stop yelling. I'm right here." He put his hand to his head. "That is one hell of a headache."

"Looks like you fell on that rock and smashed your head." Solt quickly checked his pupils. There didn't seem to be any immediate danger. "Can you tell me what happened?"

"I'm not sure. I heard a noise in the back of the mission and yelled a warning to Kari, then I remember falling. Where's Kari? Ask her what happened—"

"Kari's been shot. She was hemorrhaging and may have already died. Chief, who shot her?"

"I don't know. I yelled and tried to warn her." The chief seemed to crumble. "I can't believe she's dead."

Solt helped the chief to his feet. "Let's get out of here before somebody shows up again. And we've got to get your head injury evaluated. It's going to be a tough scramble getting back up that cliff."

"You and the dog make your way up if you can. I'll get the horses and ride back to the village."

"Chief, I don't think you are in any condition to ride—"

But the chief had already made his way through the trees to find the horses. Solt knew the old Indian was in no condition to ride a horse back, but he also knew there was no way he could get the chief up the cliff to the Jeep. With a great deal of effort and cursing, he and Tequila finally managed to scramble through brush and loose rocks back up to the Jeep. Out of breath, he looked down the cliff they'd just climbed. There were several small cuts and scratches on his legs and arms from the climb. He was glad he hadn't tried to drag the chief up the cliff. They wouldn't have made it. He and the dog climbed into the Jeep, spun in a wild circle, then raced back toward the hospital in Parker.

Solt had been a doctor his entire adult life and had seen death far too many times. But these were his two best friends in the world, and one of them was probably already dead—or soon would be. If Kari died, the devastation to both him and Brett would be beyond repair, and he knew they'd never fully recover from their loss. As he pushed the old Jeep to its limit back to town, he didn't know what he'd face when he arrived. Whatever it was, he was sure it wouldn't be good.

Twenty minutes later, he raced into the parking lot next to the ER and slid to a stop. The helicopter sat off to the side. Afraid of what he would find when he went in, he jumped out of Jeep and raced through the ER electric doors. He went to the receptionist. "Where's the emergency they just brought in?"

"Excuse me, who are you?" she asked.

"I'm Dr. Solt. Where the hell are they?" he shouted.

Martin came down the hall and grabbed his arm. "Dr. Solt, I'm glad to see you." She noted his torn shirt, along with multiple cuts and bruises. "What happened? Were you in a wreck or something?"

"Kari was shot and has nearly bled to death. Where are they? Has she—" he asked, his lip trembling.

"She's going to surgery as soon as our on-call surgeon gets here," Martin said.

"No, she's already in surgery," the nurse said. "Dr. Carson is already operating on—"

"Dr. Carson? Is he crazy?" Martin asked. "Does he think he's actually going to try to do surgery on her?"

"He's not going to try—he's going to do it," Solt shot back. "We can't wait for your surgeon to arrive."

"He's an internist. What could he possibly know about surgery?"

"An internist? Who told you that?"

"I just assumed he was an internist, specializing in infectious diseases or something like that."

Solt smiled and shook his head. "He was chief surgical resident at Duke before he joined the EIS division six years ago. Kari's in good hands—probably the best hands."

Martin stared at him in disbelief. "Is there anything he can't do?"

"Call the OR and see if he needs any help," Solt said. "I can scrub up."

While Martin was on the phone to the OR, the surgical door opened and Brett came out, wearing scrubs that were covered in sweat and blood. Before Solt could get to him to ask about Kari, another man in scrubs and a white coat stepped between them and confronted Brett.

"What's going on here? Who are you?" the man asked rather rudely. "And what were you doing in the OR?" He looked at his blood-soaked scrubs. "Did you perform surgery in there?"

Brett looked around the man and said to Solt, "She made it through surgery, Ross, but she's not out of danger yet. We'll have to wait and see."

"I'm Dr. Stitzlein, the surgeon here. I asked you a question," the man said.

Ignoring the man, Brett turned to the nurse as he peeled off his gloves. "Start her on Augmentin IV, give her another unit of O-negative, then get her to CT to see if there's any intestinal damage we may have missed."

"I don't know who you think you are," the man continued, "but you can't just—"

"I just performed a splenectomy, repaired a kidney, and hopefully saved a very special young woman's life," Brett said, staring at him.

"You don't have any privileges here. Are you even a doctor?" He turned to Martin. "Call security. I'm getting to the bottom of this."

Just then, a scrub nurse came out of the OR and walked up to them. "What the hell do they teach you guys at the CDC, anyway?" she asked Brett. Then she turned to the other man. "Dr. Stitzlein, this is Dr. Carson. He just did the most incredible splenectomy I've ever seen. That surgery would normally take up to two hours. He did it in less than thirty minutes. Never saw anything like it. She was nearly dead when she arrived. Without his quick action, there's no way she would have survived."

"Who was the anesthesiologist?" Stitzlein demanded. "I need to talk to him."

"That's the amazing thing," the nurse said. "Anesthesia wasn't here yet, so he did it using just lidocaine."

Brett started to walk away, but the surgeon grabbed his arm. "Where do you think you're going?"

Brett grabbed Stitzlein by his tie and pulled him up inches from his face. "You touch me again and they're going to have to page an ENT surgeon to come repair your face. That woman in there would be dead by now if we'd waited for you. So, take your cockamamie hospital privileges and stick 'em up your ass. Now get out of my face."

Then Brett walked over to the nurses' station and wrote post-op orders for Kari. Solt walked up and asked, "How is she doing, Brett?"

"She almost exsanguinated on the mountain when you found her and was in shock. We gave her five units of O-negative and repaired all the torn vessels in addition to a splenectomy. Her vitals are stable. Because of the massive blood loss and severe shock that she sustained, we don't know yet what damage there's been to her brain or to her kidneys."

Solt noticed that Brett's hands were shaking and sweat dripped from his face. He put his hand on his friend's shoulder. "You saved her, Brett. That thing you did on the mountain to clamp her splenic artery—"

"No, I'm the one who nearly got her killed by asking her to

come out here. She nearly died—" His voice broke, and he couldn't finish.

"But she didn't die. She's going to make it. Now, go take a shower and find some clean scrubs."

"Ross, did you find her down on that bluff?" Brett asked him. "How'd you know where to look?"

"Tequila found her. I heard yelling and what sounded like gunshots, but with the echoing from the canyon cliffs, I couldn't place it. I didn't know where it was coming from. Tequila charged fearlessly down the cliff and led me to her. He saved her life," Solt said.

"You're a bloody mess. Get cleaned up, then let's go find something to eat."

"Go ahead. I'm going to check on Kari."

58

The following morning, Kari stirred, moaned, and opened her eyes. She saw Brett sitting in a chair next to her bed with tears running down his face. "What happened?" she asked. "Why are you crying?"

He leaned over and kissed her forehead. "You're alive. Oh, babe, I'm so sorry."

She winced once from pain, then said, "What do you have to be sorry for?"

"I thought I'd lost you. For a while, there was a good chance you might not make it. I'm responsible for bringing you out here and nearly getting you killed."

Just then, Solt walked in. "Hi, Kari. How are you doing?" He walked over to them, then said, "God, Brett—you look like shit. Looks like you haven't slept in days, and when was the last time you had anything to eat? Get a shower and change into some clean clothes. And you must eat something. I'll stay with her."

Brett looked at her, then stood and left.

Solt leaned over and said to her in a low voice, "He's been

sitting here for the last twenty hours. He refused to leave your bedside until you woke up."

A nurse entered. "Hi, Dr. Solt. I'm here to check on our patient. Kari, would you like some ice chips? You're not supposed to drink anything for a few hours." She spooned in a mouthful of ice chips, then adjusted the flow of the IVs. "Get some sleep, dear."

As soon as the nurse left, Kari smiled at Solt, then closed her eyes and fell asleep again. Solt sat down to wait.

The next day, Kari woke to find the nurse adjusting one of her IV lines again. "Could I have some more ice chips?" she asked. "And how long before I'm allowed to sit up.? And any idea how long it'll be before I can get out of here and get back to my boring life?"

"You'll have to ask your surgeon about that. He should be here shortly."

Just then, Brett walked in with her chart.

"Here he is now," the nurse said. "Good morning, Dr. Carson. Your patient's doing fine. No fever, and her blood pressure's normal."

Kari's mouth gaped open in surprise. "You?" she asked, with a huge grin on her face. "You're my surgeon? Seriously, you operated on me?"

"You didn't know?" the nurse asked. "His emergency surgery saved your life. Everyone's been talking about it. You were as close to death as anyone I've ever seen."

"You did surgery?" she repeated. "On me? So now I owe you my life again? How can I even begin to repay you?"

"I've been thinking that over," he said, smiling at her, "and I have a few ideas. How are you feeling this morning?"

"I want to get out of here. Another day lying here, and I may have to jump out the window."

"Well, we can't have you jumping out of a window, so I'll

discharge you in a day or two if you continue to improve. Of course, you'll have to be under my strict supervision."

"For how long?"

"Maybe forever." He leaned over and kissed her, then left.

"I think he's in love with you, Kari," the nurse said. "You're a lucky woman."

———

The next day, Kari opened her eyes slowly and looked through the forest of IVs hanging by her bed to see Brett still sitting there. Every time she woke even briefly during the night, she saw him sitting beside her. Finally, she said, "You know, hanging around you has been dangerous, terrifying, and most of the time, plain uncomfortable. But life with you has never been boring."

"Kari, I'll never let anyone hurt you," Brett said.

She glanced down at her bandages, then back up at him and tried to laugh, but winced instead.

"Point well taken. I'll never let anyone hurt you *again*," he said. "I'm going to find that son-of-a-bitch chief who shot you and—"

"Wait—what? The chief didn't shoot me."

"What?"

"No. He yelled to warn me. I think he might even be dead," she sighed. "I saw him fall at the mission at the same moment I heard a shot. Brett, you've been wrong about the chief. He is a good man."

"I'm not so sure about that. He's the one who took you to that abandoned mission where you were nearly killed."

She mumbled something, moaned softly, then fell back to sleep.

Brett left the room and found Solt in the hospital cafeteria.

After grabbing a tray of eggs, sausage, and toast, he sat down beside Solt.

"How's the patient?" Solt asked.

"Sleeping. She's going to make it. Now I going to find out who shot her."

"I thought she said it was the chief who shot her."

"No, she says it wasn't him. When she mumbled the word 'chief,' she wanted us to look for him. She thinks he could even be dead back at the abandoned mission. We need to send someone out to check. The question is, who shot Kari and the chief? And why?"

"Because they think she knows something," Solt said as he forked in a bite of pancakes.

"Does she?"

"Does she what?" Solt asked with a mouthful of pancake.

"Does she know something?"

"Maybe. I don't know. Maybe she found something important."

"That means they could still—damn!"

"What?" Solt asked.

"I should have thought of this earlier. We need to have security outside her room in case whoever shot her comes back for her."

Brett grabbed his phone and called the hospital operator. "Get me the nurse's station, second floor."

"Hello, how can I help you?" a nurse asked.

"This is Dr. Carson. Have someone go to Kari Wheeler's room now to check on her. And we need to get security—"

"I'm sorry, Dr. Carson. She's not on this floor any longer. She's just been moved to another room."

"When did this happen?"

"About ten minutes ago."

"Who moved her? Where is she?"

"The doctor wore surgical scrubs and a mask. I'd never seen him before. He was mostly hidden by the mask. Oh—and he did have some kind of limp."

"That was no doctor! Call security now and have them lock all exits."

"What are you talking about?" the nurse asked. "I don't have the authority to—"

Somebody behind him reached around him and grabbed the phone. "This is FBI Special Agent Davis. Connect me to security." After two rings: "Security? This is FBI Special Agent Davis, and I'm ordering you to lock all exists now!"

He turned and handed the phone back to Brett.

"Call all the nurses' stations on every floor and have them check every room," Brett said to one of the nurses. Then, he turned to agent Davis and said, "Thanks. Did Higgins send you?"

Davis merely nodded.

"Thanks. We could use some help finding her," Brett said. "We have to stop them before they take her out of the hospital." After another ten minutes of frantic searching with no results, he was starting to panic.

Solt came down the hall. "Security has checked the kitchen, storage rooms, meat lockers—nothing."

"They're going to kill her, Ross."

"No, I think you're wrong. They could've killed her in her room without the risk of moving her. They want her alive," Solt said.

"Why? Did she see something? Does she have the information they need?" Brett started toward the front entrance when a nurse called out, "Dr. Carson, there's a phone call for you!"

"This is Davis. We've found her, Dr. Carson. She's on a gurney near the food delivery ramp."

"How is she? Did he—"

"She seems fine, considering that she's had recent surgery and took a wild ride through the hospital on a gurney."

"Did anyone see him?"

"No. Nothing. It was like he just disappeared."

"Thanks for your help," Brett said to the agent. "By the way, how did you happen to be here? Tell Higgins he has my full gratitude."

"Our friendly ghost again?" Solt asked, who'd caught up and heard some of the phone conversation.

"He's not a ghost," Brett said. "And he nearly killed Kari. I want to go find the son-of-a-bitch. The problem is, I don't really know who it is or where to start looking for him."

"When I was on my way to Shadow Mountain," Solt said, "I saw what might have been some kind of makeshift camp on a small bluff halfway down the cliff. It may be nothing, but you might want to look there first. It's too late to go now. It'll be dark in an hour."

"Stay and make sure Kari gets back to her room safely, then stay with her till I get back."

"Don't do anything stupid," Solt said. "And don't take any unnecessary risks."

"I'm going to find him, Ross, then I'm going to kill him," Brett said.

"How do you intend to do that?"

"I'll figure it out as I go," he said, heading to the door.

Solt grabbed his arm and stopped him. "Think about what you're doing. You're a doctor. You save people; you don't kill them."

"He shot Kari, and just now tried to kidnap her." Brett left the hospital and went outside to his Jeep where Tequila sat patiently waiting. "Hey fella, wanna go on a ride?" The dog barked once and wagged his tail.

Just then, Chief Jack walked up.

"Chief!" Brett exclaimed. "What happened? Are you okay?" He saw a nasty cut and a large bruise on the chief's forehead. "Let me look at that." He stared at the chief's eyes to make sure the pupils were equal. A nasty blow that severe to the head could easily result in an intracranial bleed—possibly fatal.

"When I dove to get out of the way," the chief said, "I hit my head on a rock or something, and it knocked me out. I came to later when Dr. Solt found me. I was dizzy and disoriented. How is Kari?"

"Someone shot her. That's all we know. Did you see anyone?"

"No, I never saw anyone. I don't know who shot at us. I was able to round up the horses and ride back to Supai. I heard she had surgery, and I'm here to see how she is doing."

"Kari will be relieved to see you. She wasn't sure what happened to you. Before you go to see her, stop in the ER, and have someone look at that cut on your head. You're going to need sutures."

The chief nodded, then started to leave.

"Chief Jack, do you have a gun?"

He stopped and turned around. "Everybody here has a gun. Why do you ask? Do you intend to shoot someone? And do you even know how to handle a gun?"

"Yep, I'm familiar with guns. On my uncle's ranch, I've shot rattlesnakes, jackrabbits, coyotes." Brett knew he wasn't a killer—at least until now. He'd shot a mountain lion once after it attacked his uncle's dog, then nursed the cougar back to health before releasing it on the opposite side of the mountain range. This time, it would be different. He wouldn't be nursing anybody back to health.

"So, are you going hunting?" the chief asked.

"More like taking care of a problem."

"Humph," the chief said. Then he walked over to his pickup

and pulled a Winchester 30-30 out of his truck, came back, and handed it to Brett. "Six rounds with one in the chamber."

"Thanks," he said and shook the chief's hand. "Now, go to the ER and get checked out. That was a nasty blow to your head."

Brett grabbed the rifle and climbed into his Jeep.

At that moment, he knew he'd gone from healer to hunter.

59

With the evening light fading, Brett, with his dog Tequila and the chief's rifle, sped out of town in the Jeep, heading toward Shadow Mountain. Three miles out of town, using a rough map that Solt had sketched for him, he spotted the tree indicated on the drawing. He drove slowly to the rim of the canyon and stopped.

He jumped out, walked to the edge, and looked down into the canyon. He spotted something partway down the cliff. A plateau formed a narrow tabletop bluff that could conceivably hide a camp of some sort. He couldn't be sure because the sun was nearly down, and the bluff and canyon wall were cloaked in shadow. He squatted and watched for several minutes with Tequila at his side, but he saw no activity. If that was a camp, whoever stayed there was either away or asleep.

After waiting and watching for another twenty minutes, the sun had set, and a near-full moon oozed its way over the horizon. It was time to check it out. He went to the Jeep and grabbed a large coil of rope and the chief's Winchester. He motioned for Tequila to jump up on the back seat, then gave the 'stay' command. Tequila would warn him if any danger appeared. He tied the rope to the Jeep's bumper and let the rope drop. He secured the Winchester with a leather strap, pulled on his gloves, then, with some trepidation, slipped over the edge, and started down.

He was aware the rope didn't quite reach the bluff—he guessed it was at least twenty to thirty feet short of the ground. If he got to the end, he would have to fall the rest of the way to the ground, and there'd be no way to get back up. For now, he was content to go most of the way down and scout out what was going on there.

After ten minutes or so of belaying his way down slowly so as not to alert anyone below, his hands ached, and his arms felt like they'd been seared by fire. His body was not used to this kind of stress. After descending a significant distance, he paused. He needed to give his hands and arms a rest. He looked up and noted that at this angle, the moon could be seen just above the cliff edge.

The night was quiet. Almost too quiet.

Could someone below in the camp have spotted him? He was a sitting duck—no, more like a swinging duck—dangling on a rope partway down a cliff. He was ready to continue his descent when Tequila started barking wildly. Not good. Something was going on at the top, and if anyone was below him, they'd be checking it out as well. None of it was good.

The smart move was to get back up as fast as he could. He started climbing back up using hands and arms that were already burning with fatigue. Tequila was in a frenzy barking, mad about something. He continued climbing as fast as his spent body let him. Obviously not fast enough, definitely slower than going down had been.

Suddenly, he heard a shot that echoed through the canyon. It came from the top. Tequila howled and whimpered as if in pain.

The dog was no longer barking. Brett could just make out a distressed, faint whimper.

Damnit! Someone had shot Tequila.

Then a silhouette of someone appeared at the top, kneeling beside the rope. Brett felt a slight movement, and the rope subtly rotated.

Someone was cutting the rope! He had to stop them. Hanging dangerously from the rope using just his left hand, he pulled the Winchester up with the other arm, tried to steady the rifle while dangling from a rope, aimed, and fired. The silhouette fell back out of his view. If he hadn't hit the person, he hoped at least it would chase the person away from the rope.

He started to slip and frantically reached for the rope with both hands to keep from falling. The rifle fell from his grip and bounced off rocks against the cliff wall as it dropped. After several more seconds, it finally smashed onto rocks below, generating a racket of splintered wood and steel against rock. For sure, if anyone was in the camp below, they were definitely awake now.

He continued to climb as fast as he could. With at least fifty feet still to go to reach the top, he had to pause. His hands and arms burned with fatigue, and his lungs ached. What the hell had he been thinking? He was a doctor, not a mountain goat. While he paused, he could feel fine vibrations in the rope. The rope had probably been cut partway through and now was unbraiding and coming apart a strand at a time.

If the rope broke, he'd fall more than several hundred feet to his death. He started scrambling up as fast as he could. The edge was now in sight, only ten feet or so above him.

Then, he felt the rope go slack in his hands when it finally broke.

60

Grabbing desperately at rock layers, he slid down several feet before he managed to wedge his gloved fingers into the rock in for a hold. He swung there for a few seconds, using only the tips of his fingers to hold himself, on the brink of failing. He had to find a way up now or fall to his death. He started painfully clawing his way back up, one rock layer at a time using his fingertips. He finally pulled himself over the edge and collapsed, completely drained. His hands and fingers were raw, bleeding, painfully cramped, and nearly useless. He wanted to just lie there, but knew he had to move. If the person who shot Tequila was still there, Brett was a dead man. He had no way of defending himself.

He slowly looked around. Faint silvery moonlight bathed the ground. There was no one in sight. Tequila's painful whimpering brought him upright, and he staggered to the Jeep to check on his dog. Tequila was sprawled on the back seat, panting, eyes only half open. Then he saw the blood—lots of it, coming from a nasty shoulder wound.

He grabbed his medical kit, applied a pressure dressing over the shoulder wound, and wrapped it tightly in place with an elastic Ace wrap. Tequila whimpered and licked him once before his head dropped back down. "Hang on, buddy. I'm going to fix you up." But he didn't know if he could keep that promise since he had no idea the extent of the dog's injury. All he knew for certain was the dog had lost a lot of blood. And there was no blood available for a dog's transfusion.

He started the Jeep, spun around, and raced back to the hospital. He'd lost his rope, the chief's Winchester, and his dog had been shot. He could barely handle the steering wheel with his cramped and bleeding fingers. He picked up his phone, dropped it twice, and after several attempts, finally managed to dial the hospital.

"Parker Medical—"

"I have a wounded dog who's been shot," he shouted, interrupting her. "I need—"

"I'm sorry, but we don't treat animals. You have to—"

"You do now," he interrupted. "This is Dr. Carson. I need a surgical setup and a portable X-ray unit available."

Silence.

"Just get everything ready. I'll take care of it." His face turned red with rage. First Kari, now Tequila.

———

It was déjà vu all over again. Brett had just finished emergency surgery on Tequila's shoulder. Luckily, the bullet had torn through a shoulder muscle but missed hitting any bone. An artery had been severed, which accounted for the massive blood loss. Brett figured the dog, like Kari, had nearly exsanguinated. He had no way to give him a transfusion, but he kept his vascular volume up with IV fluids and Plasma-Lyte. He put an oxygen mask over the dog's nose.

He listened with his stethoscope and heard a feeble, weak heartbeat. Tequila was tough. Tequila had been through a lot in his short life and always managed to pull through. Brett could only hope his dog would make it. Finally, he pushed an antibiotic through the IV tubing.

He collapsed in a chair, completely exhausted, sweating, and covered in dust and Tequila's blood and fur. A nurse came over to give him a bottle of cold water but stopped when he snapped off his surgical gloves and she saw his bleeding, torn fingers.

"My god! What happened to your hands?"

"I was just hanging around and this happened." She looked puzzled, but he didn't explain further. "Thanks for the water," which he gratefully gulped down.

"Sorry to say this, but you look like shit in more ways than one. Go take a shower and put these on." She tossed him a pile of clean scrubs. "Then come see me and I'll dress your hand injuries."

"Thanks," he said, "that's a good idea."

"Also, you need to get some sleep."

"And another good idea." Every muscle in his body rebelled as he stood slowly and took the clean scrubs. He hadn't caught a break. The nurse was right, he needed sleep. Even just an hour or two...

As he left the room, he smiled when he heard the nurse say, "Stitzlein's going to have a seizure when he finds out you operated on a dog."

61

The next day, Tequila was still mildly sedated, but managed to raise his head and wag his tail. Brett gently slid him over onto a gurney, threw a sheet over him, and wheeled him down the hall to the elevators. He passed a stern-looking man storming down the hall toward the ER treatment bay.

A nurse stepped in front of Brett as if she were shielding him from someone. "Put this mask on," she said, pushing a surgical mask against his chest.

"Why? Am I hiding from somebody?"

"Yeah, you are," she said, nodding her head toward the man who'd just passed. "That was Jefferson Heinz, the hospital assistant administrator. He likes to bully—"

"I hate bullies."

"Who doesn't? Anyway, he's on the warpath to find out who supposedly operated on a dog in *his* hospital."

"A dog in a hospital? Don't be ridiculous," he said as he slipped the sheet over Tequila's tail.

She winked at him. "Be careful."

"Thanks for your help." He continued wheeling Tequila down the corridor.

He entered Kari's room and pushed the gurney up beside her. She'd been walking the hallways and was sitting up, anxious to leave the hospital.

"I brought a friend in to say 'hi.'"

Tequila popped his head out from under the sheet, thumped his tail, and furiously licked her face as he whimpered with delight.

"Tequila!" she said with a huge smile. "My hero. You saved me." She put her arm around the dog's neck and hugged him.

"I thought my two favorite people should get together again," Brett smiled.

She nuzzled her face into the dog's furry neck. "You're my favorite best friend in the whole world." She looked at Brett. Most of his fingers were taped and there was a cut and bruise across his cheek. "My god—look at you. I heard what happened. You've been a busy man. Doing surgery, hanging off mountain cliffs, shooting..." She didn't finish.

He knew what she was asking. "No, I didn't kill him, but I wanted to. Pretty sure I wounded him. But remember, you shot him first. Now each of us has probably put holes in him— whoever he is. Hopefully, he won't be back."

"Thanks for letting me see Tequila, but you better get him out of here before the hospital security takes him to the Humane Society or something."

"Nope. Wouldn't want that. I wanted to cheer you up, and I knew he'd be excited to see you. I forgot to mention that Quinn has ordered us to leave and get back to Atlanta as soon as possible. I'll discharge you this afternoon and we can go back to our room at the Laredo." He leaned over and kissed her, then covered Tequila back up and pushed him out of the room and down the hall.

———

That afternoon, Brett settled Kari and Tequila into the Jeep, and they headed back to their room at The Laredo Inn. Tequila limped up to the room, still sore from the surgery. Once inside, the three of them took a much-needed nap. A few hours later, they went down to the dining room and joined Solt for dinner.

"Well," Solt said, "it looks like everyone is back to normal. How do you feel, Kari?"

"A little sore, but otherwise I'm doing fine. My doctor took special care of me," and she winked at Solt.

"He's a mean, narcissistic, son-of-a-bitch, from what I've heard."

"Yeah, you're probably right," she smiled. "He likes to boss people around."

"What I want to know," Solt said, looking at Brett's bandaged fingers, "how did you manage to do surgery with those banged-up hands?"

"Magic," he said. "Tomorrow, I'll make arrangements for us to get back to Atlanta. Quinn's ordered us back ASAP now that the FBI has taken over the criminal aspect of all this, and we don't want him going apeshit when we don't show up when he expects us to."

"Brett, in case you forgot," Kari said, "I'm not going to Atlanta. I've got to get back to Chicago."

"I already told you, you can't go back to teaching for at least two weeks. You're coming with me. I'm going to take care of you and make sure you heal as good as new. Besides, there's something I need to discuss with you."

She looked down at the floor for a moment, then looked up and said, "Brett, they've made me a full professor. They made a big deal of me being the youngest full professor at the university. I have to go back."

He stared at her. The color drained from his face. "Well, congratulations. You deserve it. Your help out here has been incredible. We couldn't have done it without you."

"You said there's something you wanted to discuss with me."

"Not important, since you're going back to Chicago."

The tension at their table was palpable. They stared at each other, waiting for the other to speak.

Finally, she spoke. "Since I've been out here after living full time in Chicago, I've come to realize that I want to have my own life, make my own history instead of teaching bored students about someone else's previous life's history. I told you how I've grown tired of living my life alone, having nobody to share it with. I think I might want to have a family someday. And Chicago is not a place to raise children."

"So, you and George…?"

"What?" she stammered. "No, not George. I have to go back to the university to work out new arrangements regarding my position as a full professor. *Not* to marry George."

Speechless, he found himself struggling to interpret what she was saying.

Kari straightened, paused, and asked slowly, "What was it you wanted to discuss with me?"

Brett glanced over at Solt in hopes of sensing that he thought he was doing okay as he moved forward. He turned toward Kari and sighed. With a deep breath, he reached into his pocket and retrieved a small velvet-covered box. He opened it, took out a ring, gently held her hand, and slipped it onto her finger.

"Kari Wheeler, will you be my wife?"

She started to tremble, her shoulders shook, and she began to sob.

Brett glanced questioningly at Solt as if to say, *huh?*

"You're a little dense, Brett. But I think that's a 'yes.' Pretty darned sure."

Kari leaned into Brett and sobbed against his chest.

He held her gently. "I love you, Kari Wheeler," he whispered in her ear. "I want to spend the rest of my life with you."

"Well," Solt said, "I wonder what they're serving for dinner tonight?"

Kari and Brett straightened from their embrace and looked at Solt as he reached for his beer. That broke the tension, and they all laughed.

62

The following morning at breakfast, Solt said, "Let me be the first to congratulate the new couple with a hot cup of coffee."

"G'morning, Ross," Kari said. "We're not a 'couple' yet. We've got to work out some details and kinks about our jobs and schedules." She looked over at Brett with a big grin on her face. She held out her hand to show off her new diamond ring.

"Wow. Sell that and you can retire," Solt said.

"It's beautiful," she said, "and it's not for sale."

"It was my mother's, and I know she would've wanted you to have it," Brett said.

The waitress came and took their orders, commented on Kari's beautiful ring, then left.

"I spoke to Chief Jack this morning," Kari said, "and the tribe has arranged a ritual celebratory dance tonight. Bonfire, dancing, music, chanting, the works."

"Outside in the cold night air?" Brett asked. "Are you sure you're up for it? Remember, you just had surgery five days ago."

"I wouldn't miss it for the world," she said. "This is their way of saying goodbye and well wishes to friends. To us."

"I thought it might be to honor those friends and relatives who died recently. Kind of an Indian version of the Day of Dead celebration we saw in Guatemala," he said.

"No—absolutely not. Actually, it's just the opposite. The Hispanic *el Dia de los Muertos*—or Day of the Dead—welcomes back deceased relatives for a day with food, drink, and festive celebration. They believe the gates of heaven open, and spirits of family join them for that day.

"According to Native American beliefs, life and death are just an ongoing cycle. It's the nature of things. Demonstrations of grief for the dead are never done. They have a great fear of the dead. Bodies must be buried soon after death to ensure the dead will never come back. Native Americans don't want to disturb the dead; they avoid them at all costs. Grieving or even saying the name of the deceased will slow down their journey to the afterlife.

"No, this ceremony is for us," she continued. "A way for them to say goodbye. It is not about honoring their dead. It's to celebrate the living."

Both men looked at her in amazement. As if to answer, she said, "It's what I do. I'm an anthropologist."

"Speaking about the dead," Solt said, "that could be us. You do remember that there's a shooter out there who is trying to kill us, don't you?"

"No, I haven't forgotten. Both Kari and I had close encounters with him. I'll do some checking this morning to make sure it's safe for us tonight."

Their breakfasts arrived, and they began eating, then chatting about everything that had happened to them as they finished. They spent the rest of the day packing, making arrangements to return home, and to get ready for the evening's big event.

———

That night, they drove to the area where everyone had gathered around a roaring bonfire. The full moon cast silvery shadows, and sparks from the burning wood popped and flew into the night air to be blown away in the breeze. They approached and sat down to join the large circle already formed. Men were dancing and chanting in their native tongue, while boys played drums in rhythm with the dancing.

Solt leaned over and quietly asked Brett what had been done to assure their safety. He was still worried about the shooter somewhere out there.

"Chief Jack asked the Navajo police to provide security to the area. They have several men around, as well as three trained dogs patrolling the area. The dogs will smell any anger way earlier than any humans could. I think we're okay."

Dr. Martin and her nurses, Kit and Julie, came over and sat down with them. "How are you feeling, Kari?"

"As you might expect—sore and tired, but excited to be here for this. I wouldn't miss it for the world."

Martin leaned over to Brett and asked, "Should she be out here so soon after surgery?"

"No, definitely not. But do you want to be the person to tell her that?"

They looked at her sitting there, a smile on her face, glowing in the light of the fire.

"Good call," Martin said.

When the dancing stopped, everyone was quiet as Chief Jack took center stage, wearing his eagle feather headdress and war paint on his weathered face. They watched silently as he raised his arms to the heavens and chanted something, then he spoke in English.

"A great enemy came to our village. We have all suffered in our own ways. But tonight, we celebrate our new friends who came to help us. And to say farewell to them and to wish them peace in their journey back to their own homes."

A few drums sounded, as if to mark approval of the chief's words. Brett kept his eye on Kari to make sure she was holding up in the cold night air. As far as he could tell, no one would guess that she'd nearly died and had undergone major surgery just six days ago.

Chief Jack motioned for Brett to come forward to stand beside him. The two men stood facing each other, then hugged as if they'd just found their best friend. When they separated, Chief Jack took a long leather necklace with a hand-carved bear hanging from it and placed it around Brett's neck.

"The path of the bear will show you the way, my friend."

"I'm honored and will treasure this," Brett said. "Chief Jack, I will never forget you. Thank you for everything you've done for us." He gave him a firm handshake, then went back and sat down.

The chief then nodded to several women who stood and carried a box over to Kari. Brett could see tears in her eyes as she accepted the box and opened it. It was a hand-woven shawl with the image of the blue Princess of the Mountain woven in the center. Kari stood, wrapped the shawl around her shoulders, raised her hands toward the burning sparks shooting into the sky, and said, *"Kepada putri dari gunung,"* a prayer to her father. The cold night breeze blew her hair, and the shawl blew behind her, and for just a fleeting moment, in the light of the fire and cascading sparks, she was the Princess of the Mountain.

The women chanted back to her, and they all smiled and clapped.

As the fire was slowly dying down, Brett carried his guitar to the center and sat down on the ground. He began to play a beautiful Spanish melody. Everyone sat quietly, captivated by the music echoing off dark canyon walls. The sound of snapping and popping of the dying fire were the only other sounds that night. He finally stood up and motioned to the women and girls that they should dance as he played a rhythmic Spanish dance. Everyone danced in the dirt, then clapped and laughed when he finished.

Before they headed back to their rooms, there were lots of hugs as they said goodbyes to everyone and promised to return.

The three friends drove quietly back to the Laredo in crisp moonlight air, each with their own thoughts. Their journey had come full circle, and they would be leaving in the morning. It was always hard to say goodbye after completing assignments, but this time, it was different. It was an experience that would remain with them the rest of their lives.

————

From more than a mile away, Ghost watched through binoculars the night's celebration of fire and dancing. Orange flashes from the bonfire reflected off the rock cliffs.

Then a new text message came in. It was from a number he hadn't seen for over a year. He reread the message three times to make sure he'd read it properly. But the message was short—decisive—and left no room for any misunderstanding.

He blew out a deep sigh and stood. It was time to leave. He had a new assignment, one more suited to his talents.

————

One week later, Brett was in his office working on his report. Kari was staying with him at his condo, watching Tequila and taking much-needed long afternoon naps. They enjoyed dinners out and nights cuddling on his balcony, watching moonlight flickering through leaves while they made plans for their future. They were both dreading when she would have to return to Chicago and her teaching.

He was happy, and life for him finally seemed peaceful. He had reached his 'angle of repose,' like a boulder, finally coming to rest after a lifetime of tumbling and falling from one problem to another. Then his phone rang.

"Hello."

"I need to see you. Come to my office."

It was Quinn, tossing out commands in his usual brusque manner. Brett put his papers aside and headed to Quinn's office.

He knocked, then went in. He was surprised to see FBI Deputy Director Higgins sitting there. Brett noted that the aluminum case sat on the floor beside him. He walked over and shook his hand. "Director Higgins, nice to see you again. Thank you for all your help."

"Have a seat," Quinn said. "There have been developments that I wanted to bring you up to date on."

"I see you have the case," Brett said to Higgins.

"I'm personally delivering it back to the DSTL."

Brett waited. He knew there was more to come.

Higgins continued. "First, we weren't able to discover who stole the virus, or who took it to the Supai village. We are watching Secretary Wainz and have tapped all his phones, both at his home and at his office. However, we've not turned up anything, and we doubt we ever will."

"So basically, we failed at everything," Brett said, somewhat dejectedly.

"Hardly," Higgins said. "First, you isolated and identified the virus, no small accomplishment. And as we've learned, it was a virus engineered using CRISPR and then gain-of-function to create a lethal bioweapon. As you pointed out to me when we first met, that's against the 1973 Geneva Protocol treaty agreed to by more than twenty nations. Thanks to your work in uncovering this, all research at the DSTL has been halted immediately, and every project is being reviewed.

"Also, the military bio labs in several countries—including ours here in America—are being thoroughly scrutinized. Any gain-of-functions which are aimed at obtaining a lethal bioweapon have been stopped. All future research and development will be reviewed by their respective governments."

Brett didn't know how to respond. "So," he finally said, "everyone gets off scot-free."

"Not at all," Higgins said. "Some of the scientists at DSTL have been charged with violation of an international treaty and illegal research. The masterminds behind the virus development have been fired and are facing stiff fines. The DSTL, as well as other bio labs worldwide, have relieved personnel and severely restricted future research until further review. It's difficult to express how beneficial your work has been."

"What about the man who shot Kari and is probably the same person who planted the virus?" Brett asked.

"Poof—gone. Disappeared. He left no clues. I doubt we'll ever find him or even know who he was. There have been rumors in Washington of some kind of mysterious assassin. It's probably just another myth. Then again—maybe not just a myth."

"Are we still in danger?" Brett asked.

"Can't say for certain," Higgins said, "but I doubt it. Now that the problems at the reservation and the DSTL are over, there'd be no reason to have any further interest in you."

"But—you're not sure," Brett said.

"No, I can't be certain. But it seems unlikely."

Higgins finally stood, shook Brett's hand, and said, "Thank you. To repeat what I said earlier, I wish you worked for me." He took the case, said goodbye, and left.

After Higgins was gone, Quinn asked him, "So, how are you doing? Have you recovered from your experience out west?"

"Hardly. The Havasupai are the ones who suffered the most. They seem to have been forgotten," Brett said.

"Not so fast," Quinn snapped back. "The British government has given one million pounds as payment to the tribe for their mistakes in all this." Quinn reached across his desk and handed him a large, sealed envelope. "There's a bank document for that payment. I want you to personally see that the Havasupai receive all of it. Not diluted out through bureaucrats and government agencies. Every penny to the tribe. I'm trusting you to see that is accomplished."

Brett took the envelope and started to say something when Quinn slid another envelope across the desk to him.

"We're paying for a two-week vacation for both you and Kari to see that it gets done. Plane tickets, hotel reservations, and a bonus check are in there." Then Quinn looked at him with a smile. "And I'm glad you work for me."

63

Secretary Wainz relaxed in his office at their home in the wealthy McLean district of Washington, DC, while he waited for his wife to finish getting ready. He was treating her to dinner at La Chaumière, a renowned French restaurant in Georgetown. He went to the liquor cabinet and poured a glass of Macallan Edition No. 2 single malt Scotch whisky, a rare and expensive scotch he only drank on special occasions. And tonight was one of those times. He sank into his soft leather chair to savor his scotch.

These weeks between Thanksgiving and Christmas were his favorite time of the year. Georgetown would be festive, with lights and pine boughs adorning the streets. And to add to the ambiance of the season, feathery snowflakes had begun falling that afternoon. The snow wouldn't stick, but that didn't matter. It was a night to celebrate, highlighted by the addition of the lights and snowfall.

The FBI had completed an extensive investigation into the tragic deaths of twelve Native Americans but failed to prove anything. There'd be no fallout or blame involving him, his department, or the White House. The White House had also backed off and no longer pressed him for answers. As was usually the case in Washington, every problem or scandal eventually would be forgotten, only to be replaced with another.

He was pleased with himself. He'd pulled off a complex operation that extended from a lab in England to the Grand Canyon. Everything had worked out in the end, as it usually did. Not always with the desired result, but that was also to be expected occasionally. Chief Jack was the only possible loose end remaining, and the old Indian didn't seem credible enough to even worry about.

He savored another sip of his scotch and was looking forward to an evening out with his wife.

Suddenly, his office door swung open. A man appeared inside the room as if blown in on a gust of wind.

Wainz jumped up, splashing scotch on his sleeve and Rolex. "What the—who are you? What the hell are you doing here? How'd you get in here?" he demanded.

The stranger was a nondescript man of medium height and build. There wasn't a single distinguishing feature about him. Except for his eyes, which were cold and threatening. Moving silently and nimbly as a shadow, he turned, closed the office door, and locked it.

At that moment, something clicked in Wainz's mind, and the sudden realization gripped him with an icy, paralyzing fear. It wasn't possible, was it? His heart raced and the hair on the back of his neck stood up. His stomach twisted in a painful knot that even the Macallan couldn't cure.

"Who are you?" he repeated in a voice that had grown weaker.

After several seconds of silence, the man said, "Some people call me The Ghost."

64

The Black Canyon Tributary
Grand Canyon National Park, Arizona

Two months later

When the authorities finally reached an agreement with the Havasupai tribe to do exploration only, geologists from around the US spilled into the Black Canyon and combed the walls and floor for nearly a month. They chipped away at various layers and swept dust and dirt from the canyon's floor. They brought in ultrasound equipment to explore the layers during the day, and ultraviolet lights to examine them at night. But no hint of the strange blue stone was ever found in the canyon.

They finally had to accept the obvious—that because of constant erosion and shifting of rock layers, the ancient two billion-year-old blue stone layer had once again been buried beneath hundreds of layers and millions of tons of rock.

Then they turned their attention to the bluffs and canyons around the mission, which were explored in minute detail, also with no success. No evidence of the blue stone could be found. Government officials debated whether to take ownership of the thirty-inch statue with a plan to cut it into cones that could provide the energy to power several electrical power plants for more than a decade. That plan generated a fierce debate as to who owned the priceless statue: the US government or tribal nations.

After much discussion and arguing, clearer heads prevailed, and the statue—now known as the Princess of the Mountain—was left intact. It was moved to the Denver Museum of Nature and Science, where it now resides under protective glass beside a famous thirteen-pound gold nugget, the largest gold nugget ever discovered in Colorado.

The legend of the blue stone became well known and to this day, tourists, hikers, campers, and geologists alike visiting this unique place, are compelled to occasionally glance down, with hopes of seeing a glimpse of a blue stone.

Buried again. Somewhere beneath it all.

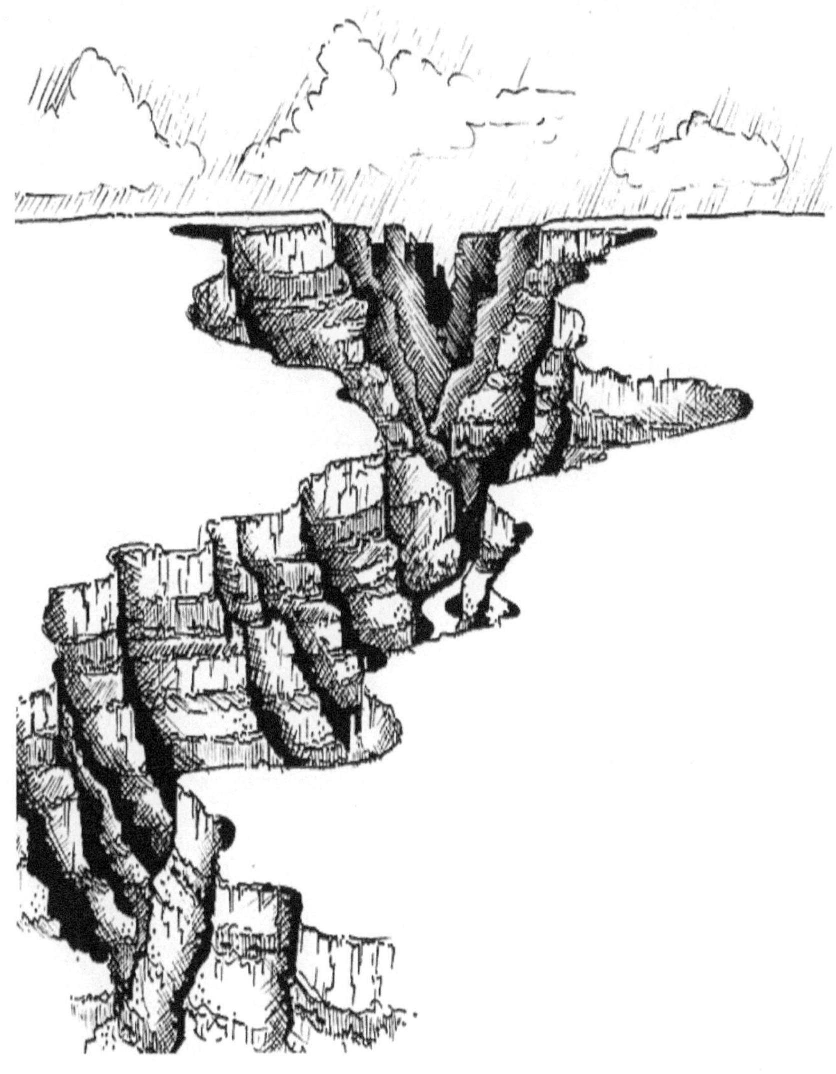

ABOUT THE AUTHOR

Dr. Keith Wilson is a graduate of the Ohio State University College of Medicine, where he earned several academic honors, and was chosen outstanding senior student in medicine and graduated cum laude. He was elected to AOA Medical Honorary Society both Junior and Senior years. He completed his residency in Denver, Colorado.

In addition to five published books, Keith has also written several short stories and has won awards, among them the Hemingway Short Story Contest and The National Writer's Club Contest.

His recent novel *Plunder* won the Global Book Gold Medal award.

Since retiring, he and his wife Cathy now divide their time between Ohio, Cape Cod, and Florida. Besides writing, his interests include golf, sailing, flower gardens, and driving his beloved Jeep.

ALSO BY KEITH WILSON

Nonfiction

Cause of Death

A writer's guide to death and dying

Code Blue

Inside the modern hospital

Fiction

The Mystery of the Blue Stone

Life Form

Plunder

Gold Medal Winner

Global Book Award